WHT U DON'T KNO CAN HURT U: This is a work of fiction and this statement is included to inform the reader that any celebrity name(s), business name(s), location(s), product(s), and organizations that are stated in the content of this book are real. However, they are used in a way that is purely fictional.

JAZZY KITTY PUBLICATIONS

PRESENTS

Wht U Dont Kno Can Hurt U

JERZ TOSTON

Wht U Don't Kno Can Hurt U

By Jerz Toston

Cover Art Created by KREATIVEGRAFIKS.COM

Logo Designs by Andre M. Saunders/Jess Zimmerman

Editor: Anelda L. Attaway

Co-editor: Jerz Toston

© 2021 Jerz Toston

ISBN 978-1-954425-17-0

Library of Congress Control Number: 2021904231

ACKNOWLEDGMENTS

First, I'd like to thank Allah (SWT) wit out Him this would not be possible.

A special thx to my kids Lil Jerz, Sakai, Meesh, Riya, Ceer and Deivyan.

My mom and especially my wife Tambra for puttin' up wit me during my writing process; I can b difficult when I'm writing but she deals wit it and is my biggest fan & critic.

DEDICATION

I book is dedicated to Mom-Betty, Ericka, Moe, Mase, and Jannie.

Ya Fav Author!

TABLE OF CONTENTS

TABLE OF CONTENTS

INTRODUCTION

This book is about the game and who will be the top kingpin runnin' everything. It won't be easy; it will be lying, scheming, shooting, comas, and murder.

Hakeem needs to figure out what friends he can trust. In the end, he realizes that he can only trust his wife, Laysha aka Lay. However, they both have been keeping a secret from each other.

In the end, Keem and Lay both reveal their secrets and hope the love can survive because they both have broken trust. Keem and Lay thought they both would be hurt because trust was broken. But the love will survive. but they realize what you don't know can hurt you!

CHAPTER 1

Finishing Up

I could remember it like it was yesterday.

"Put your hands on tha steering wheel don't move! Hakeem, we have a search warrant! Are you going to give us tha key or do we have to kick tha door down?!"

"Ain't no sense kicking tha door down if you got a search warrant!"

I looked over at my girl and couldn't believe this shit was happening to me, or should I say us. They told us to get out tha car and put tha handcuffs on us.

"Keem, Keem."

"Yo."

"Damn Nigga, you was out there."

"Nah, I was just think'n about some shit."

"Nigga it's over now; you got 3 weeks left."

"Damn Wali, it's over."

Wali was my celly, I knew him from the street, but since we have been celly's tha last 18 months we have gotton real close. We were waitin' on code green so we could do our Saturday ritual, which was clean our cell.

"Code Green 08:23, Code Green 08:23." As soon as Smith cracked tha door I went to look at tha visiting list.

"Keem, you know you got a visit today at 2:30."

"I know but I need to see it in black and white."

"What up Keem?" Smith asked.

"I can't call it Playa."

"You short now, ain't you?"

"Yeah, matter of fact punch my status sheet up for me."

When he did, I couldn't believe it; they had me maxing out next Saturday. Since my time was mandatory, I didn't earn good time.

"You sure that's right Smith?"

"Yeah, why?"

"I was pose' ta max out tha week after next. Shit, I ain't complaining though, Imma jus tell my wife today that she needs to pick me up next week."

After me and Wali cleaned our room we played handball. As usual I put an ass whoopin' on him, he would remember even after I max out.

"Imma bust ya ass before you leave Keem."

"You think so?"

"Count time!"

"Damn Imma have to sit in my chair til code green."

I hopped in tha shower, no soon as I got in shake down came. They never come in and do their work, they alwayz sit around. When I got out, they were just starting. Kado and Cannon came to our room.

"Step out Fellas." We didn't keep any contraband in our room, so I wasn't worried about them.

"Who's on tha bottom bunk?"

"I am, why what's up?"

"You can't have this pillow."

"Why not?"

"These bread ties on tha end."

"Are you serious? I had that pillow jus like that for 3 years."

"Well not anymore," Cannon said.

"Yo you crazy as Shit."

"Excuse me?"

"I said you..."

Wali cut me off, "Keem you got a visit." I went back in and got ready for my V.I.

"Keem you ready?" Smith asked. I grabbed a couple of Jolly Ranchers then headed to tha door.

"Keem you still goin' to visits; ain't you short?"

"Yeah, I'm outta here next week."

"Keem."

"What up Pug?"

"Who comin' to see you, Kita?"

"Yeah."

Tha C.O. let us know who was up and who was down. By tha time we got there our visits were already waiting on us. Laysha, Shaniya, and Shanay were in their usual booth.

"Hey Daddy," they both said as I picked up tha phone.

Niya was 2 ½, my wife was 3 months pregnant when I came to jail. It was hard watching Niya grow up behind this dirty scratched up glass.

"Damn, tha visits over already? I'm glad this is my last one."

I didn't tell Laysha that I max out Friday. I figured I would tell her that Wednesday or Thursday.

"Wali Imma make sure I keep in touch and do what I can until you hit tha bricks."

"Did you tell Laysha to pick you up tomorrow?"

"No, but I'm goin' to call at code green." When they cracked tha door, I jumped on tha phone.

"To accept this call press 5 now."

"Hello."

"Hey Nay, where ya mom?"

"Right here, hold on."

"Hello."

"Hey Beautiful wife of mine."

"Hey Baby."

"I need you to do me a favor."

"What, you nuisance."

"I need you to be up here by 8:15 tomorrow mornin', they letting me go."

"AAAAGH!" she screamed dropping tha phone. I heard Nay ask what happen Mom?

"They letting ya dad come home in tha morning." I could hear them getting excited.

"Well, I love y'all and I'll see you in tha a.m."

"I love you more and I'll be there when you come out." (CLICK) Tha phone went dead.

I couldn't go to sleep by tha time I did it was 6 o'clock. I was right back up at 8 o'clock.

"Code Red"

As soon as they called code green, I heard Brown call my name for bag and baggage. Those are 3 words every inmate wants to hear.

When I got to booking Cpl. Mays said, "Damn they finally letting you go."

Yeah, it's my time."

"Your wife should be out front; she's called here about 10 times already."

"That's my baby, she wanna make sure y'all not try'n to keep me."

After I changed Cpl. Mays walked me to tha gate where Blackson was waiting.

"Ya wife in tha visiting parking lot."

I walked around there just as she was pulling out her parking spot. Both my daughters jumped out tha car and ran into my arms.

"Daddy, Daddy!"

It felt so good to hold them especially Niya since it was my first time. When Laysha finally got out she had tears in her eyes.

As she hugged me, she said, "Please don't leave me again. These are tears of joy."

"I know Baby, I know."

CHAPTER 2

Free at Last

When I got in tha house Nay and Niya wasted no time showing me around tha apartment. When I got back to tha kitchen I let them know we're moving.

"Yeah, Yeah, no we not I like my house."

"That's tha thing, this is an apartment."

"Well, I'm not ready to move yet. Are you hungry?"

"Fo' Sho. Where my clothes at?"

"In those 2 closets."

Since it was still hot out, I picked out a pair of jeans and my Joe Namath throwback on wit tha green and white Adidas to match.

"Imma jump in tha shower." Laysha came in tha bathroom to let me know breakfast was done.

"Umm, Umm, I can't wait to get some of that," she said grabbing my man.

"You better stop, he ain't been touched in 3 years, only by me."

"My brother and his wife are comin' to get them later. Stacks want you to hit him up," she said handing me a cell phone.

"I'll call him after I eat."

Lay had put together a hell of a breakfast, beef bacon, waffles, eggs, and toast. After 3 years of eating that shit, they call food, this was five star. As soon as I finish eating, I called Stacks but didn't gets an answer. I couldn't front, I was impressed wit tha crib; Lay did know how to hook shit up.

"Baby you really want to move?"

"Yeah, but that can wait. I jus want to get this year of probation over wit."

"Well, my uncle said he would give you a job if you need one."

"Lay I can't see me cleaning nobody's house."

"I know, but if you can't find no other job you gotta do what you have to to keep ya P.O. off ya ass."

"I know. I'm going to go to motor vehicles Monday to get my license."

"Why don't we go now?"

"Come on then; Niya, Nay, let's go!"

"Where we going Daddy?"

"To D.M.V. so I can get my license."

"Yeah."

"Why y'all so happy?" Lay asked.

"That means Daddy bout to get a fly car wit some rims and a banger," Nay said smiling. We headed outside into tha warm morning sun.

"It's only 10:30 so hopefully it won't be crowded." Lay had an Audi A-4 Candy Apple Red on a pair of 22's.

"Nay you don't like ya mom's car?"

"Yes, I love mommy's car. I just know you gon' get something real nice."

"So, from tha looks of things that stock you invested in is doin' really good."

"Yeah, as a matter fact tha broker told me we went up 6 points this morning."

"I have no idea what you're talking about, but you can school me later."

"Put it like this, we made another 300,000 this morning."

"WOW!"

"Our bank account is 7 figures now."

"Well, why haven't you bought a house yet?"

"I wanted to wait for you so we could pick out one together."

"Until I get off probation, we gonna stay where we at."

"Fine wit me. Keem, I hope you meant what you said about not hustlin' no more."

"I am." *At least that's what I thought anyway.*

I got a number then took a seat.

"I see or should I say, I hear Layla got tha city on lock wit that weed."

"Yeah, remember when we went to Jamaica and brought back that KiKi?"

"How can I not? That's tha best weed ever."

"Well, that's what she pumpin'." My facial expression must have said it all.

"She got a connect from tha islands."

"That means she making a lot of doe."

"Damn, if he only knew I was really the one runnin' this Shit; Layla was just my front. I did tell Luddy once Keem got home I will be fallin' back and Layla would be tha Bitch to see." As bad as I wanted to tell him that I was doin' my thing while he was down, I didn't. Especially since he stressed how much he didn't want me hustlin'. He said if tha money got low to just call Stacks. Instead of callin' Stacks, I invested in some weed which was over a 2-year period made me very, very wealthy. I took 50,000, put that in some stock that also has been extremely profitable.

Keem came out wit a paper and a smile.

"Baby I passed; I have to come back in 10 days to take tha road test."

"Here," she said handing me her keys.

"Here we go again."

"What you talkin' bout?"

"Always wantin' me to drive."

"Boy, I been driving for 3 years straight."

"Well, I don't know what to tell you cause in 10 days, I'm gettin' me a car."

"Oh yeah? Does Layla still mess wit that Clown Nigga Star?"

"Yeah, and I told her to leave his leech ass alone!"

"Stacks told me in a letter he beat his ass for say'n he was tha police."

"That Shit was funny, he had Star runnin' like a track star."

"Fuck 'em! Jewlz told me them niggaz ain't gettin' no money."

"Nope. That's why he don't fuck wit 'em. It seems like they alwayz over Layla's free loading."

"Who be over there?"

"Star, Big Head, Chulo, Hov, and Perk."

"Fuck all them niggaz, as much as I was lookin' out for them when I was home. They didn't even so much as send me a card."

"WE STILL HUSTLE TIL THA SUN COMES UP. CRACK A 40 WHEN THA SUN GOES DOWN. IT'S A COLD WINTER, Y'ALL NIGGAZ BETTER BUNDLE UP."

"What's up Layla? Unh huh, he's right here. We just left tha D.M.V. he got his permit."

"Yeah, on tha first try?"

"A'ight, we on our way."

"Mom, we goin' over Layla's house?" Niya asked.

"Yes, we are, she wanted to see you. Did you have somewhere to go?"

"Only people I need to see are already wit me."

"Did Rachel know you was comin' home today?"

"No, I never told her. I'll call her later if I'm not too busy," I said winking at her.

When we pulled up there were police and Vice everywhere.

"What is going on out here?"

We got out and Maxi, Black, Candy, Blondy, and Whitey were all standing outside.

"Oh Shit, Keem when you come home?" Maxi asked.

"He came home this morning," Niya said.

"Boy if she not ya twin," Black said. Everybody else agreed.

"Keem they got ya cuzin' Push over there." I went over there as they were picking him up off tha ground.

When he saw me, he said, "Call Rachel and tell her to call tha bail bonds."

I pulled my iPhone out and dialed my sister's number.

"Hello."

"Push said call tha bail bonds, they lockin' him up."

"Who is this?"

"Damn, you don't know ya own brothers voice."

"AAAAAGH!" she screamed, "I thought you weren't comin' home til next week?"

"So did I, call tha bail bonds then call me right back."

10 minutes later Rachel was calling me back.

"Hey Brother."

"What's up, Lil Sis?"

"Everybody has been askin' about you."

"Sis, besides you, Lay, Stacks, and Jewlz nobody ain't get at me."

"I knew you was goin' to say that cause that's what I said."

"Sis, I'll be by there a little later."

"Boy stop lying, I probably won't see you til tomorrow. Just make sure you call me."

"A'ight, love ya."

"Love you too."

"Come on Daddy," Niya said grabbing my hand pulling me towards Layla's house.

When we walked in, Star, Big Head, Hov, Chulo, and Perk were sitting in tha living room.

"Layla!" Niya yelled running to her.

"Keem, what's up?" Layla asked.

"I can't call it; jus happy to be home."

"I know you are. Come 'mere, I got something for you." I walked back to her bedroom, "I know you can't smoke so here's a few one's for you." She handed me a stack of hundred-dollar bills.

"This good lookin' too."

"Keem as much as you use to look out for me before you went to jail; this is tha least I can do. Can I ask you something wit out offending you or you gettin' mad at me?"

"I know what you're goin' to say but go head."

"Lay told me how you keep lookin' out for Star. I think that he's dead weight and you need to get rid of him."

My phone started to ring, when I looked at tha caller ID I saw it was Stacks.

"What up Big Homey?"

"I'm over Layla's."

"15 minutes a'ight." (CLICK)

"Stacks said he beat Star up because he said he was police." (Ha! Ha! Ha!)

"I know it was over you though."

"Keem you are crazy. You and Stacks still be doin' y'all thing?"

"Yup, you know that's goin' to always be my baby." Lay came in tha bedroom.

"What y'all talkin' bout in here?"

"None ya biz-ness."

"Well excuse me." There was a knock on tha door.

"Keem, Stacks here for you."

"Baby, I'll be right back."

"Don't be all day either."

I walked into tha front room where Stacks was standing in a pair of Loui V. sneaks, jeans, and a shirt to match.

"Keem."

"Stacks." We gave each other a brotherly hug.

"You need to go shoppin' but we can do that tomorrow. Where's Lay?"

"Back there wit Layla." I saw Star looking at Stacks wit hate in his eyes.

"What up Keem," Star said try'n to be petty.

"You a funny dude," I said to him.

"Why you say that?"

"Nigga you should have spoke when I first came in."

"Nigga don't nobody owe you nothing," Perk said standing up.

"Mafucka, I know don't nobody owe me Shit. And I definitely wouldn't expect none of you Broke-Ass Niggaz to give me Shit!"

"You got it Fucked up! Ain't nobody broke!" Hov said. Maxi went in tha back.

"Y'all better get them for this get ugly."

"Keem what's goin' on out here?" I told her what had happened.

"Layla, I don't know why you got these freeloading ass niggaz in ya house."

"Come on Keem, I got a surprise for you."

"You niggaz better not be here when I come back." And we walked out.

Star said, "Layla, you better check that Mafucka."

"Don't talk that Shit when he leave," Lay said.

"Look, y'all gotta leave."

"They here wit me."

"What that mean? I pay these bills. Matter fact, you can leave too." They all got up and went outside.

"Come 'mere Layla. Did Star pay you that 10,000 he owe you?"

"He said he would be ready in a few days."

"A few days! It's already been a month! You let him know if he doesn't have that by next week, I would hate for him to end up like P.J.," she said and walked out.

Any doubts I had, she just confirmed it. Tha young boy P.J. had hit me for 15 pounds and 50,000. I told my aunt and she said she would handle it. Two weeks later they found him naked in an abandon house wit his penis cut off and shoved in his ass. Tha writing on tha wall said play pussy get fucked. Them clowns was try'n to be petty. Stacks and Jewlz were tha only ones holding him down besides me and Rachel. Not that he needed them for real, for real. They thought he was goin' to come home and put them on. He's not even hustlin' anymore.

"Where we goin' Stacks?"

"I got a surprise for you." We pulled up to this nice 3 car garage house.

"Who crib is this?"

"Mines and stop askin' so many questions."

We got out and he hit tha button on his keychain. When tha garage opened, there was a pretty black on black 850 wit 22s.

"You got enough whips, don't you?"

"That's not mines, it's yours."

"What?"

"Yup, you heard me. Me and Lay went half on it for you. She made me promise not to let you drive til you get ya license."

"Well, you better give me tha keys," I said, pulling out my permit I just got hours earlier.

"Nigga that Shit is fake."

"Me, Lay, and tha kids went to D.M.V. this mornin' and waala." Wit out any more words, Stacks handed me tha keys.

"So, what you gonna do?"

"On some real shit Stacks, I ain't try'n to get back in tha game."

"Right now, I got tha whole tri-state in a chokehold."

"I knew you was doin' ya thing but not in that magnitude."

"My connect Pablo hits me wit like a 100."

"A 100 bricks?"

"Yeah, it only takes me 2 weeks to dump that, though."

"Damn, you make a nigga want to jump back in."

"On some real shit, I could definitely use your help, but I'm not goin' to rush you back into this game, Keem."

"When Mafuckas see me pull up in this, they gon' think I'm back at it anyway. How many people do you know do 3 years and come home tha first day to an 850 on dub dueces?"

"None, only tha one wit a wife name Lay and a best friend name Stacks."

"Nigga I think you outgrew that name."

"Nah, because now I got stacks and stacks of money." (Ha! Ha! Ha!)

We both started laughing at that.

I now knew it would only be a matter of time before I was back in knee deep. Stacks took me on tour of his mini mansion. When ever you're ready jus let me know. Do you and Lay have plans for tonight?"

"I don't know, not that I know of."

"Maybe we can go to Palmers so I can inaugurate you to my man Zoro. I gotta handle some biz-ness so call me and let me know what' up."

"A'ight, you got that and thanks again for tha whip."

"You don't have to thank me for doing what I suppose to do. Keem, I know you're grown but here's a little advice for you."

"Un Oh."

"No, seriously. Lay is a good woman and she has held you down as a wife should. I can't front, I even had a few niggaz from outta town go at her jus to make sure she wasn't cheating on you. All she did was flash her ring on them and step off." That made me smile.

"I said all that to say, do right by her and if you do cheat, do it outta town." I just nodded, gave Stacks dap as we both got in our vehicles and went our separate ways.

My phone started ringing, when I answered it Stacks told me there was a few dollars in tha glove box for me then hung up. I pulled over to see how much money was in tha glove box. I could not believe Stacks had 20,000 in tha glove box for me. I pulled off headed to Layla's.

As I was pulling up Lay was calling my phone.

"Hello Foot Locker, may I help you?"

"I'm sorry, I dialed tha wrong number." She hung up before I could say anything. She called right back.

"Foot Locker, may I help you?"

"Is this 287.4455?" (Ha! Ha! Ha!)

"Keem."

"Yeah."

"Boy stop playing, where you at?"

"Outside, I jus pulled up." As soon as I got out tha car Niya spotted me.

"Daddy, Daddy! Oh Daddy, is that ya car?" Nay asked.

"Yeah, Mommy and Stacks got it for me." Star and tha rest of them were staring at me wit envy and jealousy in their eyes.

"Dad, you got a system in there?"

"Let me guess, you wanna hear it?"

"Pleeeease."

I put tha key in then said, "Plies Real Testament, track 3, volume 15."

"My Dog went to court dey gave him 15. Crackers ban my little nigga he was 16. Don't they know what all that time mean. They hollering mandatory, they want him to do tha whole thing."

"What ever Stacks got in here got this thing quaking."

"Mommy system ain't got nothing on yours Dad." I popped tha trunk to see exactly what was in there.

"Shit!" I said when I saw tha 3 15-inch solar bearics.

"What you doin'?"

"Jus wanted to see why this shit was so loud. Thank you," I said grabbing her and kissing her passionately.

"OOOOOOH! Mommy and Daddy kissing," Niya said.

"This tha car you was talkin' about?" Layla asked Lay.

"Yeah, but Stacks put tha rims and system in it."

"Baby, did you have anything planned for tonight?"

"No why?"

"Stacks wanted to go to Palmers."

"It's cool cause me and Layla are goin' too."

"I need to get something to wear."

"Only place you can go is up town to Sneaker Villa. It's only 4 o'clock so they still open."

"Well, let me run up there then."

"Daddy can I go?"

"Me to Daddy."

"I don't care, get in and put y'all seat belts on."

"Imma meet y'all back at tha house."

"When I get to 7-Eleven, I make a left or right?"

"Daddy I know which way to go."

"I gotta pack their clothes; my sisters said to drop them off at 6 o'clock."

I got in tha car then pulled off. I ended up buying 2 pair of jeans wit 2 shirts wit 2 pair of Air Ones for myself. Nay wanted these Pastry sneakers so I bought her and Niya 2 pair and these jeans that were called Pastry.

I rode thru 8th to see if Jewlz was out there. Jacob tha only one out so I rolled down tha window to see if he knew where Jewlz was.

"Oh Shit! Keem is that you?"

"Yeah."

"When did you get home?"

"This morning, you seen Jewlz?"

"He in tha park wit Bundles."

"A'ight, Imma holla at you." I drove around to tha park it was packed out.

"Daddy can we get out?"

"Yeah, but don't go nowhere because we're not staying long."

"Aunty Sandy," they said running to her.

"Where is ya mom at?"

"She's home."

"Well, who y'all here wit?"

"My daddy," Niya said all smiles.

By this time, I was getting out tha car. I spotted Jewlz sitting on tha wall wit Beanz.

"Keem what's up?" Sandy asked.

"Same Shit different smell, happy to be home."

"I know that's right. Where tha kids at?"

"Down in tha park?"

"Lay said you was coming home next week."

"I was suppose to but they let me go today and I'm not complaining at all."

"Gettin' outta jail a week early, I don't think nobody would complain about that. I like that car," she said wit a smile.

"Thanks, I'm sure you already know who got it for me." She just nodded.

Sandy was Lay's best friend; they told each other everything.

"Keem, what tha Fuck is up Nigga?"

"Let me holla at Jewlz. What up Lil' Nigga," I said giving him dap and a brotherly hug.

"Fresh out tha box pushin' a 850 on dueces. Back at it already?"

"Naw, this was a gift from wifey and Stacks."

"What up Keem?"

"I can't call it Beanz."

"You see Hov and 'nem yet?"

"Fuck them Mafuckas!" I told him what happen over Layla's

"You shattered their dreams; they jus knew you was goin' to put them on."

"Even if that shit didn't happen, I wasn't Fuckin' wit 'em!"

"I tried to tell 'em that. You know what's so funny? I use to say; I'm bout to send Keem a money order, everybody give me $10. Man, I ain't got it or I'm Fucked up or Shit real tight right now."

"So, what you doin' for 'em?"

"Keem, I ain't never been one to front, I'm just keepin' my head above water."

"9 or 18?"

"Neither 4 ½."

"Why didn't you say something? I would have told Stacks to hit you."

"Stacks is good peeps, but that's ya mans."

"I feel you. How much you pay'n for that?"

"4,050, I only make 4,500, but I cop 4 ½ every day."

"Imma have something for you tomorrow. What's ya number?" I asked pulling out my iPhone, "that's me callin', lock my number in."

"I got it."

"Let me take them home; I'll hit you in tha morning. Nay, Niya!"

"Keem they went in tha center; I'll get 'em."

"Dad you ready?"

"Yeah, Nay you don't got a cell phone?"

"No."

Before we went home, I went to Adams Four to get Nay a cell phone.

"Come on, pick out which phone you want."

"You getting me a cell phone?

"Yeah, we need to be able to find you at all times. She picked out a nice phone $60 a month unlimited everything. You gon have to pay ya own bill. Dad how Imma do that, I'm too young to work? You're going to earn $15 a week doing chores. Now if you spend the money that's on you. Thank you, Dad. You ain't been home for a day and I already got a cellphone two pairs of pastries sneakers and jeans.

I had Meek Millz banging when I pulled up in front of tha crib. When Nay and Niya got out all these kids came up to my car.

"Nay who that?"

"My dad."

"Is that Niya's dad too?"

"Yeah, Dummy. Dad can you take this stuff in tha house for us please?"

"No."

Lay was on tha phone when I walked in probably wit Sandy.

"I know you didn't buy them those sneaks and jeans. You not going to start this."

"How do I put numbers in here?"

"I know you did not buy her a cell phone?"

"She needs one, that way if we can't find her all we got to do is call her."

"I'm not pay'n that bill."

"Mom, Imma pay my own bill wit my allowance." Lay looked at me.

"It's teaching her how to be responsible. If she does her chores, she earns money, tha money she earns she can pay her cell phone bill. Now, if she spends her money, then her phone will be off til she pays her bill."

"We gonna see how long this works out. How did you end up buying them something?"

"They saw those Pastry's and went crazy."

"I should've known, all tha girls are rockin' them."

"Mom, can we go outside?"

"Yeah, but don't go far. I'm bout to drop y'all off over Aunt Jonda's."

"If we not out front, just hit my phone."

"I don't even know tha number."

"Daddy has it," she said going out tha door.

"Don't say anything, jus trust me on this one Lay."

"I wasn't goin' to say nuffin about tha phone, but like I said, don't start that buying them what ever they want shit."

"Lay you already know how I am wit my kids and I've been gone for 3 years."

"All, your kids have been well taken care of while you were gone; I made sure of that."

"Baby I know you did, and I thank you for that. I really do."

"Keem, you don't have to thank me for anything. I did what a wife is suppose to do when her husband can't. Speaking of which, you owe me a wedding."

"I told you to wait until I got out, but you're tha one who insisted on going to tha Justice of tha Peace, remember?"

"Of course, I do, I wanted to show you how much I loved you and that I would be wit you through thick and thin no matter what!"

"That's why I love you so much Lay. What would I do wit out you?"

"No, tha question is, what would we do wit out each other?"

"Let's hope we never have to find out, and that wedding is goin' to wait until I get off this probation."

I took tha outfit that I was wearing out of tha bag and put it on tha bed.

"Nay told you to get that didn't she?"

"No, I picked it out."

"How did you know that's what all tha dudes be wearing?"

"I didn't, I jus like it wit these white ones."

"I don't really care for black label, but I like that. Are you gonna ride wit me to drop tha girls off?"

"If you want me to."

"You know I do," she said, throwing her arms around my neck.

Next thing I knew, we were tongue wrestling, and I had my hand all over Lay's ass. My wife was one of tha baddest females in tha land. 5' 7", brown skin, brown eyes, hair to tha back of her neck, and a ass like tha broad Key Toi from that Outkast video Tha Way You Move.

"We better go before I rape you," Lay said wit a big smile on her face.

"It's not rape if tha other person is willing."

"Before I forget, what's Nay's number?" I pulled my cell out and gave her tha number.

"Come on before I forget Jonda changes her mind. You know how she does."

"When did she move?"

"A few months ago."

"I know y'all better get y'all asses off my car," I said to Nay and her friends.

"She know better, didn't I tell you about sitting on people's cars?"

"This is ya first and last warning. Don't be sitting or leaning on my car cause none of y'all can pay for a paint job if you scratch my car."

"Nay ya dad mean just like ya mom."

"No, he ain't, my dad da man."

All I could do was smile and said, "Damn Lay, tha kids called you mean." Ha! Ha! Ha!

"That's because I don't let them run over top of me and do what they want to do."

"Neither do I."

"Yeah right. I don't know what you doing, you driving."

"Yeah Dad, we want to ride in ya car."

"Stacks said I need to go shoppin' so that what I'll be doing tomorrow morning."

"Shit!"

"What's wrong?"

"I need to get their bathing suits; Missy said they going to a pool party tomorrow."

"Pool Party? OOH, OOH, Pool Party OOH, OOH."

Volume 15 Meek Millz came out sounding like a concert. Jonda and Missy were out front when we pulled up.

"Hey Keem," Missy said giving me a hug.

"Hey, look at you, all tall."

"What's up, Jonda?"

"I see you gained some weight while you was locked up. Laysha what you do, trade ya other car in for that?"

Before she could answer, Nay said, "That's my dad's car."

"Stacks got this for me."

"Must be nice."

"Lay you ready? I wanna go holla at Rachel for a few minutes."

"Did you put their swimsuits in their bag?"

"Sure did."

"They gon' need spending money."

"Spending money?"

"Yeah, we going to Splash World."

"Imma have to bring it back."

"Here," I said, pulling out tha money Layla gave me, "$300 should be more than enough for both of them."

"They only need 100 apiece," Lay said.

"No, they need this tha way Nay eat plus games."

"I'll call you when we get back."

"Mom you said they can stay all weekend."

"I did, didn't I. Well, drop off another set of clothes for Sunday."

"A'ight and Niya behave ya self."

"I am Mommy."

"Come give daddy a hug. Love you."

"I love you Daddy."

"Nay don't take that phone wit you."

"You got a cell phone?" Missy asked.

"Yeah, my dad got it for me today."

While we were on our way to Rachel's, me and Lay talked. She let me know she was serious about me not spoiling them. I called Rachel to see where she was at; she let me know she was on 9th & Lombard. I pulled up; she was out there wit her girls.

"Damn, you act like you didn't know who I was."

"Brother, I didn't, gettin' out of that pretty ass 850."

"Where my nephew at?"

"You know he wit his peeps. Damn Boy, ya hair got longer."

"I know, I was thinkin' bout getting it cut."

"You better not!"

"Paris, you still be braiding hair?"

"You know it."

"Can I hire you? You know how we do."

"Sure can. Is that my sis in tha car?"

"You know it is."

"Lay, I know you ain't acting like that since ya husband home."

"No, what's up Rachel?"

"Where y'all headed?"

"I'm bout to go home and get dressed."

"And where you goin' at tonight?"

"Stacks is taking me to Palmers; he wants me to meet his peoples."

"I know you not back hustlin', and you just came home today."

"Nah Sis, I ain't makin' no noise."

"Explain that then," she said, pointing to my 850.

"Stacks and Lay got it for me."

"You don't even have ya license."

"Why don't I," I said showing her my permit.

"Oh Shit, go Brother."

"I jus wanted to stop by and see you. Do you have some money?"

"No, I won't be able to hit you until next week when I get paid." I went in my pocket and peeled off 3-hundred-dollar bills.

"Here, take this."

"You're tha one who just came home; you need it more than me."

"No, I don't, I got hit wit 25,000."

"Damn Keem, you come home to more than a nigga who has been hustling for years. I don't need any money."

"Well, buy Pete some sneakers. I'll call you tomorrow, love ya Sis."

"Love you too and don't be gettin' all drunk."

I got in tha car and apologized to Lay for taking so long.

"You Ok?"

"I was on tha phone wit Layla, she told me she was putting Star out when he came back."

"She should've been put his broke ass out."

"He owes her some money that she wanted to get back before she put him out."

"Did she get tha money?"

"I don't know? I'm guessin' she did if she's putting him out."

"I hope she ain't keepin' all that weed and money in her house."

"No, she got another place where she keeps it. I'm hungry as shit."

"Me too."

"It's only 8 o'clock, what do you want to eat?"

"It doesn't even matter to me."

"Imma call Top Choice and order some curry shrimp."

"I want tha same thing wit extra shrimp."

While she called Top Choice, I called Jewlz to see who had some E-pills. He let me know Beanz had 'em. I told him to get me two and I was on my way.

"There you go wit them E-pills."

"I can't smoke no weed, so E-pills and Bombay it is for me." By tha time, we went over Westside and back to Top Choice then home to eat; it was 9:30.

"What time is Stacks comin' to pick you up?"

"I don't know? Let me call him."

After 3 rings, he picked up. After a few minutes of conversation, we hung up.

"He said he'll be here by 11:30 at tha latest."

"So, we got time for a little sex then."

"Listen to you."

"Boy I've been waiting for this for three years."

I took a sip of Bombay and threw one of my my pills back. When Lay walked into tha bedroom, Lay was taking her jeans off. Just seeing her ass in a thong, brought me to an instant erection.

"Are you goin' to stand there or are you going to take ya clothes off?"

"It's been 3 long years since I saw you naked."

I took my clothes off and got into bed. It didn't take long before we were licking all over each other.

"Umm, Daddy, I miss you so much."

I had one titty in my mouth as I caressed tha other one. I worked my way down to her inner thigh. Then I slowly jabbed at her love nest wit tha tip of my tongue driving her crazy.

"OOOOH, AAAAGH, YEEES! Right There Daddy," she said, grinding my face.

Within a few minutes, she was shaking and screaming.

"OH MY GOD! I'M CUUUMMING! OOOOOH SHIIIIIT!!! Once I felt her cumming, I moved my face and replaced it wit my 10 inches that was now 11.

"OOOOH Daddy, I've missed you so much!"

"Lay, I missed you too."

She was giving me all that she had. By now my pill had kicked in and

Damn did she feel so good. We did it in every position possible, even ones that weren't, we made possible. It was as if we were makin' love for tha first time.

After Lay came a few more times, I told her we could finish tonight when I came back from tha club. We took a shower together then got dressed. Lay put on these black Derion jeans and shirt to match. Those jeans didn't do her any justice at all. While I was putting my clothes on, I could hear Lay on tha phone.

"I know he's goin' to be there tonight, so I'll let him know that Keem came home a week early so it's over."

I couldn't believe it, I thought she was keepin' it real. I guess I was wrong. I couldn't front, I was truly hurt; I'm cool, Imma do me. Fuck being faithful!

CHAPTER 3

Clubbin'

When Stacks came Lay and Layla had already left. As bad as I wanted to tell Stacks what I heard. I just couldn't bring myself to tell 'em.

Stacks was pushing a Mercedes R350 white/white sitting on dub dueces and a system that sounded like he had a marching band in tha trunk.

"Damn Nigga, I see you got a real nice collection of whips."

"One for every day of the week." Ha! Ha! Ha!

"That's how you doin' it Nigga?"

"Hey if you got it then do it; you know that. Do you got 4 bricks?"

"Is it for you?"

"Nah, it's for Jewlz."

"He coppin' like that? I knew he was gettin' at a dollar."

"Nah, he only grabbin' 4 ½ a day for 4,050. I did tha math, he spendin' 121,500 a month; that's 4 bricks a month. How much you chargin' anyway?"

"25,000 but I'll give 'em to him for 23,000 apiece."

"That's cool, Imma need 'em first thing in tha A.M."

"How much you paying?"

"15,000 apiece."

"That's kinda steep."

"Shit that's sweet."

"Imma make a few calls tomorrow. I know I can get better numbers than that. I gotta connect in Miami wit some pure purico (cocaine) si' (yes)."

"I'm wit that, gracias (thank you)."

"De nada (your welcome)."

"I see you was studying that Spanish book I sent you."

"Yup, and my mans Diablo from Miami. He gave me his numbers told me to hit him up when I touched. He would have some good numbers as well as something me to get started."

"Hope he wasn't bullshittin'."

"I seriously doubt that."

"Hold up, so that means you back in tha game?"

"Thanks to Lay," I thought to myself, "yeah, I'm back; everybody needs a sidekick. Batman had Robin, Fred had Barney, Jordan had Pippen, and Shaq had Kobe."

"Say no more. We gon' expand, I'm talkin Chicago, DC, North & South Carolina, Atlanta, and VA; that's jus for starters."

"Damn, I see tha line still be long as shit."

He pulled in a spot right next to Lay. When I saw her car, I couldn't get that phone conversation out of my head.

"I know he's goin' to be there tonight, so I'll just let him know Keem came home a week early, so it's over! How could I have been such a fool to think she would've been faithful." We paid tha attendant then headed across tha street to tha club.

"Stacks what's up, Zoro is waitin' on you."

"Here you go Muhammad."

"Nigga put that Shit back in ya pocket." He let us in.

"Oh yeah, this my brother Keem." He extended his hand, which I shook and said, what's up.

As soon as we got in, we went to tha bar to get a drink. On our way upstairs, Stacks stopped to talk to some light-skin green eye dude.

"Stacks wat gon' My Youth?"

"I can't call it Zoro."

"Ery thing ivory?"

"Yeah, this my brother Keem."

"I heard lots bout you from ya bredren."

"All good, I hope."

"Nuttin but good. Ya jus come home, huh?"

"Yeah."

"Well, me want you ta drink free. Put dese pun ya wrist. So, Stacks, did ya tink bout wat me said?"

"Imma talk to my brother and let you know in a few days."

"His niece got tha city on lock wit tha weed. Tha price I give you; she'll have to buy from you."

"Give me a few days." We shook his hand and headed up to tha third floor.

"I would have never thought he was Jamaican."

"Me either, when I first saw him."

When I got upstairs tha first thing I saw was Lay talkin to some Jamaican dude. I could tell that tha conversation was tense. He brought her a drink then gave her a hug. *"That must be tha nigga she was talkin to Layla about."* I felt somebody grab my arm, when I turned around this pretty ass broad was asking me my name.

"Keem," I said smiling.

"Yo, here come Lay, Keem." I was so mad I didn't even give a Fuck.

"Excuse me, what's goin' on over here?"

When I didn't answer she grabbed my arm.

"I know you hear me talkin to you." I snatched my arm away.

"Don't start no Bullshit Lay!"

"You must be drunk," she said, now in my face.

"Yo Stacks, I'm goin' back downstairs." I started walking out.

"What's wrong wit you?"

"Go finish talkin to ya friend."

"Is this what's this about?"

"I should have known you couldn't be trusted."

"That's my peoples," Layla said, try'n to cover for her.

"Layla don't lie for her; I seen how they hugged. That was a hug as if you were ending a relationship or something. All I'm sayin' is you should've been done that and please don't grab me again." Stacks finally came down.

"What's goin' on?" he asked.

"Nothing was just about to get another drink," I said poppin' my other pill and drinkin' tha rest of my drink.

"Lay, go enjoy yaself, I'll see you at home."

"Just throw in the bag. See I know what Ima tell her. The same thing that the bank robber told the teller. Just throw it in the bag." Some broad grabbed me and headed to tha dance floor. While I was dancing, I could see Lay crying, but I didn't give a Fuck!

"I need to go to tha bathroom." Once in tha bathroom, I cried my eyes out.

"Damn Layla, he thinks I was messing wit Luddy."

"Tell him what it was really about then."

"I can't, he'll really be pissed."

"If he can't understand that you had to do what you had to do to make sure you, him, and tha kids were straight, then hey. I would rather him be mad about that then to think I was unfaithful. He'll probably be a'ight in tha morning. I'm riding back wit Stacks; we got a date." When we walked out of tha bathroom some Bitch was all in his face.

"Excuse me, can you buy me a Long Island?"

"No, he can't," tha broad said. He must of knew I was about to snap.

"Yo, that's my wife."

"Oh, My Fault, I thought you was lying when you said you was married."

"Well, he wasn't," I said wit an attitude.

"No need to get hostile." She didn't know I was about two seconds off her tall ass.

"Well, it was nice meeting you."

"Yeah, you too," he said wit his face frowned up.

"Did I mess ya play up?"

"Listen Lay, I would never disrespect you no matter what," he said looking me directly in my eyes.

"Baby I swear, it's not what..."

He cut me off by saying, "Listen, whatever it was it was. You held me down and truth be told that's all I could ask for."

Then he surprised me by say'n, "What y'all had is over, keep it that way."

"But Keem..." He shushed me by kissing me.

"Now go enjoy ya self," he told me, wiping my eyes.

"You just keep those bitches out ya face."

I couldn't be mad at Lay, during my bid, I'd seen a lot of broads roll out on niggaz after a few months. If tha shoe was on tha other foot, I would've probably done tha same shit.

Stacks let me know that I was riding back wit Lay. It was about 2 in tha morning and I was drunk and ready to leave.

"Yo, I'm ready to bounce."

"Me too. Let me find Layla and Lay."

"I'll be outside; I need some fresh air."

Shit, it was packed outside; I made my way over to tha parking lot and waited for them. After about 15 minutes I spotted them coming out.

"Listen Shorty, I don't mean no disrespect, but my wife is coming."

"Just tell her I'm an old friend," she said wit a smile that would melt a snowman in a blizzard.

When I heard tha alarm, I got into tha car leaving her standing there. She waved and went about her biz-ness.

"Yo, we going shopping in tha morning cause we don't do Black Label."

I just nodded my head and laid my seat back. Lay put on that dude Drake and had it crankin'. I must have fell asleep because Lay was tapping me on my arm saying, get up we home. I half walked half staggered into tha house. Lay headed to tha microwave to heat her food up while I went straight to tha bedroom. By tha time she was done, I was knocked out cold.

CHAPTER 4

Shoppin'

I woke up to tha smell of beef scrapple, French toast, scrambled eggs, and hash browns. I went into tha bathroom to brush my teeth and wash my face. I walked into tha kitchen where Lay was fixing our plates.

"Good morning, I was just about to wake you up," she said kissing me.

"How do you know I brushed my teeth?"

"Cause that's tha first thing you do when you get up." We sat down at tha table to eat.

I wasn't going to bring up what I saw last night at tha club.

"I love what you did to tha place," I said referring to tha house.

"Well, you know I always wanted chocolate furniture so when I saw this, I just had to have it." The living room and dining room was chocolate.

"We need a bigger house Lay. Niya and Nay need their own rooms."

"I thought you said when you get off probation."

"I did, but I was thinkin' instead of buying, why not get a house built from tha ground up. If we start now, then it will be done by tha time I'm done wit probation."

"I like tha sound of that."

"How much money do we actually have Lay?"

She stood up walked to tha bedroom and came back with an envelope that she handed to me. Right away I knew it was a bank statement. When I opened it up my eyes immediately got big.

"Is this right?"

"Yes, give or take another 300,000 that we just got this morning. Every time we hit wit tha stocks, tha broker puts it in tha bank. That way, if it crashes, we won't lose out on too much money."

"Lay that's very smart to do it like that, I guess that's why you have all this money."

"No, why we have all this money is because it was ya money that started it. We have enough money to last us a lifetime. After you see ya PO Monday, we can talk to a realtor and get tha ball rolling. Since we are doin this from tha ground up, I can build my dream house."

"How much do you plan on spending on this dream house, Lay?"

"Uhh, maybe a mill."

"A million dollars?"

"Yeah, you don't think that's enough?"

"Lay that's more than enough. Shit, for that much it better come wit a pool. Well, let me hop in tha shower."

I called Stacks to see what time has was coming and to make sure he was still giving me tha 4 bricks. Next, I called Jewlz to let him know I would holla at him within tha next 2 hours. I was looking through all my stuff try'n to find Diablo's number. Just when I was about to give up, I found it. I dialed tha numbers and waited for somebody to pick up.

"Ola (Hello)."

"May I speak to Diablo, please?"

"Speaking."

"Yo, this Keem."

"Oh Shit, what up Primo (Cousin)?"

"Ain't shit, jus checking in wit you."

"When you touch down?"

"Yesterday."

I got right down to biz-ness. By tha end of tha phone call, not only did I have better numbers, I also had a free 10 bricks which would be here later on today.

I jumped in tha shower and put on tha other set I had bought yesterday.

"I hope you and Stacks don't mind, but I'm going wit y'all."

It was all good cause Stacks pulled up wit Layla on tha passenger side. We climbed in tha back and made our way to King of Prussia.

"Shit, I forgot to call Jewlz." When I did, I let him know that I had something for him when I got back.

We let Lay and Layla go their way while we went ours. I fell in love wit Nieman Marcus; I knew from this moment on all I would wear would be Gucci, Prada, Louis Vuitton, and Ralph Lauren. When it was all said and done, I had spent all tha money Stacks had given me. We met back up wit Lay and Layla at tha Food Court.

"Damn, did you leave anything in tha stores?"

"Not in my size, I didn't. I even grabbed a few pairs of designer frames. I was never big on sunglasses, but Stacks talked me into buying them. I called Rachel to see if Paris could do my hair.

She said, "Yeah, what time?"

"I'm about to leave King of Prussia, so about an hour."

"A'ight, we'll be on 9th."

I only had six braids, so that wouldn't take me long to take out.

"Lay, you need to learn how to braid so I don't have to keep pay'n people to do my hair." I finally got my braids out.

Layla said, "Damn Keem, ya shit is long as a Mafucka. It didn't look that long when it was braided."

"That's because his ends curl all tha way up. If I practiced, I could probably learn how to do it."

"Keem has more than enough hair for you to practice wit."

While I was gett'n out my phone began to ring, but because I had my hands full, I couldn't answer it. Once I got inside and put my bags down, I pulled my phone out.

"Fuck!"

"Baby what's wrong?" As I was about to say that I missed an important call, my phone rang again.

"Hello."

"Ola (Hello)"

"Diablo, what's tha deal?"

"My primo (cousin) will meet you in 30 minutes at this place he calls K.F.C., sí (yes)."

"Sí (Yes)."

"You take that free of charge, you like, we do biz-ness."

"Gracias (Thank you) Diablo."

"De nada (You're welcome) Keem. We will make mucho (a lot) of money together; I have tha best purico (cocaine) in tha land by far."

"Diablo, I'll call you in a few days."

I called Stacks to let him know it was going down in 30 minutes. He told me about tha stash spot in tha car.

"Lay, I'm about to go get my hair done and see if I can get a shape up."

"I'm going to take a nap; I'm tired."

When I got to tha car, I did what Stacks told me to do and stash spot came open. I shut it back and pulled off, headed to K.F.C. Diablo's cousin was already there when I arrived. I nodded then went inside to order something to eat. After I got my food, I went back to my car. Diablo's cousin was gone and there was a Gap bag on tha passengers' side floor. I opened tha stash spot and put tha bag in closing it back. I called Jewlz to let him know to meet me on 10th & Madison.

I pulled over in back of Jewlz's car; he got out then got in my car.

"What's up Keem?"

"You got some work?"

"Nah, I was about to call my peeps when you called me."

"Well listen, I did tha math. If you cop 4 ½ every day, that means you pump 4 bricks a month."

"Damn, I neva thought about that." I opened tha stash spot.

"Grab 4 bricks outta there. Matter of fact make it 5. Hit me wit 120,000 and call ya folk and let him know he can cop off you from now on. That's new shit, so try it out. My peeps said it's tha best on tha east coast so you might be able to get 7 from tha 5. Once you do it, let me know."

I called Stacks, told him to meet me at 9th & Lombard. When I got over the eastside, Rachel and her crew were sittin' on Paris steps.

"We thought you changed ya mind."

"Nah, I had to get somethin' to eat."

"I BROKE BREAD WIT YOU I KEPT IT TOO REAL."

"Yo, I'm right here; go around tha block." I went and got tha Gap bag out tha car.

"Rach what's up?"

"Hey Stacks."

"Yo, this 5, let me know if it's really what he says it is."

"What's tha numbers?"

"Imma tell you when you hit me."

"What was in that bag?"

"He left his shirt in my car."

"Umm huh, yeah right."

"Paris you got sum rubber bands?"

"Yup, already got 'em. What am I doin?"

"You already know, ya favorite style."

"Damn Keem, ya hair is long as shit. Wow Brother, look like you got a weave-in."

"You got a lot of jokes."

"I'm just say'n cause ya hair is so long."

"EVERY DAY I'M HUSTLIN, EVERY DAY I'M HUSTLIN."

"What up Jewlz?"

"You said this Shit is tha best on tha east coast, right?"

"Yeah."

"Nah Keem, this Shit is tha best on tha planet! This Shit is so pure I put 36 on 36, brought it back to two and it's still top quality."

"Are you for real?"

"Yeah, Imma sell these for 36 apiece; all 10 of them. Imma hit you wit 200,000."

"Nah, just hit me wit 120,000 I ask for."

"Naw Keem, I gotta hit you wit tha 200."

"A'ight, just take ya time and be safe." When I hung up, Rach was just staring at me.

"I knew you were back at it."

"You better not tell Lay either."

"Brother, just be safe."

"Sis, I ain't doin shit; I'm jus tha nigga wit tha connect."

"So you spent 20,000 at Neiman Marcus?"

"Damn, ain't nobody tell you that but Lay."

"I called her to tell her to pick me up a shirt. When she got back, she told me when she woke up; she would drop tha shirt off."

"What that got to do wit me?"

"Because I asked her what you got, and she told me that you spent 20,000 on all that Gucci, Prada, Louis Vuitton, and Ralph Lauren shit."

"That was tha money I said I had yesterday. Plus, that's all I'm wearing this go-round." When Paris done, I paid her $20.00.

"I don't got no change."

"I wasn't look'n for none."

"Thanks. Brother, are you going to Doc B's party tonight?"

"Yeah, I gotta report to my P.O. Monday, so I'm goin ta party all weekend long."

"Where you going now?"

"I need a shape up. Here," I said handing her a couple hundred dollars.

"Unh, Unh, I'm cool."

"Rach ya brother home now, so you know Imma make sure you straight, no matter what."

"You always do. When you gon' let me drive that car?"

"When you get ya license."

"I got 'em," she said pulling them out.

"Why don't you have a car then?"

"I will when I get my taxes back."

"Ya taxes? That's about 6 months."

"So, as long as I get one."

"You work Monday?"

"No, I'm off."

"After I see my P.O., me and Lay gotta see a realtor."

"For what?"

"We gett'n a house built."

"Damn, you ain't play'n no games."

"They say if you got it, do it!"

"I know that's right."

"When I'm done that, me and you going car shoppin'. I don't want to hear Shit." Now I wasn't going to say nothing about that.

"I'll see ya later."

"Rach he been home 24 hours and he Fuckin' it up already."

"I just want him to be safe; you know they alwayz try'n to rob him."

"Shit, I wish I had a brother like that."

"Tha funny thing is, me and Keem aren't biological brother and sister, but you would never know. I use to mess wit his use to be friend Perk. And we been brother and sister since; 30 years plus. But I love him as if we came out tha same womb and he feels tha same way. He just left, now what he want? Hello."

"Rach, what's up wit Cream? He ask'n about you."

"Call him and give him my number; tell him to call his big brother."

"Imma call him now."

Since I didn't know Kyree's number, I decided to just go by there. Kyree was standing out front when I pulled up.

"Oh Shit, when you touch?"

"Yesterday, can I get hit up?"

"I was about to roll, but you know I got you." My phone went off as I was sitt'n in tha chair.

"Hello, who dis?"

"It's ya lil' brother."

"What up wit you Cream?"

"You know me, a little of this a little of that. How you want it Keem?"

"Just bring me back; don't cut my beard, just shape it up."

"You want some dye?"

"You know it."

"My fault Cream, I'm at tha barbershop try'n to get right for tonight."

"Oh, you goin' to Doc B's party?"

"So, you messin' wit them Timbs still?"

"Yeah, that's all I mess wit."

"What ya numbers like?"

"1,200 a pound."

"I might have a better number than that; give me a couple days."

"Let me finish wit this shape up and Imma come holla at you."

"A'ight."

"Damn Nigga you back at it already?"

"Shit don't stop Ky."

"I feel you on that."

"Do you still Fuck wit them Timbs?"

"You know it."

"What you pay'n?"

"1,200 a pound."

"I might have some better numbers and it's top of tha line exotic."

"Hit me up and let me know."

"Let me get ya number." He gave me his number and told me tha cut was on him.

On my way to holla at Cream, I called Stacks.

"What up, I was just about to call you. Where ya peeps get this Shit, Columbia?"

"I don't know."

"You can put a brick on a brick and it's still better than what my peeps got. You need to call him and tell him we locked in."

"I'll do that when I hang up. But I was callin' to ask, how much Zoro try'n ta charge?"

"Funny you ask that; I jus talk to him about that. He said if we get at least 100 pounds, we can get them at 500 apiece."

"Put a order in for 400."

"I'll do that as soon as we hang up. I already talk to Layla; she can keep doin' her thing; we gon' do out of town and a few in town."

"As far as my end, we can get them at 10,000 apiece."

"Keem, we about to be billionaires."

"You didn't tell Layla I was involved, did you?"

"Come on, now you disrespect'n me."

"My fault Big Homie. Stacks alwayz remember, 'Death B-4 Dishonor' and 'Trust is Ery Thing!' Those are tha codes we live by no matter what. This Shit is about to be in full swing."

I called Kyree to let him know I could let it go for 900 a pound and it's exotic. He said he would take 20 when I was ready. Since it was now 9 o'clock, I called Cream and let him know I want 900 but since he was my brother he could get 'em for 800.

"Are you serious Keem?"

"Dead serious."

"Well, when you ready, I need 40."

"I should be ready by Friday and I'll throw you another 40 but Imma need 36,000 for those."

"That ain't bout shit. Is tha weed good?"

"Yeah, it's exotic. I'm bout to get dress; I'll see you later."

"Ok."

"Cream, what you drivin?"

"I got a Crown Vic on 24's."

"Ok, I was makin' sure you had a whip. You do still got ya L's, right?"

"You betta know it. See you later."

I was pulling up at tha same time as Lay was.

"Damn Sexy, Imma have to watch you tonight. Where you comin' from?"

"I had to drop tha girls clothes off. Who cut ya hair?"

"I went to my barber."

"Kyree brought you back."

"Damn, you said that like I looked real bad."

"I didn't mean it like that, you know you alwayz look good no matter what. Ha! Ha!Ha!"

"What's so funny?"

"I remember tha time I came to see you and that lady asked me if you were Dominican."

"You act like that's ya first time hearing that."

"Who you going to tha party wit?"

"Like you don't know tha answer to that already."

"I don't know, maybe Jewlz and Beanz might be goin'."

"You know what, let me call him and see." Jewlz answered on tha second ring.

"What up?"

"You Fuckin' wit that party tonight?"

"Yeah."

"Well, I'll meet you there around 11:30."

"Keem, this is like ya debut so come wit that shit on."

"Nigga you talk'n to me not some noodle ass nigga! I know ya whole crew goin'."

"Yeah, I wasn't try'n to drive but me and Layla are tha only ones wit cars."

"Don't say Shit."

"What? I didn't say shit."

"You didn't have to; your face said it all. Hey, let me see what I'm going to wear."

"While you do that, I'm jumpin' in tha shower."

"Can I join you?"

"You don't need to ask me that."

Watching her get undressed and walk into tha bathroom, I knew we were going to be a minute.

Three orgasms and an hour later, we both were getting out tha shower.

"Baby which outfit do you think I should wear?"

I told her to put on tha brown Gucci dress wit tha Gucci sandals to match. I opted to wear tha brown linen Gucci Capris wit tha shirt to match and tha Gucci slip ons.

"Lay you look real good." She had her Gucci frames on wit her diamond necklace and bracelet that said 'Mrs. Bell'.

"Well, I'll see you later," she said giving me a kiss.

"Behave yaself," I said tappin' her on tha ass.

"I always do," she said walking out tha door.

Once I was dressed, I put on some Furdose and grabbed my shades. Stacks called to say he was out front. When I got out front Stacks was sitting in a white-on-white Aston Martin DBS on dueces.

"Damn, you wasn't Bullshit'n when you said you had a car for every day of tha week."

"This DSB is top of tha line."

"We gon' have a ball tonight."

"Jewlz and Beanz said they would meet us there."

"Damn, look how packed it is out here."

We pulled up in V.I.P. and let tha valet park tha car. Jewlz and Beanz was waiting on us at tha V.I.P. line.

"Oh Shit Bitch, when Keem come home? Damn, he's even sexier." Those were a few comments I heard while going in.

"Yo, let's take a few pictures first."

Lay and her crew were taking pictures when we got there. We took a few wit them then took some of our own. I took a few wit Lay and by myself.

"Here Baby, hold on to these for me."

"Keem, get in this picture wit us." I turned around to see who had said that and it was my daughter's mom.

"Nah, I'm good."

"So, you gon' act like that? How long you been home you ain't even called to check on ya daughter?"

"Damn, he just came home yesterday," Whitey said.

"I don't think I was talk'n to you."

"Look Shante, just give me ya number and I'll call you."

"Unh, Uhn, you can give me ya number, though."

"Look, I'm not goin' to play this game wit you."

"Ain't no game to play; you want to see ya daughter give me ya number." I could see Lay was gett'n pissed.

"Listen Shante, since that blood test came back, Hafiza has been well-taken care of so I hope you're not about to be petty."

"I appreciated everything you've done, but I just want Keem to be in Fiza's life."

"Check this out, here's my number cause I didn't come here tonight for this Bullshit!" I walked off, headed to get a drink.

- 49 -

"Beanz, did you bring those pills?"

"Yup, here," he said, handing me two.

"Do you be makin' a lot of money off these?"

"Yeah, but tha nigga I be deal'n wit only sells me 200 at a time for 5 dollars apiece. Keem, I run through 200 in like 2 of 3 hours."

"Damn, so you could sell like a 1,000 a day?"

"Definitely, maybe more."

"Imma see if I can get my hands on some of them for you." We all got our drinks, then walked to tha dance floor.

"You try'n to corner tha market, ain't you?"

"Stacks ain't no boundaries. Plus, I met a nigga from New York who said he has them by tha boatload. He told me if I got at least a 1,000, I could get 'em at $2.00 a pill. Beanz sells them for 15, I'll charge him $7.00 a pill so off every 1,000 we make 7,000 and he makes 8,000. That's an easy 140,000 a month just off pills. A lot of money to be made, so why not make it. We will not under any circumstances sell any heroin. We don't want or need that type of heat."

"I'm definitely wit you on that."

"Lay, look at all them Bitches in Keem's face."

"I'm not worried about that and neither is he; look at his face. I do know I'm going to end up beat'n that Bitch Ass again!" I said pointing to Shante, "look at her just watch'n him. Watch this," I said walking over to my husband grabbing his hand and dancin' wit him.

"Thank you."

"Why you thanking me?"

"Because you saved me from tha vultures. Bitches just don't respect a nigga being Fuckin' married!"

"When did they ever," I said while turning around to put all this ass on him.

"Lay, I think I'm goin' to deal wit Shante through tha courts. She's been stalk'n me all night."

"I know, cause I've been looking at her looking at you."

"Lay, we've been together for 15 years; married for 10 Don't they know by now we ain't goin' nowhere?" Her only response was to kiss me passionately.

"Hey, Hey, do that at home," Blondy said, "tha haters are really hating now."

"Good! Baby, I'm bout to get a drink; you want one?"

"Yeah, please."

"Blondy, walk me to tha bar."

While we were stand'n there Star, Big Head, Hov, Chulo, and Perk walked up.

"What up Jewlz?"

"What's up?"

"You, from what I hear."

"And what's that suppose to mean?"

"Word is, you got tha best coke since tha '70s."

"Oh yeah, that what's up."

Star asked, "What tha numbers look like on it?"

"Damn Nigga, what you wear'n a wire?" We all started laughing which made him mad.

"Jewlz don't disrespect me like that!"

"I'm just say'n, let's be real, you don't got no money."

"Damn Jewlz, Keem come home now you act'n brand new," Perk said.

"Hold up, let's get one thing straight. I wasn't Fuckin' wit you Niggaz before he came home. One thing about me, I ain't no Fake Ass Nigga like y'all!"

"What?"

"You heard me; you niggaz is fake. Every time I asked you Niggaz to give up 10 or 20 dollars toward a money order it was alwayz tha same story."

"Man, Keem didn't need no money."

"First off, you Niggaz don't know what I needed. And even if I didn't, it wouldn't have hurt to send it. Tha funny thing is, none of you came through that door my whole bid. So how can you be fucked up?"

It looked like they were having a heated conversation wit Hov and them. I walked up handed Keem his drink and just listened.

"That means you Niggaz is in tha way."

"We not fortunate enough to have a Mafucka give you nuffin," Star said, looking at Stacks.

"Nigga a Mafucka ain't give me Shit! Every Fuckin' thing I got, I bust my Ass for. When I went to jail, a nigga ain't have to do shit for me cause I had my own!"

Rach and her crew had walked over.

"Brother what's wrong?" I was so mad I ignored her and kept talking.

"Tha only people who kept it real and held me tha Fuck down was my wife, sister, brother, Jewlz, and Stacks," I said point'n to all of them, "Shit,

Beanz even sent me some flicks. Not because I needed it, because they knew I didn't, but because real people do real Shit!"

"We don't or didn't owe you Shit," Hov said.

"You right, you didn't and don't get it wrong; I ain't mad at y'all."

"Fuck you Nigga," Perk said.

Rach got mad and said, "Perk you so fake; you tha same Mafucka that said you couldn't wait til Keem came home so he could put you on!"

"Bitch mind ya Fuckin'!" Before he could get tha rest out, I punched him in tha mouth.

"Nigga if you ever disrespect my sister again, I promise you you'll be on a T-shirt!"

"You gonna wish you never did that," Star said stepping up.

"Nigga you don't got Shit to do wit it," Stacks said gett'n in his face.

"Stacks No!" Layla said hold'n him back.

"Get ya Dumb Ass over here!"

Star it's over, so get ya shit out my house. Now even though we got money, niggaz know we wouldn't hesitate to send a Mafucka to tha boneyard. Not to mention, Jewlz and Beanz were guns."

"Tha best thing to do is let it go before somebody gets hurt," Beanz said.

Two bouncers came over to see what all tha commotion was about.

"Everything cool over here, Stacks?"

"Yeah, P.J., Shit straight."

When they stepped off, Rach asked me why I hit Perk?

"He disrespected you."

"I would have put him in his place."

"Well, I did it for you."

"When this is over, why don't we all go out to eat. We going to tha Guards when we leave here."

"So are we," Lay said, "y'all not goin'?"

"Nah, I ain't doin' tha Guards. I'll be home when you get there."

"Boy, you gon' be sleep."

"Fuck it, let's go to tha Guards," Jewlz said.

"It's up to you Keem."

"If y'all really wanna go, I guess we can go."

After we left tha Chase, we went to tha Guards. We never got to go in because somebody started shooting. Next thing we knew there were police everywhere.

"Beanz said he thought it was Perk shoot'n in tha air."

"Do you think it was meant for me?"

"I don't know, but there's only one way to find out," Jewlz said pull'n out his phone.

"Yo, what tha Fuck was that about?"

"It wasn't about nothing."

"I hope it wasn't, cause you not ready or built for this."

"I'll be tha judge of that," Perk said and hung up.

"So, what did he say?"

"He said he'll be tha judge of that. That's him lett'n that Remy talk for him."

"You know what? Imma holla at him tomorrow when he sober up."

CHAPTER 5

Beat Down

"I'm not try'n ta hear that Shit! Get tha Fuck out!"

"You must be Fuckin' Stacks again!"

"If I am or not doesn't matter, I want you out!"

"So, you are Fuckin' that Bitch Ass Nigga!"

"You wasn't say'n that when he had you runnin' like Jesse Owens!"

"Fuck you and that Nigga! Do you got my money you owe me?"

"Since you want me to leave, I'm not givin' you Shit!"

"Oh, you gon' give me my money," I said pulling out my phone.

He tried to snatch my phone. When I pulled away, he smacked me.

"Imma kill you!" I ran into tha kitchen to get a knife.

"Oh Shit," he said ran out tha door.

I called Lay to let her know what had just happened.

"He did what?" (Click)

"Layla, let me hit you back."

Before I could say a word, she hung up.

"Keem!"

"Damn Baby, why you yellin'?"

"Where you at?"

"On my way to holla at Jewlz."

"You know that Mafucka put his hands-on Layla."

"Who?"

"Star, she just called crying say'n he smacked her."

"I'll handle it, don't worry about it."

I pulled up on 8th and it was packed. I spotted Jewlz talkin' to Blondy and Whitey, while Star, Hov, and Perk were standing on Bossy's steps. I got out, walked right pass Jewlz.

"Keem what up?"

"Hold on y'all somethin' about to go down."

I walked right up to Star and smacked tha shit out of him. He stumbled back.

"How does it feel to get smacked. Nigga if you ever put ya hands on Layla again I swear it will be..." He swung at me before I could finish my sentence.

"That's what I wanted you to do. Jewlz hold this," I said handing him my .40 cal. I caught him wit a right jab and it was a wrap after that. I beat tha shit out of him, literally.

"EEEL! He Shit on hisself!" Blondy screamed while laugh'n. Perk and Hov acted like they wanted to jump in it.

"Please don't do that," Jewlz kindly let them know wit my .40 in one hand and his .38 in tha other.

I was still stomping him when I heard Niya and Nay screaming daddy. Before I could say anything, they were kicking Star too.

"Niya, Nay get over here!" Jonda yelled, "Keem what is going on?" I didn't have to say shit because Lay and Layla were now standing on tha corner. Layla's lip was swollen.

"I know he didn't do that to ya lip," Jonda said, "I bet he won't do it no more." Hov and Perk helped him up then they walked up tha block.

"Is that shit on his leg?" (Ha! Ha! Ha!)

"He beat tha Shit out of Star." Everybody was bagging up.

"Next time you two better not do that Shit again. Do you understand me?"

"Yes."

"What did they do?"

"Girl, they ran over there when Keem was stomp'n him and joined in."

"Are you serious," Lay said laugh'n even harder now.

"It's not funny Laysha, anything could've happen."

"I just seen Daddy fighting so I ran to help him."

"Me too Mommy, I said boom right in his face," Niya said demonstrating wit her foot.

"Y'all heard what I said."

"My God child is something else," Blondy said smiling, "I wish I had a camcorder. Huh, I ain't neva seen nobody literally get shit beat out of 'em."

"It's a first time for ery thing."

CHAPTER 6

No Sweat

We dropped Niya off at daycare then headed to Cherry Lane so I could see my P.O.

"I want you to come in so when he calls me, you can see what he looks like."

I checked in and then went into tha waiting area. 15 minutes later my name was called, my P.O. was a female and she was bad as shit. She looked familiar but I couldn't put my finger on it.

"Mr. Bell you just did 3 years for trafficking cocaine, correct?"

"Yes."

"I'll be your officer for tha next year."

"Lindsey?"

"Excuse me," she said wit a puzzled look.

"Ya name, it's Lindsey, right?"

"Yes."

"Saturday night at tha Chase Center, my brother Stacks introduced us. I had 72 hours, so I wasn't out past curfew." She had a smile on her face then got up to close tha door.

"Stacks is my Baby; I've been dealing wit him for 2 ½ years. I know he does his thing, but I still love him," I sat there and listened while she talked, "all I ask is that you pay your fines and come see me every Monday. Can you piss right now?"

"Yes."

"I'm going to take your urine today that way; you can blow if you want. I'll also let you know when I'm going to send Safe Street to your house so you can be home. If you play your cards right, you'll be off in 6 or 7 months," I couldn't hold my smile back any longer, "let me go get a male officer to take your urine." After I gave up tha urine, I left.

"Damn, she must be a Bitch, you was in there damn near an hour."

"I had to give up some piss."

"Already?"

"Yeah, but you not goin' to believe this."

"What?"

"My P.O. is one of Stacks girls. She told me to just pay my fines; she said I'll be off in 6 or 7 months, tops."

"How did you know she mess wit Stacks?"

"I met her Saturday at tha Chase. When I first went in there, I kept try'n to remember where I saw her before then it dawned on me. Before we go see tha realtor, I need to stop by Layla's."

"Look at you, ready to smoke already."

"She said I could, that's why she took a urine. Plus, she said she'll tell me in advance when she needs another one so I can get my shit clean."

"Rach called you too. She probably just wanted to make sure we were still going car shopp'n. I told her you would call her when you came out, so make sure you call her." I pulled out phone to call.

"Damn, did you let tha phone ring?"

"Boy shut up; I was try'n to call Cream."

"I'm on my way to tha realtor's office; then I'll be to get you so we can grab you a hoopty."

"A'ight."

"I'll call you when I'm on my way."

"I know you not buy her a hoopty, for real."

"Yeah, she can find something nice for $2000."

"Yeah right, for that she better hope it makes it from A to B. I'm not say'n you have to spend 20 or 30,000, but you need to get her a dependable car."

We let tha realtor know what we wanted and how much we were willing to spend. He said it would not be a problem.

"Baby go to tha B.M.W. lot on ya way back in town."

When we pulled up Lay said, "They still got it."

"Got what Baby?"

"That navy blue 325I Wagon."

"You bout to get that?"

"No, you are for Rach."

"How much is that?"

"It was 10,000."

"I'm not spend'n no fuckin 10,000, I was only try'n to spend 5,000 at tha most."

"Boy, come on."

"Hello, may I help you wit something today?"

"Yes, how much is that 325 over there?"

"We were asking 10,000, but now we only want 8,000. It's all power, low miles, and one owner."

"We'll take it."

"We will?" I said running game, "why don't we just get tha Ford Focus; they only want 7,000. She doesn't need a B.M.W."

"Are you sure?"

"Yeah."

Tha salesman didn't want this sale to get away, so he said, "Hold on, let me talk to my boss," he left then came back, "my boss says tha lowest we can go is 7,500."

I knew he was lying, so I said, "Nah, we goin' wit tha Focus, but thank you for your time."

When we started walking away, he said, "Ok, he may chew me out, but for 7,000, it's yours." I smiled, knowing I just called his bluff.

While he was doing tha paperwork, he wanted to know if it was cash or check. Lay pulled out her checkbook and wrote tha check. Ery thing was in Rach's name.

"I'm going to shoot to Dunrite's to get some shoes on it."

"I'll be home but Imma get somethin' to eat, you hungry?"

"Yeah, just get me anything."

When I got to Dunrite's there was only one person in front of me. They said that I could only get a dub on it. When they finished, it look like a whole another car.

I called Rach to let her know I was on my way and she had to take me home since I already had her hoopty. She said she was in front of Paris's house. I called Cream to see if he were at tha crib so I could put the factory tires in the basement.

"Damn, this shit nice as shit. How much you pay for this?"

"They wanted 10,000, but I talked them down to 7,000 and I paid 2,000 for tha rims. Imma tell Rach I paid 12,000 for ery thing. That weed will be in Wednesday."

"I'm wait'n on you."

When I pulled up in front of Paris's house, I rolled tha window down.

"Are you just goin' to sit there?"

"Oh My God! Is this tha hoopty?"

"Yup."

"Brother, this is not a hoopty."

"Well, to me it is. I even tried to put some shoes on it to make it look like somethin'."

"And this is my car?"

"You see tha T-tag, don't you? Come on, you got me hold'n up traffic."

"Paris ride wit me."

"I'll pick it up in tha morning to get tha alarm and system hooked up."

"Brother I don't need no system."

"Sis you can't have shoes wit no music."

"Does tha factory work?"

"Yes."

"Well, I got music then. Stop at tha house so I can get a couple CDs."

She came out wit a handful of CDs. I was now in the back; I told Paris to get upfront.

"Why you get in tha back?"

"So all I have to do is get out and y'all can keep it movin." She put in a Meek Millz CD.

"Now imagine that in a system."

"This ride like a new car."

"UUGH, UUGH," I said clearin' my throat, "this is a new car, we got this from tha dealership. So, when you need an oil change, tune-up, or brakes, take it to tha dealer."

"If I got dealer money."

"If you don't, I do."

"Brother, you do too much for me as it is and you only been home 4 days."

"This for all tha collect calls you accepted while I was down."

"I did not accept ya calls for you to pay me back."

"I know, this is just tha love I have for you. Sis, you better not Fuck wit Perk either."

"I don't, he calls me from time to time."

"Change ya number then. All you got to do is call ery body and give 'em ya new number, unless you want to talk to that Sucker! Turn here."

"I know where you live."

"Excuse me."

"Oh, is ya P.O. cool?" I put her down with my P.O.

"Boy you lucky."

"I left a couple dollars in tha glove box for your insurance."

She opened it then said, "This is too much."

"No it ain't, pay that shit up for a year."

Lay came outside, "Damn Sis, I need to step my game up."

"Yeah right Lay."

"Oh yeah, she picked this out for you."

"Thanks Sis."

"You more than welcome."

"She all siked for her hoopty."

"Brother, this is not a hoopty."

"Tell him to stop disrespecting ya car Rach."

"It won't be no hoopty once I put that voice-activated system in."

"I knew what I had to ask you Brother. Did you beat tha Shit outta Star?"

"Sure did, ya nieces had tha nerve to stomp him."

"You lying."

"No he not," my sister said, "they saw their dad fighting and ran over there."

"I told them if they ever do that again I was gonna bust their asses."

"Yeah right, you ain't beat'n nothing."

"I know, but it sounded good. Well, I'll talk to you later and tell my nephew I'll be by to see him later."

"Yeah, cause he asked when you was coming by."

"And don't be having no whole bunch of people in ya car."

"Rach, tell him that is ya car."

"Hey, a flat gon' cost her 250.00. She can ride four deep."

"I know."

"He think he ya dad."

"Bye Sis, bye Paris."

"Bye Brother, Lay."

"Bye y'all."

"Rach, Keem love you like a mafucka. I would kill to have a brother like that."

"I know, I got 2 loving brothers."

"Cream said he about to have some Exotic."

"I know, he gettin' it Keem."

"When Keem do it, he do it."

"I just want him to be careful this time. That's why I'm glad he gett'n a house built out of tha city. Bitch guess how much his house cost?"

"100,000."

"Add another 900,000."

"Bitch a mill!"

"Yes."

"Oh, he hold'n if he spend'n that on a house. Not to mention, he just probably spent 20,000 on this car. You know he gonna put a hell of a system in here."

"I know."

"Bitch we roll'n now," Paris said giving her dap."

"Hi Haters!" they both said at tha same time.

My mom called to tell me she had already picked Nazir up from school.

"Mom, you have to see tha hoopty, as he calls it, that Keem brought me."

"Where are you at now?"

"Coming pass tha Gulf on Governor Printz."

"Come by tha house so I can see it then." We pulled up, my mom and Nasir were in tha backyard.

"Mommy that's a hot car, who car you driving?"

"It's mine, Uncle Keem bought it for me."

"Where Uncle Keem at, he ain't come to see me yet."

"He said to tell you he would be by later."

"He better, he ain't seen me since he been home." We all laughed; Nazir was 6 but thought he was somebody's dad.

"Rach, I like this, my mom said, Keem called this a hoopty?"

"Yeah, he said once he puts tha alarm and system in it that it won't be."

"He must of paid a couple dollars for it."

"12,000," Cream said coming out of tha house."

"How you know?"

"He told me; how else would I know? Mom you still need to use tha car?" Cream asked holding out his keys.

"Uncle Cream, you know we going food shoppin."

"Mom you taking Nazir wit you?"

"Yes. I have to go up Maryland Avenue to tha insurance company. Paris you gon' ride wit me?"

"Sure but run me by my house so I can give my daughter this money."

"Let me catch a ride wit y'all."

"Where's Jungle at?"

"Around tha corner. This ride good, I know I'll be pushing this."

Brenda, Kelly, and Shonda was sitting on tha corner when we pulled up.

"I know this ain't tha car Brother got you?" Kelly asked.

"Yes it is," I said getting out.

We were all girls, but Kelly was my best friend.

"I thought he said he was buying you a hoopty?"

"Bitch this a hoopty to him. Lay picked this out."

"He had tha nerve to call this a hoopty?"

"That's cause he drives a 850 and his wife drives an Audi A-4."

"You got a good point on that."

"Well, I don't care what he say, this ain't no hoopty."

"I know, tha system is ridiculous."

"I don't have one."

"Yeah right," Shonda said looking inside.

"He's gonna get it hooked up tomorrow morning."

"I wish I had somebody to buy me a car and do tha thing to it. Shit, I be bustin' my ass."

"Bitch you don't work so somebody doin' something for you," I thought to myself, "I'll be back, I need to pay my insurance."

"I'm surprised Keem didn't give you tha doe for that."

"Actually, he did, told me to pay it up for a year."

"Rach, let me ride wit you."

"Come on."

On our way, Paris said, "Shonda is a hater."

"Girl yes, don't want nobody to be doing better than her," Kelly added.

"That's just a shame, she's so miserable."

"She only comes around when she has somethin' new and try'n to show it off."

"Misery loves company!"

CHAPTER 7

Not Stop'n My Money

Everything came in today. We got 100 birds from Diablo, 400 pounds from Zoro, and 7000 E-pills from my man Tiger from New York. I want to meet things. Lucas you can dump a thousand a day is 7000 pills. Every Monday I'll hit you with 7,000 unless you knock them off before then. I want 7.00 a pill, you're gonna make 105,000 a week. I take 49,000 and you keep 56,000. So, you stand to make 224,000 a month. Is it fair enough for you?"

"Hell yeah, I'm gettin' dizzy just thinkin' bout all tha money I'm about to make. Keem, I'll be a millionaire in 4 months."

"There's only one thing, work off ya phone. Go buy another phone for your personal calls, use tha one you got for strictly biz-ness. Before I roll, remember we live by 2 codes. Death B-4 Dishonor (D.B.D) and Trust is Ery thing (T.I.E). Anything after that Fuck It!" I pulled off leaving him wit all tha pills.

I made sure we all had Stash Spots in cars, I even made Beanz and Jewlz get their L's. Next stop to tha barber shop to get wit Kyree.

"Damn, I thought you was bullshit'n when you didn't come through tha other day."

"Come on, you should no I don't play no games."

"You got 40 for me? I got some folk that need 20."

"I got what ever you need," I said pulling out 40 pounds.

"Shit, that thing stink and it's lime green. You can sell this shit for 2,500 a pound easy."

I put tha money in tha bag then let him know I would see him Friday for a cut. I pulled up off headed to holla at Jewlz. I hit him wit 10 birds, told him tha 2 codes, and kept it moving. My last stop was at my sister's house to holla at Cream. I also let him know about tha codes we lived by and that he needed to find someplace else to keep his weed cause Rach's house wasn't gonna work. I gave him 100 pounds instead of 80. I got wit my cousin from Fayetteville, North Carolina, he said that for 25,000 he could take 20 off my hands. But he also had folk in South Carolina who would take 20.

"Kin Folk if this Shit is what you say it is Imma need plenty more; I control tha whole N.C. My folk I deal wit charge 32,000 a pie, and I could turn you on to some other folk. Between me and my folk, we can rid you of 160 a month easy, especially at that number."

"Ok Smiley, let me know if it's a go which I know it will be."

Biz-ness was going much better than I expected. I even had a couple of cops on tha payroll just a insure that tha workers we had pumping tha little shit would be safe. My cousin had called back to let me know that everything was a go. I also let him know I would only deal wit him and that his peoples would go through him. Which he was cool wit because it made him tha man, not to mention, he was charging his folk 27,000.

I had just called Diablo to let him know I needed to increase my order.

"Ola (Hello) Keem."

"Ola (Hello) Diablo. I have a problem."

"No entiendo que pasa (I do not understand, what happened)?"

"Not a bad problem son solo negocios (only business)."

"Ai gracias a dios (Oh, Thank God)."

"I need more purico (cocaine)."

"How much more?"

"All together, I need 300."

"Whew."

"You can handle it, can't you?"

"Of course, I control tha purico (cocaine) on tha east and west coast. There's not an order I can't fill. Did you not think I was tellin' tha truth when we were in that place you call prison."

"I know you wouldn't lie to me Diablo, as you know I wouldn't lie to you!"

"Keem, I have something even better for you. How about I give you tha 300 you buy and throw in another 200?"

"Diablo, I need to be honest wit you, I know I can get rid of 300 but I don't know about 500."

"Keem, I also have a proposition for you. Do you think you can come to Miami for a few days? I'd rather discuss this face to face."

"I don't know if tha wife will go for that."

"Bring her and tha girls."

"Diablo, she doesn't know I'm back in tha game."

"All tha money you have been makin' in tha past 2 months and she doesn't know?"

"No she doesn't, and I'd like to keep it that way for now."

"Well, she knows how close we were in tha prison; I'm sure you can think of something."

"Let me talk to her, I'll call you later."

"Bring ya brother and tha other 2, I'd like to meet your team."

I called Stacks, Jewlz, and Beanz to let them know we would be going to Miami in 3 days on biz-ness.

That night while we were eating dinner, I asked Lay if she wanted to go to Miami.

"Go to Miami for what?"

"Diablo called and wanted me to bring you and tha kids down to his place for a few days."

"What about your PO?"

"I don't have to see her for 2 weeks. You'll be Ok because Layla, Whitney, and Maxi are going too."

She looked at me then asked, "Keem are you back in tha game?"

"No, why you ask me that?"

"Why would Stacks, Jewlz, and Beanz be going to Miami wit us?"

"I'm not goin' to lie, Stacks asked me to introduce him to Diablo. Diablo sells a lot of cocaine so why not hook him up wit my peoples. Especially, if it could take him to tha next level."

"So, this is a biz-ness trip?"

"Not for me."

"Well, when are we leaving?"

"Monday morning."

I called Diablo to let him know that everything was a go and we would be there Monday. He said he would have a few cars at tha airport waiting.

CHAPTER 8

Miami

When we arrived in Miami it was warm for it to be November. "Damn y'all, just imagine how it feels in tha spring and summer if it feels like this now."

"Baggage claim is this way," Maxi said point'n to tha sign.

Whitney had brought her kids so that Niya and Nay could have some kids to play wit.

Once we had our luggage we headed outside where we were met by signs that read "KEEM". We put our bags in tha trunk then pulled off heading to Diablo's.

15 minutes later, we were pull'n up to this mansion.

"Wow! Look at this big house, Daddy. Who's house is this?"

"It's a friend of mines."

When we got to tha end of tha driveway we were greeted by 2 armed men and a few house maids. Tha ladies and children were ushered into tha house while we were patted down.

"Mr. Diablo is waiting for you by tha pool."

"Wow Lay this one hell of a house," Maxi said. We were showed to our rooms that we would be staying in, tha kids shared a room.

"When you get settled in, you can join them pool side."

"OOOOH Mommy, can we go swimming, Pleeese? Pleeeease can we Mommy?" Niya asked. I wanted to say no, but how could I resist those puppy dog eyes.

It was 79 degrees but tha humidity made it feel much hotter. It's a good thing Diablo told us to pack our swimsuits. They said tha temperature never drops below 60 degrees here. We went out tha pool and tha fellas waved us over.

Diablo, this is my wife Laysha."

"You can call me Lay though."

"Keem tha girls wanted to go swimming."

"They can swim wit my grandkids."

"Niya can't swim by herself."

"She can get into tha little pool."

After all tha introductions were done, we went to where his wife and daughter were so they could talk. Before I walked off, I gave Keem a serious look that Diablo caught.

"Lay you have nothing to worry about," Diablo said smiling.

"Oh, you caught that, huh? Women, you know they only want tha best for us."

"Let's get to tha reason I asked you to come. I have a small problem that I could easily handle on my own, but I want to see where we stand."

"Diablo you should already know where we stand. We were cell mates for 18 months; for tha first 3 we didn't even speak to one another."

"My Friend, that's because we were feeling each other out."

I was never one to beat around tha bush, so I asked, "Who do you want us to kill?"

He pulled a briefcase from under tha table and sat in front of us. Placing 2 photos on tha table.

Diablo said, "These 2 men are tha Jimanez Brothers. They control tha 10 percent of tha purico (cocaine) that I don't. Now, don't get me wrong, I have no problem wit that but when you start try'n to take over my territories then I have a problem." He gave us all tha information we needed on them.

"Don't worry, they'll be distant memories by tha end of tha week."

"Well, tonight we party and have a good time."

Diablo had a stable of cars, he let us know we could drive any one we wanted. I decided to take Lay and tha girls out to sightsee and to also do a little shopping.

"Daddy can we stay and play wit Marisol and Madi?"

"No."

"Pleeease, Pleeease Daddy!"

"You guys go ahead, they'll be fine."

"A'ight but you better behave and listen; do you hear me?"

"Yes Daddy."

"We will Daddy," Niya added just for good measure. I couldn't help but laugh.

"Lay your daughters are something else."

"Oh, so now they my daughters?" Since we all were going out, we decided to to take two cars tha Rolls Royce and tha Bentley.

After sightseeing for more than an hour I was ready to do some shopping. To my surprise they had a Gucci store. I grabbed everything in my size that I didn't already have. They had a Gucci store for kids, Lay went berserk, she got tha girls damn near tha whole store. She even picked them up a few pair of Gucci shades.

"Baby we gon' have to come up here once a month. Before you say anything, tha clerk said they get a new shipment in once a month."

"I'm not going to be flying here once a month just for that."

"Well, I'll come by myself then. Miss, excuse me."

"Yes."

"Is there any way we could set up an account and you can just send us all tha things in their size? We're not from here, so it would really be great if you could help us out."

"How about if you give us your number, then when it comes in, we can let you know how much it is and do it over tha phone."

"Baby do you think it would be easier to get Diablo to do it for us?"

"Did you just say Diablo?"

"Yes, that's my tio (uncle)."

"Why didn't you say that this is his store?" I pulled out my phone and dialed his number.

"Ola (Hello)"

"Why didn't you say you owned a Gucci store?"

"I didn't think it was of importance."

After I explained it all to him, he told me not to worry about it and that dinner would be ready in tha next hour.

We met up wit everybody else.

"Leave it to y'all to buy out tha stores."

"Come on, Diablo said dinner would be ready soon."

"Good, cause I'm starving," Jewlz said.

"I need to smoke me a blunt Fuck dat."

"Now you talk'n my language," Maxi said, "did anybody bring some smoke?"

"Hell Nah, I wasn't bring'n no weed on no plane," Beanz said.

"I know that's right," everybody said agreeing wit him.

"Shit, I'll be tha only one smoking then cause I bought me some weed."

"Me too," Lay said wit a smile.

"Great minds think alike," I said givin my baby dap, "well, I suggest y'all ask Diablo where y'all can get some weed at cause me and Lay tha only ones smokin this good weed we got."

When we got back to tha house we put our bags up and got ready for dinner but not before we stepped out on tha balcony to smoke a blunt. By tha time we came down everybody was already seated at tha table.

"Nice of you to join us," Diablo said wit a huge smile, "that must be top of tha line weed you smoke?"

"Why do you say that?"

"Even though you were on tha balcony I could still smell it."

"That's because you have tha nose of a bloodhound," his wife said. We made small talk as we ate dinner.

"Let us all get ready so we can go out."

"Niya, Nay come on so y'all can get bathed and ready for bed."

"Awe Mommy, we wanted to finish playing."

Diablo said, "Well then, you get a bath and go play."

"Yeah, Yeah Tio (Uncle), you tha best," Nay said.

"See Daddy, I know Spanish too." I looked at Diablo who winked at me.

"You keep spoiling them like that they're going to want to come here all the time."

"They're welcome anytime they want to visit."

We headed upstairs to get showered and changed. While we were gett'n dressed Layla knocked on tha door.

"Who is it?"

"It's Layla, can I come in for a sec?"

"Come in."

"Look, I need to get high so let me buy some weed from one of y'all!"

"You must've thought we were play'n, I can't speak for Keem but I ain't selling Shit."

"Me either," I said from tha bathroom.

"Now get out so I can get dressed."

"Fine, I'll just ask Diablo."

"We told you that from tha jump." Everybody met up in tha foyer ready to have a night of fun.

"Let's go have some fun."

We pulled up to this club called Images, and tha line was all tha way around tha corner.

"Damn, this must be tha place to be." Tha valets parked tha cars and we made our way to tha front of tha line.

"Hello Mr. D, nice to see you tonight," tha bouncer said lifting up tha rope.

We were met by tha sounds of Rick Ross Maybach music. Diablo was like a local celebrity, an icon so to speak. Everyone was sending bottles to tha table, even tha Jimanez Brothers sent a bottle.

"They think I don't know what they're try'n to do," he said wit a fake smile tipping his glass to them. We partied and had a ball for tha rest of tha night.

By tha end of tha night, everybody was drunk, except me. When I saw tha Jimanez Brothers I stayed on my P's and Q's. When we got home, I couldn't sleep, so I went to tha study to go over tha information on tha Jimanez Brothers again. It was 2 in tha morning and I decided to go for a drive to clear my head. I decided to take matters into my own hands. I got out of tha car, walked up to tha door, and rang tha bell. After a few seconds, I could hear footsteps approaching.

"Can I help you?"

"Yes you can."

Spit, Spit, Spit, Spit, four shots to tha face, he was dead before he hit tha floor.

I left as quietly as I came. Thanks to tha silencer, nobody heard a thing. I pulled over to use tha payphone.

"911."

"Yes, I'd like to report a murder at 1514 South Haven." Before they could ask anything, I hung up, then headed to my next destination.

There was a small light on in tha front room. I crept around tha house looking in tha windows making sure no one was downstairs. When I was sure it was safe, I cut tha alarm and made my way inside. When I got to tha top of tha steps, I could hear tha soft moans of a woman. I eased my way down tha hall until I got to where tha moans were coming from. I pulled my gun out and slid in tha room. I didn't say a word, I just stood there while he banged this chick doggy style. When I'd seen enough, I cleared my throat causing them both to jump.

"Who tha Fuck are you and how did you get in!"

"Now, Now, is that anyway to talk to a man wit a gun pointed at you?" I cocked the gun.

"Whoo, Whoo? Is it money or drugs you want?"

Before I could answer, he was telling me where everything was at. I thought why not, get some free money and drugs. I pulled out a big hunting knife and threw it to tha broad.

"Pick tha knife up Shawty." When she didn't pick it up, I pointed tha gun at her.

"Bitch, I'm not going to ask again!"

Once she picked tha knife up, I told her to stab him in tha chest repeatedly. She hesitated until I aimed my pistol at her, then she stabbed him over 50 times. She must of had a flashback about something that happened to her tha way she stabbed him and screamed, "I hate you, I hate you! Die Mafucka Die!" I pulled out a .380, handed it to her then told her to shoot herself in tha head.

"Please don't make me do this. I won't tell, I swear."

"Either you can do it or I can." POP! That shot killed her instantly.

I made my way downstairs to retrieve tha money and drugs and got outta there. I could hear tha sirens in tha distance getting closer so I hopped a few fences and came out on tha other side. When I got back to tha mansion everybody was still sleep, so I thought. I left tha duffle bags in tha trunk and went inside. I climbed in tha bed trying not to wake Lay.

"Where have you been for tha past 2 hours?"

"Huh."

"You heard me," she said sitting up.

"I took a long drive to think about some things."

"So, you thinking about getting back in huh?"

"No, I was thinking about us gett'n a summer house up here."

"I was thinking tha same Shit."

"I saw a few places for sale." She scooted into me then told me she love me.

"I love you more."

"I doubt it."A few hours later Lay woke me up to get ready for breakfast.

"Diablo, anything interesting in that paper?"

"You're not going to believe this," he said lowering his paper.

"Believe what?" I asked.

"Tha Jimanez Brothers were killed last night. One brother was shot 4 times in tha face and tha other brother's death was a homicide-suicide. Apparently, his girlfriend had stabbed him 50 times then shot herself in tha head. Tha neighbors say they heard her screaming she hated him and to die; then they heard a single shot.

After breakfast, I went into tha study to talk to Diablo.

"Couldn't sleep last night so I took care of that biz-ness myself."

"That was you? No way."

"Yes way," and I told him all about it, "oh yeah, I'll be right back." I left and came back wit tha 2 duffle bags I left in tha trunk.

"Damn that really was you; close tha door." There was 100 bricks in one bag and 1.2 mill in tha other.

"We can split this down tha middle."

"Nah Keem, this is all yours. Don't worry about getting it back, I'll handle that for you and you now get them for 8,000 a pie." Tha next few days flew by before we knew it it was time to head home.

While we were at tha airport waiting to board Stacks asked, "That was your work on tha Jimanez Brothers, wasn't it?" My silence gave him tha answer he was looking for. We all boarded tha plane and headed back to Delaware.

CHAPTER 9

Tha Meetin'

"Stacks we need to hold a meeting wit all tha Capo's from each side of town. Diablo has dropped tha price to 8,000."

"That's definitely what's up, that'll save us a mill on tha 500."

"Actually, I was thinking to up tha order to 600 since we were goin' to hit all tha Capo's off."

"Shit, I feel like Pablo Escobar."

"This ain't even half of what he was dumping."

"I'll make a few calls and put ery thing in motion."

"You do that then hit me wit tha details."

Beanz called to tell me he needed some more pills. He was selling them faster than we could get them. He was selling damn near 2,000 a day and my man Tiger couldn't fill tha order. It's time to find a better plug. I called Cream to see if Jungles people could handle my order. He said he will call me back in about 30 minutes. I had decided to let Cream run tha weed, especially since Layla decided to retire out of tha game.

45 minutes later, Cream was calling me to say that Jungles people said that since we were buying so many, we could get them at $1 a pill. So, I decided to double tha order since we normally pay $2 a pill. I also let him know I wanted to meet this dude; I wasn't down wit tha middleman Shit! He set up a meetin' wit him for later that evening.

Stacks finally called to let me know to meet him at tha Clubhouse in 30 minutes. Tha Clubhouse was a restaurant where we went to discuss business of importance. When I walked in almost all tha Capo's were there. Tha ones who were not said they weren't interested in doing biz-ness wit us. Lil'

Tony from tha Hill was there, as well as Cheeze from Eastside, Casy from River, K.K. from 27th, Gunner from 22nd, Blaze from 30th, Yung Roco from 7th, and Praz from 5th.

"I have asked you all here to offer you a better price, as well as quality than you are getting now."

"It's a recession and I'm pay'n 32,000 a brick," Casy said. Everybody was paying between 31,000 and 35,000 a brick.

"Well, clearly that's too much, I can give you a price of 28,000." Tha look on their faces said it all.

"I'll even give each of you a brick free of charge to test tha product out. If you like it then get wit Stacks and tha ones who chose not to come they won't be able to jump aboard. They had their chance; they chose not to come their loss your gain."

When tha meeting was over everybody was given a brick. As I was getting into my car Cream called.

"What up Lil Bro, where you at?"

"Leaving tha Clubhouse, meet me at Rachel's."

"A'ight, I'll be there in 15 minutes."

20 minutes later, I was pulling up to my sister's house.

"We gotta go talk to Jungle's peoples."

"I'm riding wit you," I said. "Let's go then, we're meetin him at tha tattoo shop across from KFC."

"Is he gonna have tha work?"

"I don't know?"

"Hold up, let me grab tha money out my car just in case he does."

We walked in to find Jungle talkin to some Spanish chick.

"Cream, Keem, what tha biz is?"

"Always money wit me," I said wit a smile.

"Well, I'd like you to meet Nadia."

"Ola (Hello) Nadia."

"Al Dios Mio (Oh My God) you speak Spanish?

"Si (Yes), My Tio (uncle) is Spanish."

"I thought you were Dominican?"

"Jungle is this ya girl?" (Ha! Ha! Ha!) They both laughed.

"Did I miss tha joke? I asked smiling.

"This is my peeps wit tha e-pills."

"Oh, I'm sorry, I didn't mean to disrespect."

"No papi you good.

"Well, can we talk son solo negocios nada (only business nothing personal).

"Si (Yes).

"I'll holla at you once a month. Can you handle 112,000?"

"Al Dios Mio (Oh My God)."

"Is that too much?"

"No, and since you buy so many you get them at $1 a pill."

"I have tha money wit me."

"Let me make a call, I only was told you wanted 28,000. I can have tha rest here wit in a half hour."

"Fine, I might as well get a tattoo while I wait. Shane you busy?"

"Never for you Keem."

"I want 2 tattoos, both on my face." Everybody looked at me like I was crazy.

I told him what I wanted and where.

"$80."

"Tha price ain't about nothing."

It took him less than 15 minutes. When I looked in tha mirror I was pleased.

"Shane, let me get tha same thing," Cream said.

While he was doing that, me and Nadia conducted biz-ness. She gave me her number and I did tha same. After I was finished wit Nadia, I walked across tha street to get something to eat.

"Yo Keem, you ready? Cause I got to handle some biz-ness."

"They ain't goin' nowhere, they need what you got."

"I know, I just like to knock 'em off as they call."

"That's all fine and dandy but work at your pace not theirs. Trust me, it's better to be long-winded than to rush. Cream let me ask you a question. If they don't get it from you, who are they gonna get it from?" He shrugged his shoulders.

"Nobody, you know why? I'll tell you because you got tha best weed and price in tha city. I said all that to say, now why rush?"

I thought about everything Keem said and he's absolutely right. It was no doubt in my mind that after this conversation I would be doing things differently for sure.

"Keem, not to be in ya biz-ness."

"Then don't be. Nah, I'm jus fuckin' wit you, so don't go getting in ya baby feelings."

"Nigga I ain't worried about that cause I was gonna ask anyway."

"Ask away then, even though I know what you want to know."

"What do I want to know Big Brother?"

"112,000."

"Huh?"

"112000 e-pills is what I got from Nadia."

"Wow! You wanted to make sure you was good for a few months, I see." (Ha Ha Ha)

"No, that's just for a month."

"Damn, y'all dumpin' them things like that?"

"We dumpin' ery thing like that."

"At this rate, you'll reach millionaire status in no time."

"Stop disrespecting me Cream, I came home to that."

"Yeah, thanks to Lay."

"I never said it wasn't; I jus said I came home to it." "Before you get out, answer me this."

"I'm all ears."

"How did you know Lay was tha one?"

"Sometimes you jus do and when you find that best friend/soulmate you better hold on. Why you ask that? Don't tell me you thinkin' bout putt'n a ring on Keesha's finger?"

"Nah, I was just wondering why I can't be faithful to her."

"When I use to cheat on Lay, I don't know why I did it; I honestly don't. But when I realized that I didn't need any other woman but her, I stopped immediately!"

"So, you haven't cheated on her since?"

"Hell No! Listen Lay loves me to death. She's put up wit my cheating, she was my co-defendant, not to mention I had Fiza on her, and she's still wit me."

"Enough said Big Brother."

"You'll know," I said getting out tha car.

CHAPTER 10

Shit Don't Stop

"What up Star?"

"I can't call it Perk."

"You got some money?

"What kind of money you talkin' about?"

"Re-up money Nigga! My cousin got some good coke and numbers."

"I only got 1,800."

"That's all you need, I got about tha same. That will get us 4 ½ all day."

"Where we gon' dump it, on 8th?"

"Nah, Jewlz got it on lock over there. I was think'n we move out down Maryland. I got some folk in Salisbury. He told me to come down and get some paper."

"Fuck going down there wit only 4 ½!"

"So, what you want wait until we get more, then go down?"

"Nah, we gon' jam Jewlz for a brick."

"Tell him we need a brick when we go meet him; Imma put out on him. Easy as 1, 2, 3." He pulled his phone out and dialed Jewlz number.

"Yo, what up Jewlz?"

"Who dis?"

"It's Perk, you got some work?"

"What kind of work you talkin' about?"

"How much you want for a bird?"

"Did I just hear him right; they must all be putt'n in for this."

"For you 25,000."

"We only got 24,000."

"I knew they were all putt'n in."

"A'ight, just hit me back wit tha stack. Imma have my young boy meet you at Thriftway in a half."

"You know it's hot down there; tell him to come to 10th and Madison."

"Ok, be there in a half."

When I hung up, I let Star know this would be easier than we thought since Jewlz was sending his young boy. 10 minutes later my phone was ringing.

"Yo."

"He'll be in a black Caprice."

"A'ight, let him know I'll be in a blue Taurus."

"Perks."

"Yeah."

"Don't have him waiting!"

"I wont."

25 minutes later, I was pulling up to 10th and Madison. I let Star out in tha middle of tha block so he could get in position. When I saw tha black Caprice pull up I stayed at my car so he could walk to my car. After a couple minutes, he finally got out wit a Prada bag in his hand.

As soon as he got in he said, "Next time walk to my car."

"Just let me see tha work."

"You got tha money?"

"I got tha money, let me see tha work."

He handed me tha bag, once I saw that tha brick was there I nodded my head. On my signal Star came to tha car.

"Yo, let me get that change so I can bounce."

"You gon' bounce but you ain't gettin' no doe," Star said gettin' in wit his pistol pointed in tha young boys face."

"What tha Fuck is going on?!"

"Ain't Shit goin' on, you gon' get tha Fuck outta this car."

"Not wit out tha money!" (SMACK) Star smacked him in tha head wit tha butt of his pistol.

"Now either get tha Fuck out or get shot!" As soon as he got out I pulled off.

"Jewlz, Jewlz! Them Mafucka's robbed me!"

"Who?"

"Perk and Star."

"Where you at now?"

"I'm about to go to tha hospital. I think I need stitches; my shit is leaking bad."

"Is that you stand'n by tha pole?"

"Yeah." When I got over there to where Dump was I saw all tha blood on his shirt.

"This is all my fault Dump."

"Nah, if it wasn't me then it would've been you or somebody else."

"Imma kill those niggaz! Go to tha hospital and hit me when you get out of there."

"A'ight."

I called my cousin in Maryland to let him know we were on our way down. "Aye Perk, before we hit tha highway, shoot through Riverside."

"Why, what's over there?"

"I need to holla at Casey real quick. Stop right here, there he go on tha green box. Casey!" He look in my direction then got up.

"What tha biz is Star?"

"Yo, you got that for me yet?"

"Yeah I do," he said going into his pocket, "how much 1 owe you anyway?"

"2,500."

"I only got about 1,800 on me."

"That'll be good, I'll get tha rest at a later date."

An hour later we were in Maryland.

"Did you call ya peeps to let him know we were here?"

"I'm bout to do that now...Yo Rolo we here. What's tha address? Ok, we'll be there in a sec. (Click) Star at tha light make a right then a left. Now go down 3 blocks and make a left. Once you do that, at tha next corner make another left." He did all that and just like Rolo said they were sitting on these steps.

"Park down there," I said pointing to an open spot in tha middle of tha block.

"Damn, what up Cousin?"

"Shit, just try'n to get at a dollar."

"I can feel you on that fo' sho. It must be hot up ya end for you to come down this end."

"Yeah, they doin' that Operation Fed shit. Yo, this my ace Star."
"What up Homey?"

"Yo what up?"

"Perk, you remember Plot and tha Twins?"

"Yeah, what's tha deal?"

"Did you bring some shit wit you?" I gave him a look.

"Of course you did"

"We brought down a brick."

"Damn, you doin' ya thing up top, ain't you?"

"Just enough not to be broke."

"We be deal'n wit this kid named Grams. His work be proper, he got all tha weight around here."

"When we dump this, we probably holla at him; save us a trip up top."

"I'll introduce y'all to him later tonight at tha club."

Meanwhile in Wilmington...

"Where tha Fuck is Star and Perk?"

"Jewlz, I don't know. I haven't seen or talked to them in 2 weeks."

"Hov if I find out you lying so help me God."

"Listen, I don't know what they've done, but I didn't have Shit to do wit it."

"If they should contact you, call me."

"Hey Beans, meet me on tha block in about 10 minutes."

"I'm already here."

"Who out there?"

"Big Head and Chulo."

"Don't let 'em leave."

"Gotcha."

When I got there, they were still standing on tha corner.

"Yo let me holla at y'all for a second."

"What up Jewlz?"

"What's up wit Perk and Star?"

"What you mean what's up wit 'em?"

"Where tha Fuck dey at?"

"Why tha Fuck you askin' us?" Chulo asked.

"Mafucka because I can," I said pulling out my .40 cal, "now where tha Fuck are they?"

"We don't know and put that gun away."

"If you talk to either of them, give 'em a message for me. Tell 'em to pick out a headstone."

Back down Maryland...

"Damn Cousin, that Shit y'all got is top-notch."

"I know, they go crazy for this Shit up top, too."

"It might be better to go up there to cop."

"Maybe, but tha risk ain't worth it."

"We bout to shoot to tha mall to grab somethin' to wear."

"Y'all go ahead, Imma stay out here and get this money. Perk grab me up somethin' to wear for tonight."

"I got you."

"Don't get me no bullshit either."

"Come on Dog, don't disrespect me like that."

Over the next couple of months, we had gotten real cool wit Grams. So, we started watching and plotting on him. Within three weeks we had his whole routine down packed.

"Perk, I know this nigga gotta be holdin'."

"I know, and he's so certain that he won't get robbed that he keeps his money at his house."

Tonight, was tha night that we would find out how much Grams was really worth. He must have made a lot of money cause they partying really hard tonight. It's 3 in tha morning I'm about to say fuck it and try tomorrow. Just as we started to leave, they came staggering out. Once they were in tha car we pulled off behind them. They stopped at a few of his stash houses to collect some money.

"It's about fuckin' time," I said when he dropped Flynn off.

Since I knew where he lived, I floored it to his house so we could get tha drop on Grams.

"He's pulling up now. Remember as soon as he opens tha door we rush him."

When Grams got to tha door he couldn't get tha key in tha lock. When he did, I was on his ass like a thong on a model.

"Don't try nothing stupid and you might live to see another day! Now punch in ya code to disable tha alarm." When he didn't do, it I hit him in his mouth wit tha in butt of tha gun.

"AAAGH SHIIIT!"

"Now punch in tha code!" Once he did, I tied him to tha chair.

"Now I'm not gonna ask this question too many times. Where's tha money?"

"I don't know what you're talkin' about." (SMACK)

"Wrong answer," I said screwing on tha silencer.

"Look, y'all wasting ya time." (SSPT, SSPT) 2 shots to both kneecaps; had him cry'n like a newborn baby.

"Go upstairs and search every room. So, you don't want to tell me where tha money is?" When he didn't say anything, I shot him in tha shoulder.

"AAGH FUCK! I'm gonna kill you! AAGH FUCK!"

"Nigga you ain't gonna do a Mafuckin' thing! (SMACK) Bitch Ass Nigga if you don't start talkin' you won't make it pass tonight." I didn't plan on letting him live anyway.

"Yo ain't Shit up there, I tore all tha rooms up."

I looked at Grams who had a smirk on his face. (SSPT, SSPT) 2 more shots to his legs.

"Not smirking now, are you?"

"UUGH, UUGH, Ok, Ok I'll tell you."

"I'm listening."

"Downstairs in tha basement."

"Ok, where in tha basement?"

"Behind tha bookshelf." I nodded to Perk to check it out.

"If you're lying tha next shots will be in your head."

Perk yelled up, "What's tha combination?!"

"You heard that man."

"42-13-6." I yelled down tha combination that he had just given me.

"Holy Mother of God!"

"Is everything a'ight down there?"

"Hell Yeah! This nigga is holdin' like a Mafucka."

"Damn, I should have told 'em about tha dummy safe. 500,000 would

have been more than enough to make them happy," Grams thought to himself.

"Smart man, I thought you were going to try and give us a dummy safe."

"Damn, glad I didn't. Now I can live and find out who these niggaz are."

"We need more duffle bags; this one is not enough."

"Well, unfortunately for you Mr. Grams your end is near," I said pointing my gun at his stomach. (SSPT, SSPT, SSPT, SSPT) Grams fell over on tha floor. I went downstairs to help Perk load tha rest of tha money in tha bags.

"I kept slipping in and out of consciousness, please don't let me die. When I heard them coming upstairs, I laid as still as I could."

"Come on Star, let's get out of here."

"Damn Nigga, why are you sayin my name asshole?"

"That nigga dead as a Mafucka." I came to just in time to hear Stars name.

"Oh God, please don't let me die. I swear both of those two niggaz gonna die."

We dumped all tha money on tha bed and started to count it. "This is gonna take all morning to count."

"I don't have shit else to do."

"Neither do I, I'm just say'n."

"Nigga you ain't say'n shit, start counting."

When we finally finished it was 11 in tha morning. I was tired as shit and 600,000 richer after we split it 50/50.

CHAPTER 11

Talkin' Shit

"Hey Aunty."

"Hey Layla. Lay I was thinkin' about opening up a hair salon."

"Oh really?"

"Yeah, I want to invest my money in something I can turn a profit wit."

"You should invest in some stock."

"You still got ya money invested in stock?"

"Yup, and still gettin' paid off it. Have you talked to Maxi?"

"No not today. You know she got her lawsuit back this morning."

"That's what's up, she probably up top shoppin'."

"MMM."

"So, have you talk to Luddy lately?"

"No, not since that night at tha club. What about you?"

"I talked to him last night; he called me to see how I was doing. He did ask me how you were doing."

"There go Maxi right there," she said pointing to tha Grand Marquis that just pulled up.

"Hey y'all."

"Hey Maxi."

"Lay, I got that 200 I owe you."

"That's what's up, cause a bitch broke."

"Yeah right, tell that to somebody that don't know better."

"So, what's up on tha agenda for tonight?"

"I don't know."

"Me either."

"Well, you know Lil Wayne and Drake supposed to be at Solo tomorrow."

"Yeah, we in tha building for that."

"Is that ya car?"

"Yeah, I bought it today from a lot on Lancaster."

"It's nice."

"I'm puttin' some rims on it tomorrow."

"Go head Bitch. Don't be Fuckin' up ya money on a whole bunch of bullshit."

"I'm not, I needed a car."

"I know, I'm just say'n."

While we were sitting there talkin' 2 broads came up talkin' all loud.

"Bitch that Mafucka is sexy as Shit."

"Yeah, so is his boy. I tried to holla at him but he told me he was married. I asked him what that had to do wit me."

"I know that's right."

"Bitch you know me; I don't kiss and tell."

"Do you know his wife?"

"No, and I don't care to know her either."

"Bitches ain't Shit," I said to Maxi and Layla, "I wish a bitch would try to holla at Jewlz."

"I'm definitely feeling you on that cause tha whole city knows I'm Keem's wife. So, if a bitch try to holla, she straight disrespecting me. Speakin' of tha devil."

Keem and Jewlz were walking across tha park. Tha girl that was just talking stood up as they got closer.

"What's up Keem, I was just talkin' about you."

"This bitch just don't get it."

Jewlz said, "Damn didn't he already tell you he was happily married."

"Mind ya biz-ness Jewlz." I saw Lay looking our way.

"So you can't speak for ya self?"

"No he can't and didn't he already tell you he was a married man."

"Who tha Fuck are you and why tha Fuck you worried about it?"

"I'm his Mafuckin wife, that's who tha Fuck I am!"

"You wasn't his wife when he was all in my face."

"Bitch stop lying," Keem said. I knew she was lying because of tha conversation we just heard them having.

"Lay don't feed into that Shit," he said walking past her.

"I wouldn't dare," I said walking off.

"Bitch!" I turned around, walked up to her and punched her square in tha mouth.

"Bitch that..."

She tried to steal me when I turned around, but Layla caught her wit a nice right. Her girl tried to jump in it, but Maxi beat tha dog shit outta her. Keem and Jewlz ran over to break it up.

"Lay chill out."

"No, she disrespected me twice today! Let me go Keem!"

"You know I'm not going to do that."

"Yeah, let her go so I can beat her Ass!"

"Listen Shawty, just let this Shit ride."

"Fuck you and ya Bitch! Imma have my brother Fuck ya Punk Ass up!"

"Bitch are you threatening me? I'll have ya brother in a body bag before tha sunset!"

"Nigga you betta ask around about my brother!"

"I don't need to do Shit! I know ya brother, he ain't built like that," Jewlz said.

"He'll dead both y'all clowns!"

"I had enough of ya mouth, Lay Fuck her up!"

Tha fight was over before it even started. Lay caught her wit a 3-piece that put her straight out. It wasn't too many bitches that could see Lay or her squad.

"Damn Baby, I see you still got it."

"Never lost it and who is her brother Jewlz?"

"Tha boy Gunner from 22nd."

I looked at Jewlz wit a look that said are you serious? He just shook his head yes.

"Jewlz, let me holla at you for a sec."

"I'm already on it," he said pulling out his phone.

"Yo Gunner."

"What up?" Jewlz told him what just went down.

They talked for a few minutes then hung up.

"He said he don't get in his sisters' shit, but I don't trust him."

"How do you want to handle it?"

"Let's just keep a close eye on him for now. Imma hit ya phone later. Maybe we can go have a few drinks. Oh yeah, you Fuckin' wit Lil' Wayne and Drake up Solo tomorrow?"

"More than likely, Stacks called and asked me tha same thing."

"If you go grab something to wear, let me know."

"I don't need nothing to wear."

"Oh yeah, I forgot you got tha Gucci store in ya closet. Lay, what are you about to do?" I asked her.

"Nothing, why?"

"No reason, I was just wondering. Don't be out here in no Bullshit!"

"That wasn't my Shit."

"I know, just chill out please."

"Keem, you goin' out tonight?"

"I might slide to tha Casbar and have a drink or two."

"Let me use ya car."

"Here, where you park at?"

"Across tha park; you want me to bring it over here?"

"Please."

"I can't believe that Bitch disrespected me like that."

"Well, she got her ass beat for it."

"Imma be sore as shit come tomorrow."

"You, me too." We both looked at Maxi and busted out laughing.

"What's so funny y'all?"

"You always fighting, so you not goin' to be sore."

"Cause bitches always testing me. Lay, what y'all doing for Niya's birthday this year?"

"Keem is try'n to see if he can rent tha whole rink for a couple hours."

"A couple of hour?"

"Yeah, cause they only let you rent it for like a hour. I'll be giving out invitations in a few days."

"Well, make sure I get one for my bad ass nephew."

"I got you. Damn, here comes this bug a boo." Me and Maxi turned around to see who Layla was talking about.

"He still be try'n to holla at you?"

"All tha time."

"Hey Lay, Maxi."

"Hey Peanut."

"What up Layla?"

"What's good Peanut?"

"You, as always."

"Oh God," I thought to myself, *"here we go wit tha bullshit."*

"Lay, they said you just beat tha dog shit outta Kita." I didn't respond; I just shrug my shoulders.

"She won't try that no more. Oh, tell Keem she's telling mafuckas she gon' get her brother."

"That Bitch gonna get her brother killed; that's what she gon' do," Maxi said.

"Bitches is crazy, she was just try'n to holla at him, but because he dissed her, she wanna get her brother."

"Un Fuckin' Believable, I bet she'll think twice about talkin' Shit again. Lay you must go cause Kita can go. Have y'all seen Beanz?"

"Nope, not today."

"Damn, I need to grab a couple of E-pills for my White boy. Y'all be kool," he said walking off.

"Now that's a first."

"What?"

"He didn't talk slick."

"You sound disappointed."

"Bitch, yeah right."

"I need to go get something to wear for tomorrow."

"So, do I, let's go to King of Prussia."

"You driving."

"Unh Unh Bitch, you driving. Lay you going?"

"Hold up, let me call Keem to see if he'll get tha girls."

"What up Baby Girl, you good?"

"Yeah, I need you to pick Niya and Nay up for me."

"Why, where you going, shoppin'?"

"No, I just need to buy something for tha show tomorrow."

"All that Shit you got in tha closet wit tags on it."

"I know but..."

"But you like spending money; who even said you can go?"

"Excuse me?"

"You heard me, who said you could go?"

"In that case, Baby is it alright if I go to tha show?"

"Girl you know I'm just Fuckin' wit you."

"You better stop play'n wit me."

"Go head, I got tha girls; I'll probably take them to Dave and Busters. You think Missy wanna go?"

"More than likely, call her."

"A'ight, see you when you get back."

"Keem."

"Yes."

"I love you."

"And I you more."

"I doubt that."

"What ever, call me when you get back. Oh, you better eat too because we're gonna eat at Dave and Busters."

"Once again, I love you."

"And me you more."

"Boy bye."

"Umm, hubby say you can't go to tha show?"

"Yeah, but he was playing."

"I know he was."

"If he wasn't, I wouldn't have went."

"Damn Aunty, it's like that?"

"He is my husband; just like if I tell him not to do something, that's all it is."

"I don't think I'm ever getting married," Maxi said giving Layla dap."

"Are y'all ready or what?"

"You rushing us like you driving."

"No I'm not, but I'm also not try'n to be up there all night either."

"Let us tell you right now, you not gonna be rushing us when we get there."

"Why don't we just go to South Street?" Layla asked.

"We can since you don't have to get all dressed up at Solo."

We all got in Maxi's car headed to Philly.

CHAPTER 12

Comatose

"Damn Baby Boy, you got to come up outta this," Flynn said.

"I'm try'n, my eyes just won't open up. I've been hearing every word you have been say'n since I've been in this bed."

"What up Flynn any changes?"

"Nah, still no change."

"You might need to start thinkin' bout unplugging tha machine."

"I was thinkin' tha same thing."

"No Hell No! These Mafucka's put me in here Flynn!"

"Come on Grams open ya eyes! Wake tha Fuck up!"

"Flynn get those Snake Ass Niggaz outta here!"

"I think pulling tha plug is tha best thing to do."

"Don't listen to 'em."

"I know but I just can't do that to him. Grams is strong, he'll come out of it.

"That's right Baby Boy, let me fight."

"Flynn, Grams has been in a coma for a few months now."

"Yeah, thanks to you two faggots! Damn, I wish they could hear me."

"I think you could use our help holding Shit down until he comes out of his coma."

"Let me think about that and get back wit y'all in a few days."

"Make sure you do that," they said walking out.

"Damn Grams, I need you. You got to come back."

"I'm try'n Flynn, I'm try'n."

"I don't know what it is but I don't trust those two."

"You shouldn't trust them, they snakes."

"Grams, Shit ain't tha same wit out you. Tha money is still coming in even more than before. But it's not tha same wit out you. I know you can hear me. I miss you like a motha, you hold on and fight; don't give up."

"I won't give up; I swear I won't. Flynn just be careful and watch those two snake niggaz."

"Yo Perk, do you think he gon' come out of that coma?"

"Truthfully, Star I don't give give a shit if he do or not. Plus, by tha time he does Flynn will be dead and we'll have Maryland on lock."

"I just hope Flynn takes us up on our offer."

"If he does, he'll get a little longer to live. If not, he'll be in tha boneyard before tha sun sets."

"How we gonna cop once we kill Flynn?"

"My cousin gon' have to holla at Jewlz."

"I got something real special planned for Keem's Bitch Ass. I hope he didn't think he was gonna get away wit that Shit he did to me."

"I was wondering when you were going to handle that Shit."

"Soon real soon, and it's gonna cost him big time."

My phone was ringing off tha hook. When I got out tha shower, I picked it up wit out looking at tha caller ID.

"Yo."

"Surprise, Surprise."

"Who is this?"

"It's only been a few months, you and Perk ain't been runnin' that long."

"Who tha Fuck is this?"

"Let me put it like this, instead of 25,000, you now owe me 60,000 for tha brick you took."

"Jewlz?"

"Nah, this Keem Nigga."

"How you get this number?"

"Now that's not important, is it? What is important is that you pay me my money real soon."

"Nigga Fuck you, Fuck ya money, Fuck ya wife, and Fuck anybody who Fuck wit you!"

"You real tough over tha phone. If I didn't know any better, I would think you were a killer instead of tha Bitch you are."

"Ha! Ha! Ha!" When he laughed, it only pissed me off.

"Laugh now, but I bet you won't be laugh'n for long Pussy."

"You my friend will be in casa de los muertos (House of tha dead) Adios (Goodbye.) Tha line went dead.

"Who tha Fuck this Mafucka think he is!" I called Perk to fill him in on tha conversation me and Keem just had.

"How he get ya number?"

"Probably Layla, I'm going to put my plan in action sooner than I wanted to."

"Did Flynn call you?"

"Nah, he just hit my phone, said he wanted to holla at us. I told him we would be at tha club in a little while. He said he would meet us there."

An hour later, we were pullin' up in front of Calibers. This was one of tha clubs that be jumpin' down here.

"This line is extra-long to tonight."

"It's not like we gonna wait in it."

"I know, I'm just say'n." We walked to tha front where Debo was stand'n.

"What up Perk, Star."

"What's tha deal Debo?"

"Flynn in there waitin' on y'all." I slipped him a C-note as we walked through tha rope.

"Damn, you just gon' let them in like that?" I stopped to see who was talking.

"I said it," some bad ass chick said. She was in tha middle of tha line, I held my hand out for her.

"Shawty, you wanna get in or not?"

"Yeah, but my girls wit me," she said pointing to 3 other bad chicks.

"What that mean?"

"I'm not leaving them out here."

"Who said you had to; are you comin' or not?" They started walking to tha front of tha line.

I slid Debo another 50 and went in. I paid everybody's way then went in tha opposite direction.

"Wow Perk, you gonna let them bad ass bitches get away?"

"Nah, they'll find us."

"What makes you so sure?"

"How many niggaz you know get four bad bitches in a packed club pay their way then step off wit out even askin' their names?"

"None."

"Exactly, and neither do they that's why they'll find us; Trust me Star."

"I always do." We met up wit Flynn in tha V.I.P. poppin' bottles.

"WOOO, you gettin' it in playboy."

"I'm drinkin' for two tonight."

"Fuck it, we might as well all get it in for Grams." I signaled tha waitress over and ordered another 2 bottles of that Ace of Spades.

"Well, I thought about it and decided to let y'all roll wit a nigga."

"That's a smart move on your part." We sat there drinkin' bottle after bottle busting it up.

"Perk, Perk!"

"Yo Playa."

"Looks who's coming." I looked over by tha steps and it was tha chicks that I told him would find us.

"So, this is where y'all been hiding at."

"Nah Ma, nobody was hiding," Star said wit a smile.

Tha one that Perk had talked to said, "I didn't catch ya name."

"That's because I didn't throw it yet."

"Oh, you a smart ass."

"I'm just play'n wit you, don't take it personal."

"I won't since you said you were play'n. So, are you going to tell me your name?"

"Perk but my friends call me Perk."

"A smart ass and a comedian. Wow your tha total package."

"I already know your name."

"What is it then?"

"Angel."

"Nope."

"You sure? Cause you look like you fresh out of Heaven." She started smiling.

"Look, you got me blushing."

"Well, if it's not Angel there's only one other name."

"What's that?"

"Beauty, ain't no need to explain that, it's self-explanatory."

"How did you know that was my name?"

"Seriously."

"Nah, I'm just play'n, it's Brazil and yes that's really my name."

"Let me guess, ya parents always wanted to go to Brazil and since they couldn't they named you that."

"Wow, a smart ass, comedian, and a psychic."

"Oh Shit, I was just guessing."

"Well, you guessed right."

"Your name is just as lovely as you."

"Thank you."

She was beautiful, 5'7," bronze skin tone, hazel eyes, shoulder length hair, and an ass that would make delicious mad.

"Well, her girls name must be Tennessee." We all looked at Flynn like he was crazy.

Then he said, "cause you're tha only Ten I See." I couldn't front that was original.

After about another hour I was ready to roll. Star and Flynn said they were gonna stay a little longer.

"Well, do you think I can catch a ride home since my girls are staying?"

"Sure, come on." Long story short, we ended up stay'n at a hotel and let's just say, neither of us got any sleep.

CHAPTER 13

Niya's Day

"Keem, you still haven't heard anything on Grams condition?"

"Flynn said he's still in a coma."

"He doesn't have any idea who did this?"

"Nah."

"Lindsey ain't let you off yet?"

"Monday I'm suppose to be done, I gave up a urine last week and she came by. Just tha routine stuff they do when they about to let you go."

"What time you wanna leave for tha show?"

"It don't matter, I'm pull'n out tha Aston Martin DBS tonight."

"Well, it's 8:30, I'll be ready by 10:30 at tha latest."

"A'ight, Jewlz and Beanz are going to meet us at your house."

It was 10:45 when Stacks and Beanz pulled up. I walked outside and smiled when I saw Beanz behind tha wheel of his cream/cream Maserati Grand Terismo on 22's.

"So, this tha car you been talkin' about?"

"Yeah, I figured why not treat myself; I deserve it."

"Yes you do, I see you got ya tattoos."

"Yeah, I got 'em earlier."

Beanz didn't have any tattoos and was scared to get his first two on his face. I damn near hold him down to get 'em. I couldn't have my team wit theirs and not have mines. All 4 of us and Cream had T.I.E and D.B.D on our faces. I had my man Ralphy make 10 pieces 5 T.I.E and 5 D.B.D all icy.

"You ready Keem?"

"Cream should be here any minute. Shit," I said when that pretty maroon/maroon Bentley Continental GT Speed pulled up on dueces.

"Damn, you niggaz ain't play'n. Y'all are pullin' out all stops. Since that's how y'all rolling, I got something for you niggaz." I ran in tha house then came back out wit 5 jewelry boxes. Once they opened them, they were all smiles.

"Now this what I'm talkin' about," Beanz said.

Jungle said, "Damn Keem, I'm not part of tha unit?"

"My fault Jungle, I didn't know you were back. Last I heard, you was working."

"I'm back wit my ace."

"I had 2 extra ones made that I was gonna give to my peeps down tha Lina's. But we can't all have on ours and you don't," I said going back in tha house. We all put on our T.I.E chains and headed to Philly.

We pulled up in our 3-car caravan and all eyes were on us. We parked right in front V.I.P. We stepped out of tha car wit our Gucci, Prada, Louis Vuitton, Ralph Lauren gear on; they were sick. We looked like money in every sense of tha word. We went straight to tha V.I.P. line. I could hear bitches ask'n who we were. We got our V.I.P. bracelets then headed to tha bar.

"Damn, you look real good, are you spoken for?" I turned around to see who had just asked that question.

"Oh Shit! What's up Salina," I said giving her a big hug.

"I heard you were home but I couldn't catch up wit you."

"I been hittin' and missin', what's goin' on wit you?"

"Same shit, bust'n my ass working. What's up wit Uncle Rudy?"

"You know him, still thinks he a young boy." (Ha! Ha! Ha!)

"I would ask you what's up but lookin' at you I think I know tha answer."

"I ain't makin' no noise, my boys makin' sure I'm good."

"What does that stand for?" she asked pointing at my chain.

"Trust is Ery Thing."

"You got enough diamonds in it."

"Give me ya number so I can call you. Do you still Fuck wit Dame?"

"Yeah, he in here somewhere. Well, make sure you call me," Salina said hugging me.

"Damn Keem, who was that bad ass honey?"

"My little cousin."

"Hook a nigga up," Cream said.

"I got you, she here wit her man."

"Her man?"

"Yeah but Fuck that Nigga!" We took a few pictures then went inside tha V.I.P. room.

Lil' Wayne and Drake were sitting in there drinkin' bottles of Cristal. We grabbed a spot and did tha same. There weren't to many people in V.I.P. considering they wanted 200 for a ticket. I heard Drake say they were about to go on stage but I chose to stay in V.I.P.

"I should of known where you were. Why you not out there wit Stacks and tha rest of them?"

"I didn't want to be in tha mix of that while they were performing."

"Me either."

"I thought that's why you came, to see them perform?"

"I came for tha same reason you did, to have a good time. I saw Salina and her man."

"Yeah, I talked to her."

"Baby let's go take a few pictures."

"A'ight, come on."

I picked my bottle up off tha table and followed Lay to tha picture booth. While we were taking pictures Lil' Wayne and Drake came up. All tha females and even some males were try'n to get pictures wit them.

It surprised me when Weezy said, "I like that piece. If you don't mind me asking, what does it mean?"

"Trust is Ery Thing." We ended up taking a couple of flicks then went back to the V.I.P. Lounge. I knew Lay's birthday was coming up so I ask Weezy if he would perform and how much would he want? When it was all said and done, I had Weezy booked for Lay's party next month. Lay didn't know it, but she was going to have tha biggest birthday party tha city has ever seen.

Tha next few days we made sure Niya's party was in order. Christiana agreed to let us have tha whole building from 1 to 4. We decided to get chicken from Waltz and make some seafood salad to go wit it.

"Niya told me she wanted a bike, clothes, and Powerwheel."

"Keem, she doesn't need a bike and Powerwheel," Lay said wit an attitude, "that's her problem now, she spoiled."

"So what."

"Ain't no so what."

"Lay I'm not going to argue wit you about no petty shit like that. I'll be back."

"Where you going?"

"To Al's to get Niya and Nay some skates."

"Did you go to tha post office to get that stuff my mom and Diablo sent?"

"Yup, it's in tha closet."

It was Niya's birthday and she was excited about her skating party. Lay had given out close to 50 invitations.

That morning Lay, Niya, and Nay went to get their hair done. My 3 ladies were lookin' good as shit. Niya was real fly wit her brown Gucci dress and matching Gucci sandals.

"Shaniya, Shaniya."

"Yes Daddy."

"Wow look at daddy's little diva. Come here daddy got a present for you to put on." I took tha necklace out tha box.

"OOOOH Daddy is that for me?"

"Yes, let me put it on." She ran to tha mirror.

"Go Niya it's ya birthday, it's ya birthday, go Niya." All I could do was laugh.

"Mommy where my glasses at?"

"On ya dresser!" Lay yelled from tha front room, "Keem, you not dressed yet?"

"No."

"It's almost 10 o'clock."

"So."

"So nothing, she gonna be late to her own party."

"No she not, she makin' a grand entrance."

Niya sat in my room til I got dressed.

"Come on Daddy let's go."

"Niya, what you got on ya neck?" Nay asked.

"Daddy got it for me as a present."

"OOH Mom look at her necklace."

"Let me see Niya, Damn that's nice Keem."

"For tha money, it better be."

"Where you been getting money from? Cause instead of tha money in tha bank decreasing it's been increasing a lot. Keem, please don't lie to me."

"I'm a silent partner."

"I knew you were back hustin' again."

"Actually, I'm not. I just put up some money, I don't touch Shit! I just get paid every time they flip."

"I hope that's all it is."

"Did I tell you 3 ladies you look beautiful?"

"You told me Daddy," Niya said.

When we arrived, it was 1:30 and tha lot was packed.

"Grab y'all skates."

"Daddy I don't want to skate," Niya said.

"Why not?" She pointed to her feet.

We all started laughing.

"Ya daughter is too much," I said to Lay.

When we got inside it was packed. A few of tha kids ran up to Niya wishing her a happy birthday and hugging her.

"Oh My God! Look at God Mom's baby. Niya you are a true Diva and look at that Diamond necklace," Blondy said wit a smile.

"My daddy got it for me, he said every Diva should have diamonds."

"Girl you know she said don't wanna skate cause she don't want to mess her feet up."

"Are you serious Lay?"

"Yes."

We talked Niya into putting on her skates. All in all, she was having a blast and tha best part was yet to come. I went to tha DJ booth and got tha mic. Tha DJ stopped tha music for me.

"Excuse me."

"What is he doin' now?" Lay asked Stacks.

"Ya guess is as good as mine."

"Is everybody enjoying their selves?!"

"Yeah!" Everybody screamed.

"Shaniya come here Baby. I want to thank everybody for comin' and for tha gifts," I got down on my knees and said, "Shaniya, daddy loves you with all his heart and I wanted to make ya 6th birthday special and one to remember."

"You have Daddy and I love you," she said hugging me.

"Let me ask you a question. What song you want to hear?"

"You already know, Soulja Boy, Turn My Swag On."

"I don't have that tha song Shawty," tha DJ said.

Niya took tha mic and said, "How you not going to have Soulja Boy?"

"I know," all tha kids said mad.

"Hold on, Hold on Niya, I got tha CD in tha car. Imma get it and be right back. I didn't want nothin' to spoil this special day for my diva." All tha kids was down wit that.

I left but when I came back, I didn't have tha CD.

"I got some bad news and good news. Tha bad news is Lay took tha CD out of tha car."

"Mom!" Niya said mad.

Before Lay could say anything, I said, "Now since I don't have tha CD, I decided to have my peoples do his thing. Come on out!"

When Soulja Boy came out, Niya and tha rest of tha kids went crazy. I looked at Laysha and winked.

"Bitch ya husband is tha Shit," Maxi said, "Niya will never forget this."

"I know, how many 6-year-olds can say Soulja Boy was at their party," Blondy added, "he loves his daughter."

"Yes, and she's siked for her dad."

After he performed a few songs, he took pictures wit tha kids.

"Baby, did you get it all on there?"

"You know I did, I even got a lot of pictures wit him and Niya."

Soulja Boy said goodbye and then left. When tha party was over, everybody went their separate ways. Except Lay's click, they came back to tha house.

"Daddy you tha best! Soulja Boy was tha best present. I'm not even mad that I didn't get my bike or Power Wheels now." When she walked in tha house and saw her bike or Power Wheels she went berserk, for real.

"My dad is tha best daddy in tha world."

"Didn't I tell you she didn't need both of them."

"And didn't I tell you that if I want to spoil my kids, I will."

"I know that's right," Jonda said.

"You spent out on her for this birthday," Layla said, "I know you had to spend close to 20 grand."

"Nah, only about 17 grand."

"Damn, that's too much for a 6-year-old," Candy said, hatin' as usual.

I looked her in tha face then said, "You can't put a price tag on love."

"I know that's right," Blondy added.

CHAPTER 14

Play wit Fire Get Burned

"Yo Stacks what's up wit Gunner?"

"I don't know, I hit his phone but he ain't pick up."

"I know this nigga ain't try'n to play us."

"I don't know, but ever since that incident wit his sister; he been acting different."

"If he don't got that money by tomorrow we gon' pay him a visit."

"Yeah, cause if we let one nigga get away wit it, other niggaz gon' try us."

"Have you heard anything about Star or Perk?"

"Nah, I even called his sister to see if she knew anything."

"Damn you still got her number?"

"Gotta keep that in case one late night I want some good head.

"Shit, tha way she look she gotta have something going for herself. Well keep her, she might be our Ace in tha hole later down tha line. So, did you get up wit Freeway and Meek Millz yet?"

"I'm glad you mentioned that I talked to both of them. Free said he'll do it for 5 stacks. But Meek said he has another show to do that night."

"What about Chris or Peedi?"

"I know I can get and I got my folk hollering at Plies."

"We only got 3 weeks til tha party and I want to get flyers out A.S.A.P."

"Don't worry I'll know something by Wednesday then you can get tha flyers made."

"Is that Jewlz across tha park?"

"Yeah, that's that nigga."

I pulled out my phone to call when shots rang out.

Pop, Pop, Pop, Bong, Bong, Bong then tha sounds of tires peeling off. I could hear people screaming across tha park. Me and Stacks took off running across tha park. When we got there Jewlz was laying on tha ground wit a bullet in his leg.

"Go get a car so we can get him to a hospital, I said to Dump. When Dump came back, we put Jewlz in tha car and drove him to St. Francis.

"Imma kill that nigga."

"Who was shootin'?

"Gunner, they had mask on but I heard tha driver say hit him Gunner."

"Ok, so since they wore mask, they not gon' to think you know it was him."

"Yeah, he's right, I agree wit Stacks."

"So, we'll talk once you get outta tha hospital."

"Keem be careful, you know what this is about."

"Fuck that Bitch Nigga, he's a dead man!"

"Nah, Imma handle that nigga myself, he fucked up my jeans." (Ha! Ha! Ha!)

"Nigga just got shot and worried about his jeans. Let's get outta here. Stacks call us when they release you."

15 minutes later, we were sitting A block away from where Gunner hustles at.

"Keem this nigga must don't know who he Fuckin wit."

"We tried to help him get his money up IM GET HIS MONEY up by giving him tha coke at that number."

"I don't think he built from tha same cloth we are."

"I know he's not, Shit Stacks a lot of what niggaz."

"There he go right there coming out that house."

"Follow him."

Gunner got into his car and pulled off slowly. He had no idea we were tailing him because we stayed at least 3 cars behind. He made a few stops but didn't stay to long. Finally, he pulled up to this old two-story house and went inside.

"I say we go inside and rock that nigga to sleep."

"Nah, we gon' wait, we don't need no witnesses or unnecessary bodies.

After 45 minutes, he came back. When he came down tha steps an old lady came to tha door holding a plate.

"Kevin your forgetting ya food," she yelled to him. He ran back got tha plate then kissed her and said thank you Nana.

Gunners next stop was his baby moms house.

"Fuck this Shit!" Stacks said getting out. I jumped behind tha wheel and eased up tha street.

"Aye Gunner." When he turned around to see Stacks standing there, he immediately went into explain mode.

"You on ya way to Keisha's house?"

"How do you know my baby mom?" he asked.

"Ya baby mom Keisha told me y'all was cousins."

"She said what?"

"Yeah, I'm Fuckin' her." As soon as he turned around, Stacks pulled his .40 cal out.

Jewlz said, "He'll see you in Hell! BOOM!

A single shot to tha back of head sending brain matter all over tha sidewalk. Stacks slowly walked back to tha truck we were in as I pulled off.

"Jewlz gonna be mad at him."

"Why?"

"Because he wanted to kill him."

"He'll be a'ight."

"Now if we could only find Perk and Star."

"They'll surface sooner or later; I can feel it."

"Yeah, I hope you right."

Two days later, Jewlz was released from tha hospital. He was pissed that he had to use crutches for a couple weeks.

"I guess you won't be going to Lay's party."

"Imagine that, I'm not going to miss this party. We need to get tha flyers made."

"Already on top of that."

"So, what did you decide on?"

"On tha front, it's Freeway, Peedi, Weezy, Drake, and Plies. And On tha back it says BIRTHDAY BASH for a DIVA at tha Chase Center wit a picture of Lay."

"How much is it to get in?"

"50.00 and 125.00 for V.I.P. I have to pick tha flyers up at 4 o'clock."

"I hope you got enough made up."

"400 should be more than enough plus, Imma post a bulletin on IG and FB."

"When you going to get something to wear?"

"Been there done that."

"Damn you didn't even let ya homies know."

"I went wit Lay and we got our shit made from TOI East."

"Let me guess, you got some Gucci Shit made."

"Nah, Lay talked me into some Louis Vuitton shit."

"How did she do that?"

"She bought me these hot Louis shoes. Hit me up later, I have to pick up Nay from school."

On my way to Nay's school tha realtor called to let me know tha house would be completed in a month, but we could come by and see it. After I picked Nay up, 1 headed to tha print shop to pick up tha flyers since Lay was picking up Niya.

"Daddy why we come here?"

"I have to pick up something, I'll be right back."

I was in and out in a flash."

"OOOH Daddy is that Mommy on there?"

"Yes."

"You giving her a party?"

"Yes."

"Can me and Niya come."

"No, it's for adults but if you want, you and Niya can throw Lay a party at home. We can cook her dinner then eat cake and ice cream. We gotta keep this a secret. Don't even tell Niya until tha day before."

"I'm not, cause she'll tell Mommy not knowing she told."

"Exactly."

By tha time we got home, Lay had dinner on.

"Baby that steak smells good."

"Keem can you make that salad?"

"No problem."

I made tha salad, put it in tha fridge, and ran to get tha flyers out tha car.

"Babe, you wanna see what tha flyers look like?"

"Yes please." I handed her tha flyer and she went crazy.

"Oh My God! Baby I love it! Who thought of this?"

"Now you being disrespectful."

"I'm sorry, I should've known. Birthday Bash for a Diva, I love it.

"I'm bout to post it on Facebook. Baby, you about to have biggest party, they'll be talkin' about this party for a while."

"That what I want. Mommy you having a birthday party?" Niya asked.

"Yes, I am Sweetie."

"I'm gonna buy you a nice present."

"I know you will. Dinner is done so wash y'all hands."

"Damn!"

"What Keem?"

"I just posted tha flyer on Facebook and 6 people sent me a message say'n they're in ."

"That's a real good picture of me you got on there too."

"I know."

"You real cocky, come eat ya dinner."

Tha four of us sat at tha table talking and eating.

"So, Lay, what do you want for your birthday that you don't already have?"

"I know Mom, cause you got so much stuff," Nay added

"It doesn't matter, this party is enough for me." Lay didn't know that I had overheard her telling Sandy she wanted an old school car.

After dinner, Nay and Niya took their baths while Lay was in tha shower. I went to talk to tha girls.

"What do want to get ya mom for her birthday?"

"I want to get her some shoes and a bag," Niya said.

"Imma get her a bracelet and earrings."

"A'ight, we'll go to Philly this weekend."

I held my hands out in front of both of them.

They slapped my hands and when I didn't move them Nay said, "What Dad?"

"Give me y'all money and I'll hold on to it."

"We don't got no money."

"So how are y'all going to get her gifts?" They both pointed at me then we all started laughing.

"I know y'all better go to sleep and Keem, get outta there!"

"Buenas noches (good night)."

"Huh?"

"Good night."

"Oh, good night. Daddy we love you."

"And I love y'all more." They started laughing again.

"What did I just tell y'all? Leave them alone."

"Mom we told Daddy we love him and he said he loves us more."

"He tells me that all tha time too."

Saturday morning ery thing fell right into place.

"Keem can you watch tha girls while I go to tha salon?"

"Yeah, I got 'em."

By 10:30 we were on our way to Philly.

"Daddy we got to go to Blondies; that's where tha shoes and bag are."

I looked at Niya, "What a 6-year-old know about Blondies?"

"Daddy I know a lot about fashion." Me and Nay bagged up.

Tha girls picked up a few outfits for themselves. I decided to grab Fiza a few things since Shante had called to let me know she needs spring clothes.

"Dad I'm hungry."

"Me too Daddy."

"What do y'all want to eat?"

"Cheese steaks," they both said in unison. As soon as I heard tha ringtone of my phone I smiled.

"That's Mom, ain't it?"

"You know she got to check on us. Hello."

"Hey, y'all ok?"

"Yeah, we on our way home."

"So am I, I'll meet y'all there."

"Ok. (Click)

"We gonna leave Lay's stuff in tha trunk and Niya you better not tell her."

"I'm not Daddy, I promise." I put her stuff in tha trunk wit tha other stuff me and Nay got from Party City.

"I know you didn't take them shoppin?"

Actually, I went to get Fiza some spring clothes and they saw a few things they liked."

"They always see things they like that don't mean they have to have it. Did you get Qadir and Little Keem some stuff too?"

"No because I'm taking them tomorrow. I'll be back, I got to handle something."

"Daddy can I go please?" Niya asked

"Yeah, put ya shoes back on."

I grabbed Fiza's bags and headed out tha door wit Niya on my heels. I called Shante to see where she was at. She let me know she was at her moms. As I was pulling up Joe called me to let me know Lay's birthday present was ready. I let him know I would be out there in 30 minutes. Fiza was out front on tha steps; whenever rq we pulled up she ran to tha car.

"Daddy!" Me and Niya got out and gave her a hug.

"Sister," Fiza said, hugging Niya again.

"Why didn't you come to my party?

"My mom wouldn't bring me."

"I told her I would pick you up."

"You missed it. Daddy had Soulja Boy there."

"Aww."

When Shante came out Fiza said, "See Mom, Niya had Soulja Boy at her party."

"I don't care, I said you wasn't going."

That pissed me off; as I was giving Fiza her bags I said, "Shante, I don't care how you feel about me or Lay, but you're not going to keep my kids from knowing and spending time wit one another."

"I'm not try'n to hear that Shit Hakeem!

"Well, you are! Fiza you want to stay tha night wit us?"

"Yes."

"No, she's going somewhere tomorrow."

"What time? I'll make sure she's home tomorrow."

"9 in tha morning."

"A'ight, I'll have her home by 8."

"No."

"I didn't want to do this but I'm tired of ya Shit; I'm filing for visitation on Monday!"

"Mafucka if you do, I'm taking you for child support!" Shante's mom and sisters came out.

"Child support! My daughter don't want for shit. All I want is to be able to spend time wit her."

"What's going on here?" her mom asked.

"Mommy said I can't stay wit Niya tonight."

"Why not?" I explained to her mom what was going on.

"Fiza go get ya bag; you staying wit ya Dad. Keem she wasn't going anywhere but to church wit me and I'm not leaving until 10." I shook my head at Shante then told her mom thank you.

They got in tha back seat.

"Put those seat belts on."

"Thanks Ms. Bunny."

"You're welcome and I like that car."

"Thank you," I said getting in my car.

I hit Joe to let him know that I was on my way. 10 minutes later, I was pulling up to Joe's shop in New Port.

"Stay here, I'll be right back."

"What up Keem?"

"You Baby Boy."

"Let me show you this Pretty Mafucka."

"WHOO0 God Damn!"

"So, you like it?"

"Man, I love it! If it wasn't pink Lay would be out of luck."

I had bought Lay an old school 4 door, 72 Buick Lasore. I had Joe paint it pink wit white leather interior piped in pink, two-inch TV's in tha headrest, one in tha dash, her initials in tha headrest, 4 6x9's across tha back window. I had them make pink and two 15's in tha trunk. Oh yeah, tha top was white and a convertible.

When Joe turned tha system on, it was so loud it was sick. Tha 26's really brought tha car out. I also had ery thing under tha hood chromed out.

"Joe she gon' love this, I'll be back to pick it up Friday. How much I owe you?"

"30 grand."

"A'ight, I'll bring it Friday when I come pick it up."

"No problem Keem."

"As soon as I find me a nice old school I'll be back. Let me go, I got my daughter's in tha car."

When I got back to tha car Niya said, "Daddy ya phone was ringing."

Then went right back to playing.

I looked at my phone I had 6 missed calls. Before I went home, I rode thru tha city giving out flyers.

"Damn, I didn't think y'all was coming back."

"He was beefing wit my mom Mrs. Lay."

"What was y'all beefing for?"

"Because she didn't let Fiza come to Niya's party; then she didn't want her to spend tha night."

"Nay run ya sisters some bath water please."

"I told her I would deal wit it through tha court. That Bitch had tha nerve to say she would take me for child support."

"So how did you get her to let Fiza come?"

"Ms. Bunny she said she's tired of Shante being petty. I do have to take her home in tha morning so she can go to church."

"Baby, I'm tired of Shante."

"Me too."

"Mom tha water ready."

"Fiza, Niya get in tha tub."

CHAPTER 15

Alive

"Listen, it's been too much blood shed."

"Niggaz gonna either get down or lay down. Simple as that, anything else tha body count gon' keep going up."

"Why tha Fuck did I get involved wit these dumb ass niggaz?"

"We gon' give you a call later Flynn."

"A'ight."

"Yo Star, it's time to get rid of that nigga."

"I know, since Grams been in that coma, he's gotton soft ass shit." Perk pulled out his .38.

"What tha Fuck are you doing?" He just got out of tha car.

"Aye Yo Flynn."

"What up Perk?"

"I forgot to give you this..." Boom, Boom, Boom, Boom, Boom, Boom, Boom.

Tha first 2 hit him in tha face, tha next 5 hit him in tha chest. Just to make sure he was dead I stood over top of him and put one in tha middle of his forehead.

"Now I'm ready, let's get outta here." I looked over at Perk, he was cool as a fan. I couldn't help but smile.

"What you smiling at Nigga?"

"You done turned into a stone-cold killer over tha past few months. If you ask me Star, I think we need to pull tha plug on Grams ourselves. That nigga ain't never comin' out of that coma."

"Yeah, you probably right. You know that Bitch Lay is having a party at tha Chase Center next weekend. That will be tha perfect time to execute my plan."

"So, what's this plan that's to get us paid?" I explained it all to him step by step.

"I gotta give it to you, Star that's a winner."

"I know, I know."

"I need a doctor! I need a doctor!" Grams girl yelled.

Tha nurses came running into tha room.

"What's going on Mam?"

"He's back," she said pointing to Grams who had his eyes open.

"Get Dr. Phil in here now!" one of tha nurses yelled.

Dr. Phil came running in, "My patient has returned finally." Grams just laid there wit his eyes open.

"Nod your head yes or no to these questions, don't try to talk. Can you hear me?" He nodded yes.

"Good. Can you see me clearly?" He nodded no.

"Can you see me at all?" He nodded yes.

"Am I a blur?" He nodded yes.

"That is normal for person who just was in a coma for 4 months." Grams tried to talk but nothing came out.

"Don't try to talk," Dr. Phil said handing him a pen and a pad.

He could barely hold tha pen so his girl helped him. He scribbled Flynn's name on tha pad.

A tear fell from her eye as she said, "He was killed a few days ago." Grams threw tha pen and pad across tha room as tears fell from his eyes.

"Mr. Penn please calm down."

"Sorry doctor but I had to tell him his best friend was killed."

"I'm truly sorry to hear that but we don't want to set him back. Mr. Penn you should be able to talk in tha next few days or two. As for your vision, about two or three hours. If you need anything just push tha button on tha side of tha bed.

"Damn, I need to ask her what happened to Flynn."

I motioned for her to get me tha pen and pad I had thrown earlier. After I wrote it down, I showed it to her.

"He was shot 7 times; 3 in tha face, 4 in tha chest." Who? I wrote down.

"They don't know who."

"Do you think Star and Perk did this?"

"No."

They did this to me!

"They have been up here every other day."

Don't let them know I'm out of my coma.

"I won't and I'll let tha doctors and nurses know tha same."

About an hour later, Star and Perk came in.

"Still no change, huh?"

"No."

"So, did you find out anything about Flynn?" my girl asked.

"Word is, he owed some nigga a debt from gambling."

"These Mafuckas lying, Flynn don't even gamble. I know these niggaz did it."

"Well, I'll be back in a day or two to check on him," Star said, "yeah, and we'll keep our ear to tha street about Flynn."

"If you hear anything different, let me know."

"We gotcha."

Once they left, I wrote down what I wanted her to tell them she pulled tha plug on me.

"Why?"

I don't know if you heard me but they tried to kill me once and they'll probably try it again.

"Ok and if they think your dead, they won't be able to stop or see you coming."

You got it, tell tha doctor to put me in another room A.S.A.P.

"We need to start putting a team together. Rolo is going to cop off of Jewlz so we got that part covered. We can organize a meeting so that they know we're running shit now."

"That sounds good because I don't want anybody to think they gonna try to run our shit that we put work in for! I'll call tha niggaz I deal wit and you do tha same. Perk, this is our Shit now, this is tha come up we been waiting on." So he thought.

Little did they know there would be a price to pay for tha life they tried to take and tha one they did take.

CHAPTER 16

Happy Birthday Lay

"Happy Birthday to Mommy, Happy Birthday to Mommy, Happy Birthday to Mommy," Nay and Niya sang waking us up.

"We made breakfast in bed." I looked at tha tray, they were carrying containing a bowl of cereal, sliced oranges, and toasted bread wit jelly.

"Awe you made this for me?"

"Yes."

They wanted to give her tha gifts they had gotton, but I convinced them to wait until tha party. Layla and Sandy were coming to take her to get her hair and nails done. Last night, I had Joe bring tha car to tha house. After we were dressed, I asked Lay if she was ready for my gift.

"Keem, I told you that you didn't have to get anything tha party was more than enough."

"I know and I wasn't but I overheard one of your conversations."

"You were ease dropping?"

"No, didn't you hear me? I overheard you. Look, didn't you want a dog?" She looked at me like I lost my mind.

"You must of heard me call somebody a dog."

"Fuck!" I yelled. Niya and Nay started laughing.

"Daddy you crazy."

"Well, until we can find someone who wants a dog you better go get him out ya car."

"What! I know you didn't put no Fuckin' dog in my car," she said walking out tha door wit tha girls on her heels.

"AAAAAGH OH MY GOD!"

- 135 -

"OOOOOH Mommy!"

"WOOOOOW Mom!" When I walked outside, they were taking tha big bow off tha car.

"You overheard me telling Sandy I wanted an old school car."

"You need these," I said holding tha keys.

Lay snatched tha keys, hit tha alarm and opened tha door. When she started it up tha sounds of Stevie Wonder's Happy Birthday came bursting out. Lay tried to turn it down but couldn't.

I said, "Volume 3." And down it went.

"Everything is voice activated." I showed her tha way I had tha trunk done as well as under tha hood.

"Baby thank you. I love my new car and tha color is to die for."

"Lay, I haven't shown you tha best part yet."

"There's more?"

"Just this," I said hitting tha button to make tha top drop.

"OOOH Mommy, you got tha hottest Old School in tha city."

"How did?"

I cut her off, "I had this custom made. You like?"

"No, I love it!"

Layla and Sandy were pulling up as she was about to pull off.

"Damn Bitch! You gonna really have them hatin' now."

"My Baby got me this for my birthday."

"Shit, all I got for my birthday was a bracelet and you get a drop top Old School on 24's," Sandy said.

"Nah, these 26's."

"Excuse me."

"Excused."

"Imma park and we gonna jump in wit you."

"Come on then, my appointment is in 20 minutes."

"You want me to drive?" Layla asked.

"Hell no! See y'all later," Lay said.

It was tha beginning of spring but it was 77 degrees out so Lay left tha top down.

4 hours later, me and tha girls had tha house decorated.

"Daddy that's Mommy on that cake," Niya said.

"Yes it is Baby. Now come on let's get this dinner started it's 4 o'clock."

We decided to make Lay some macaroni and cheese, collard greens, barbeque chicken, and cornbread. When dinner was finished. I called Layla to let her know, she said they were on their way. When I heard them pull up, we hit tha lights and hid. Lay came in and called our names. When we didn't respond, she hit tha kitchen light.

"SURPRISE!" We all jumped out yelling.

"Y'all scared tha shit outta me! Oh My God, look at all this."

"Mommy we wanted to throw you a party since we can't come to yours."

"Awe, thank y'all," she said hugging tha girls." We sat down to eat.

"Me and Niya made tha macaroni and cornbread."

"It's really delicious."

"Thank you," they both said.

After we were done, we brought tha cake out. Wow, you girls went all out for ya mom. Niya ran in her room then came back wit her gift that she had wrapped.

"Here Mommy, open my gift first."

When she opened it and saw tha handbag and shoes she said, "This is tha bag and shoes I wanted."

"Yeah, that's what Niya said when she asked to go to Blondies. Now open mines."

"This is beautiful Nay."

"I knew you like it Mom."

"Nay go pack you and Niya some clothes."

"We staying over Aunt Jonda's?"

"No, y'all staying wit ya Aunt Val."

Val was my sister that I didn't really deal wit her but I wouldn't stop my kids from dealing wit her.

"How did that happen?" I asked Lay when tha girls left tha room.

"Netta called and asked could they stay tha night."

"What time you dropping them off?"

"She's coming to get them at 9 o'clock." I heard a horn and looked out tha window.

"Well, she must have changed her mind because she's out front." 2 seconds later there was a knock on tha door; Netta came in.

"Happy Birthday Aunt Lay."

"Thank you Netta."

"Is that your pink car outside?"

"Yup, it's hers," Nay said smiling.

"That thing is tight."

"My daddy got it for her birthday," Niya said.

"Come on y'all for my mom start bugging."

"Bye Mommy, Bye Daddy."

"See y'all tomorrow and behave."

"We are."

After they left Lay said, "Do you think I can get myself a little something, something?"

"Oh, you want a little Jeramiah "Birthday Sex" huh?" She just smiled and started taking her clothes off.

An hour and 3 or 4 orgasms later we were getting in tha shower. I stayed in tha shower after Lay got out.

"Keem, Stacks is calling you!"

"Answer it for me, please!"

When I got out, she let me know that she told him I was riding wit her.

"I don't want to ride wit you and ya girls."

"You're not, I told them me and you were riding together. Between Layla, Sandy, and Maxi they'll get there. Stacks said they would meet us at 10:30."

I looked at tha clock, "We better get a move on it."

"No, you better get a move on it, I'm almost ready."

By tha time we were both dressed and I rolled a couple blunts it was 10:05.

"Laysha you look gorgeous."

And she did wit her brown Louis Vuitton one of a kind dress wit pumps to match. She decided to wear tha diamond necklace and bracelet that Nay brought her.

"Damn Baby that dress showing every curve."

"Do you think it's too tight?"

"Hell Naw, it's just right."

"Thank you, looking real handsome yaself."

"Thanks to you."

"I did do tha damn thing, didn't I?"

"Yes you did."

I had these brown linen LV Capris wit tha linen shirt to match as well as my LV ons. I decided to go basic as far as my Jewels diamond necklace and bracelet.

"Baby you ready?"

"Yeah, let's go turn some heads."

We hopped in her car and dropped tha top then pulled off and headed to tha biggest party of tha year so far. Halfway there both of our phones started ringing.

"Hello," we said in unison answering our phones.

"I'm almost there."

"Yo, I'll be there in 5 minutes."

We pulled up banging Hollywood's version of Maybach music. Lay's system was so loud everybody was looking on in awe.

"Holy Shit!" Beanz yelled.

We got out and let tha valet park Lay's car.

"Oh, hold up," Lay said reaching in and hitting tha button to put tha top up.

"Damn Bitch that shit is hot," Candy said, "I gotta give it to you Keem, you snap with that Baby Boy."

"Damn Lay, you got tha hottest Old School by far; a nigga gotta step their game all tha way up," Jewels said, "look at them niggaz from 20th." They had some nice Old Schools but they didn't have shit on Lay's.

"What up Keem?"

"What up Blue?"

"Is that a 72 Lasabre?"

"Yeah."

"You want to sell it?"

"No, he don't want to sell it!"

"My fault and Happy Birthday Lay."

"Thank you but it's my car not his."

"You didn't think I would be driving a pink car, did you? Enjoy yaself tonight," I said walking into .

Lay thanked tha people that wished her a happy birthday. Shorty's back drop was a big air brushed picture of Lay.

"Let's go to tha bar and get somethin' to drink."

"Tha birthday girl has entered ," Doc B. announced over tha mic.

The party was in full swing and it was only 11:30. We still got 5 ½ hours to party. Money talks and that's how we got them to let us rock out until 5 am.

Backstage Freeway and Peedi were getting high about to perform their 2003 hit Flipside. Once Doc B. introduced them, they did their thing. Next up Drake and Weezy followed by Plies. They all tore it up something serious.

"This ya boy Plies, I wanna thank y'all for having me and my boy Keem for bringing me down. Oh yeah before I forget, let me give a special shout to Lay. Happy Birthday Baby Girl from ya boy Plies!"

They all went to V.I.P. to get drunk. We sat around wit them until they were ready to go. But before they left, we took pictures wit them. Tha picture Lay took wit them all came out nice as a mafucka. Even though it was over at 5, me and Lay left a 3:45; she was beyond drunk.

When we got home Lay went to tha bathroom and praised tha porcelain god aka tha toilet. I was hungry so I fixed a plate and put it in tha microwave.

"Baby did you make me a plate?"

"Yes, but are you going to be able to eat?"

"Yeah, I'm good now. I shouldn't have drank that Patron knowing I don't like it."

"You only drank it because Freeway bought it for you."

"I know."

We made love then fell asleep in each other's arms.

CHAPTER 17

Kidnapped

"There go that Bitch right there."

"I see her, we gonna follow her then snatch her ass up." We followed her while she dropped Blondy and Candy off.

"She's going to her mom's house."

"A'ight, as soon as she parks, we gon' get her ass."

I got out and started walking towards her car. As soon as she got out, I smacked her upside tha head wit my pistol knocking her out. Perk pulled up wit tha van, I threw her in, blind folded and tied her up.

"AAAGH, AAAGH!"

I opened my eyes but it was pitch black. When I tried to move my hands and legs, I couldn't. It smelled like mold and piss. I heard a door open and footsteps.

"Damn, my head is pounding. I must of had too much to drink tonight."

"Yo, she's up."

Then I heard another set of footsteps coming down tha steps.

"So, you finally decided to wake up."

"I know that voice from somewhere but I couldn't put my finger on it. Who are you and where am I?" (SMACK)

"Bitch we'll be asking tha questions around here! What is Keem's number?"

"I don't know." (SMACK)

"OOOW SHIT!"

"Let's try this again. What's Keem's number?" When I didn't answer he smacked me again busting my lip.

"Bitch you can make this easy or hard, it's up to you."

"Oh Shit Star, you are going to die."

I looked at Perk like how did she know. He just shrugged his shoulders. I snatched tha blindfold off her eyes.

I squinted my eyes trying to adjust them to tha light.

"Star what tha Fuck do you think you're doing?"

(SMACK)

"Didn't I tell you about asking questions? Now tha number. (SMACK)

"SHIIIIIIT, you broke ass..." (SMACK)

I could feel my eye swelling up.

Finally, he said, "We'll be back in a few hours; maybe you'll talk then."

"Don't count on it!" I yelled through swollen lips, *"how am I going to get out of this alive anyway?"*

A few hours later, I heard tha door open and footsteps.

"I thought you might be hungry so I got you something from McDonalds."

He took a pair of handcuffs out of his back pocket. Then he untied my hands. Tha minute they were free I smacked tha cowboy shit outta him.

"You Dumb Bitch!" he said punching me in tha same eye that had swelled up.

Once he had tha cuffs on me, he threw my food in my lap.

"Now are you ready to talk?"

I thought about it, *"I might as well give him tha number so Keem can find me and Kill this Bastard. 685.4322."*

"This better be tha right number." After a few rings Keem picked up.

"Who dis?"

"You might want to change ya pitch Nigga."

"Who tha Fuck is dis?"

"Somebody who has something that belongs to you?"

"Is that right?"

"Yup."

"What might that be?"

"Ya pretty niece."

"Man, whatever," he said and hung up.

"I know this faggot ass nigga didn't just hang up on me." I called right back but got no answer. Now I was pissed off. (SMACK) (SMACK)(SMACK)

"AAAGH, AAAGH! FUUUUUCK!!!"

"Baby who is that that keeps calling?" Lay asked.

"I don't know? Have you talked to Layla today?"

"No why?"

I picked my phone up and dialed her number. After about 5 rings it went to voicemail. I tried again wit tha same results.

"Call ya sister, see if she's talk to Layla."

"Why, what's going on?"

"Lay just Fuckin' call!" I said, not meaning to but raising my voice.

"Jonda, have you talked to Layla today?"

"No but she must of been drunk last night."

"Why you say that?"

"Because her car is out front and her keys were on tha ground."

"Ok, if you talk to her, tell her to call me."

I told Keem what Jonda had just told me.

"Let me call Stacks, maybe she's wit him." As I was about to call Stacks my phone rang wit that same number.

"Star call him back one more time; if he hangs up this time her blood will be on his hands." I called, this time tha phone rang once before he picked up.

"So, you are ready to talk now or what?"

"What is it that you want?"

"As I said tha first time, I have Layla. Now it's up to you if she lives or dies."

"Listen, let's cut through all the bullshit! What do you want?"

"A million dollars."

"What?"

"Nigga you heard me or is she not worth a million?"

"So, you want a million dollars?"

"Yes, and I know it's a lot of money, that's why you have 3 days to get it."

"I want to talk to Layla to make sure she's alive." I put tha phone to Layla's ear.

"Hello," she said through swollen lips.

"Are you a'ight?"

"Not really," she cried, "it's Star and..." Before she could finish I snatched tha phone from her ear.

"Now didn't I tell you you wouldn't be laugh'n for long?"

"Star I swear if you touch one hair on her body you will pay!"

"Too late for that and you'll pay first a million, that is in 3 days. I'll call you wit further instructions." I hung up before he said another word since I was call'n tha shots.

"Star do you think he has a million dollars?"

"All that cocaine he sell'n; he should; if not, he'll get it from somewhere. Shit, get her boyfriend should have it as well."

"Man, that nigga was just gettin' by til Keem came home. Nah, Star I gotta disagree wit you on that."

"Yeah whatever.

"Who Fuckin' side you on?"

"Yours, I'm just not no hater!"

"Let's take her to tha bedroom."

"Untie her feet."

"Get up Bitch and let's go!"

Meanwhile...

"I need to call Stacks and fill him in."

"I'm gonna call Jonda so she won't be worried."

"Laysha I swear Imma kill those two niggaz."

I knew that Keem was serious, he had tha look of murder in his eyes. We both made tha calls we had to make.

"Stacks is on his way over."

"Jonda is too."

After about 20 minutes, they were both there.

"Listen Keem, we'll both give up half a mill," Stacks said.

"You know tha money ain't a problem."

"I know, but that's my baby so I wouldn't see it any other way."

"Are you sure its Star?" Jonda asked.

"Positive, she told me before he snatched tha phone. I told her not to mess wit him, I didn't trust him. He said he would call in 3 days wit instructions. I have to be honest; I don't think he's just gonna take tha money and give her up."

"What are you say'n Keem?" Lay asked.

"Nothing, let's just go get tha cash."

Over tha next 2 days I didn't get any sleep and to make matters worse, Flynn got killed. They said Grams girl pulled tha plug on him. They say bad things come in 3. I was sitting in tha bedroom cleaning my gun when Lay walked in.

"What are you doing wit that?" she asked pointing to my .40 cal.

"I told you Imma kill that Fuck Ass Nigga when I catch him!"

"Why don't you just pay somebody to handle him for you?"

"Cause I can handle my own. Where are tha girls?"

"Over Jonda's wit Missy. You know you should really get some sleep."

"I'm not tired, besides, I have too much on my mind."

"Well, let me help you to release some stress," she said taking off her dress. As soon as I saw her ass in that thong, I got an instant erection. Next thing I knew, I had my face between her legs.

"OOOOOH Baby that feels SOOOOOOO GOOOOOOOD!" I slipped out of my clothes and into Lay.

"UMM Lay you feel good."

"You like this pussy?"

"I love it," I said in total ecstasy.

"UMM, OOOH, AAAAAGH YES Baby, you know right where my spot is!" I gently slipped one of her nipples in my mouth.

"UM HUH YES! I'm bout' to Cum Daddy! OOOH SHIT, I'M CUMMING! I'M CUMMING!!! She started shaking then I felt her cum all over me but I kept stroking.

"Oh My God! Baby I'm Cumming again!"

Lay came 3 times back-to-back. When she was about to cum again, I was ready to do tha same.

"Baby I'm about to cum," I said to let her know.

"So am I, cum wit me." Another 3 strokes and we came at tha same time.

"Damn I needed that."

"So did I, you been holding out on me."

"Only because of what's been going on these past 2 days."

"Star you ready to get this money today?"

"No doubt Baby, we bout to get a free mill."

"Are we going to really let her go scott free?"

"She's not going scott free; it's costing them a mill."

"Me myself, I don't think they got tha money."

"Well let's find out."

When I called tha first time nobody answered. I called right back this time Lay picked up.

"Hello."

"Bitch put ya husband on tha phone!"

"Keem come get tha phone and ya mom is a Bitch Faggot."

"Yo."

"You better put that whore in check nigga."

"Star you really testing my patience."

"Fuck you! I'm calling tha shots! I want you to meet me in one hour at tha car wash on Governor Printz. Perk bring tha van to tha side door."

"Stacks it's time."

"I'm on my way, I'll be there in 10 minutes." When stacks came I filled him in on tha details.

"Do you think I should have Jewlz and Bean across tha street at tha gas station?"

"Nah." As we were about to turn in my phone rang.

"Hello."

"Change of plans, there's a side street by Auto Zone put tha money in that trashcan. Once we have tha money you'll get Layla."

"What he say?"

"Keep going straight then turn at tha Pepsi Cola building. Turn by tha funeral home, stop right here," I got out and grabbed tha duffle bag, "got damn, I didn't realize a mill was so heavy."

"I said tha same thing when I put it in tha car." After I put tha bag in tha trashcan, I got back in tha car.

"Hello."

"Now pull off."

"Where's Layla at?"

"I told you when we get tha doe you'll get Layla." We pulled off slowly checking tha rearview tha whole time.

"Pull up next to tha trashcan."

I had my gun in my hand as I got out to retrieve tha money. I threw it in tha back and took a look inside.

"WHEEEEEEEEW!"

"Is it all there?"

"It sure looks like it." I pulled my cell out and called tha number I had gotton familiar wit.

"Yo, I just had a change of heart, I need another mill. This time you have 2 days." Perk was looking at me funny.

"What? That was to easy; we might as well get a mill apiece. I think Imma open me up a biz-ness; invest my money."

"I feel you on that."

"Yo, where tha Fuck is my neice?

"You did what and you need what?"

"Hello. Hello."

Imma kill that Mafucka!"

"What he say?"

"That Faggot Ass Nigga had tha nerve to say he wants another mill."

"Keem what choice do we have? It's not gonna hurt us."

"Fuck that Shit, tha game has changed! Call that niggaz sister and set up a date wit her."

"What are you gonna do?" I filled him in on tha plan after he called to set up a date wit Star's sister.

"I hope this shit work."

"Trust me, it's definitely gonna work."

Stacks date couldn't have worked out any better. She told us more than we needed to know.

Two more days had passed and still nigga still hadn't called yet.

"Keem don't worry she still alive."

"I know, I just want that nigga in tha casa de los muertos (House of tha Dead)."

"I know you do and so do I." When he finally called, I was fed up being nice.

"Look you Dumb Mafucka I want to speak to Layla now!"

"Nigga who tha Fuck do you think..." I cut him off.

"You Mafucka you, that's who I'm talking to." When he didn't say nothing, I thought he had hung up until I heard Layla's voice.

"Are you a'ight Layla? Don't worry you will be back home today, I promise."

"A'ight, A'ight that's enough, same spot 30 minutes."

"Let's roll, it's that time."

Tha bag was already in tha car. 30 minutes later we were putting tha bag in tha trashcan.

"Hello."

"Yo around tha corner in that ran down van."

We sped around to where tha van sat. When I slid tha door open tha sight of Layla's face made me furious to say tha least. We untied her and helped her in tha car. After about 15 minutes I decided to call Star.

"Ain't you satisfied?"

"Ha! Ha! Ha!"

"What's so Fuckin' funny?"

"I take it you have not looked in tha bag yet," I said and hung up.

"Perk look in tha bag, make sure that money in there."

Perk opened tha bag then said, "Oh Shit." As I was turning to look he was taking tha tape off.

"Star they got Mommy, please give them tha 2 million they want!" When I saw my sis pop out tha duffle bag I damn near crashed.

"What tha Hell!"

"They got Mommy, they said you have one day to get their money." I picked my phone up and called Keem.

"Yo you like tha gift I sent you? Ain't no fun when tha rabbit got tha gun, is it?"

"Please don't hurt my mom."

"Ya pleas and cries fallin' on deaf ears. You should have thought about that when you put ya hands on my niece you Fuck Ass Nigga," I looked back at Layla who was smiling, "now I want tha mill you took back wit a mill interest."

"A'ight, so you want 2 mill?"

"Yup then I want another for ya moms safe return."

"I don't have that type of money."

"Well at least I know you got a mill (Ha! Ha! Ha!)"

"I need longer than a day though."

"You tell me how long you need."

"At least a week."

"You have 5 days to come up wit my 3 mill."

"So do y'all really got his mom?"

"Yup but she came willingly after we explained what he did."

"You know they don't have that type of money."

"We gon' take our money then give his mom tha rest. She said she's tired of his Shit always falling back on her and her daughter. You need to go to tha hospital to make sure nothing is broke or fractured."

"I'm good, I'll be fine." We pulled up to tha house Lay and Jonda came running out.

"Oh My God! Look at ya face," Lay said wit tears running down her face.

"Y'all didn't kill that Mafucka?" Jonda asked.

"Naw, not yet." We all went inside; Layla's face didn't look so bad once she cleaned herself up.

"I still think you should go to tha hospital."

"I am, Lay gon' take me after I smoke me a much-needed Dutch."

"Lay you good? I'll take her."

"You sure?"

"Yeah, I don't got nothing to do."

"Layla that nigga was going crazy too; I ain't never seen Stacks like that." (Ha! Ha! Ha!)

"Me either."

"Oh, you don't need to laugh, you was Fucked up too."

"I know I was, that's my Baby and that's why that nigga going to tha boneyard."

"Are you sure?"

"Yes Ms. Williams, you're 9 weeks pregnant besides that everything else is fine. Tha swelling will go down in a few days."

"Thank you Doctor, I didn't know what to think."

"Wow, I'm 9 weeks pregnant and there's only one person who could be tha father."

"So, is everything a'ight?"

"No."

"What did they say?"

"Just that I'm 9 weeks pregnant."

"So, what are you gonna do? I know you don't want to have Star's baby?"

"No, I don't and I'm not because it's your baby."

"Are you serious?" he asked wit a smile.

"Positively, you're tha only one I been fucking tha past 3 months."

"So, are you going to keep it this time?"

"Yes."

It had been 4 days and I decided to give Star a call.

"Hello."

"Times up."

"I still have one more day to come up wit tha money."

"You're not calling tha shots, I am. I want my money in 2 hours, no excuses. You hold your mother's life in your hands. 2 hours, nothing more nothing less and don't try to short me because I will count it before I tell you where your mom is. Tha time is 2 o'clock at exactly 4 o'clock meet me at tha Dollar Tree on Miller Road." I decided to take a nap so I told Lay to wake me up at 3:30.

"Damn this nigga wants tha money in 2 hours."

"How much do we need?"

"We about 700,000 short."

"How much we got on tha streets?"

"Close to 300,000."

"So, we gonna be 400,000 short?"

"Yeah."

"Fuck him, it's not like he going to count it."

"Actually, he is, he said he was going to count his money before he gave Mom up."

"He's bluffing."

"I don't think I'm willing to risk my mom's life on it."

"Well time is ticking; we better get a move on it."

For tha next hour we scrambled to come up wit tha rest of tha doe.

"Fuck it Perk, Imma just let him know we a quarter mill short."

"That's up to you, I think you shouldn't tell him."

"I feel you but I can't take that chance."

When we pulled up Keem was sitting in his 850.

"Yo we here."

"Pull on tha side of me then both of y'all go into tha store."

Once they did that, I got tha duffle bags and put them in my trunk. I could be wrong but one of tha bags was a little lighter than tha other two.

I called Star, "Yo, I didn't even count it yet but I know you're about 200 grand short."

"Nah, it's only 100 short."

"Well, Imma be nice and let you slide. You can find ya mom at home. (Ha! Ha! Ha!) Oh, and just in case you try something like this again I know where everybody who means anything to you lives."

With that being said I called Star's mom to let her know I was on my way wit something for her. When I pulled up, she was standing on tha porch.

I got out and carried tha duffle bag that I was sure didn't contain a mill.

"Ms. Diane this is courtesy of your son," I said sitting tha bag on tha living room floor. When she unzipped it and saw all that money, she was more than happy.

"Lord Jesus, thank you I'm moving to Atlanta."

"That's enough to buy you a house and start a biz-ness if you want. Well, I believe you deserve this for all tha trouble Star has caused you."

"Thank you, Baby, is Layla ok?"

"Yeah, her face is swollen but she's fine."

"Baby can I ask you a favor?"

"Sure."

"Please don't tell Star I'm moving to Atlanta."

"You don't have to worry about that. No offense but I don't even like your son."

"Believe me, none taken. I don't even like him and I carried him for 9 months."

"Here's my number Ms. Diane, if you ever need anything don't hesitate to call me."

"Thank you again and God will bless you. Tell Layla I'm sorry."

"You don't have to apologize for what ya son did."

"I know but I just feel so guilty."

"Don't," I said giving her a hug then leaving.

CHAPTER 18

PAYBACK

"Baby don't overdo yaself."

"I'm not, I promise.

I had been working out since I left tha hospital. I needed to be 100% so that I can take back what I built. Star and Perk aren't going to know what hit them. Tha money they took wasn't nothing compared to what I was really worth. Nobody knew about this house except Flynn; this is where I keep all my money.

"Baby I need to handle some biz-ness, I'll be back later."

"Grams please be careful."

I pulled up to tha stop sign then pulled over. I turned the car off then leaned back. After about a half hour he finally came out. I knew he was going to tha block so I got out and followed him.

"Aye yo Rolo, let me holla at you for a sec. He turned around.

"Who that?"

"Ya peeps, hold up for a sec. When hen he slowed up I knew I had him.

"Oh Shit, I-I-I-I-I thought you were dead," he said studying my face.

"I am, you're just imagining this," I said playing off his high.

"Damn that wet got me trippin' I need to sit down," he said, sitting on tha steps.

"So why did they want me dead?"

"Hold on," he said, rolling another wet blunt, "you weren't suppose to get killed, just robbed."

"Is that why you brought them here?"

"Hell Naw! But ya boy Flynn was, I wanted to do him myself."

I pulled my Glock out and put it in his face then emptied tha whole clip. Before I walked off, I kicked him in tha stomach. One down, two to go.

CHAPTER 19

Surprises

Biz-ness was at an all-time high. We had even expanded to a few more cities, thanks to niggaz I met in jail. Since school was out in two weeks, we decided to take tha kids to Disney World.

"Do you think Shante will let me take Fiza?"

"I don't see why not."

"Hand me my iPhone please." I went to my phone book, found tha number I wanted, and touched dial.

"Hello."

"How you doing Ms. Bunny?"

"Fine."

"This is Keem."

"I know who this is."

"I wanted to know if you could ask ya daughter if Fiza could go to Disney World wit us in two weeks?"

"Sure, she can go; I know she'll be happy to go."

"Well, I'll call you tomorrow wit all tha details."

"How long y'all gonna be there?"

"Two weeks."

"I'll get her stuff ready."

"All she needs is under clothes."

"I know you not buying her more clothes; she has more then enough already."

"Ms. Bunny you never can have too many clothes."

"I'll let Shante know she'll be going."

"Ok thank you Ms. Bunny."

"Keem you don't have to thank me for being a father to your daughter."

"I'll call you wit tha details tomorrow." I respected Ms. Bunny for allowing me to see my daughter when Shante was on her bullshit which was all tha time.

"Lay did you tell tha girls yet?"

"No, I was going to do that today. I have a doctor's appointment in a hour."

"Do you want me to go wit you? I had to feel his forehead.

"What are you doing?"

"Just making sure you don't have a fever."

"I can't accompany my wife to tha doctors?"

"Sure, but any other time you always say no when I ask. I don't have anything to do and I want to spend some time wit you. After we leave tha doctors we can go to T.G.I. Fridays and have lunch."

"Well let's go so I don't be late and you're driving."

We were in tha doctors office for what seems like an eternity before they finally called Laysha's name.

"This way please."

"Come on," she said looking at me.

"I was only here for my yearly checkup."

"Dr. Sasillo will be wit you shortly Laysha."

"Ok, thanks Londa."

"We'll be in here for another hour."

"No we won't." Just as she said that Dr. Sasillo walked in.

"Hello Laysha, how are you doing?"

"I'm doing fine and yaself?"

"I can't complain. What's up Hakeem haven't seen you in a while."

"Yeah, I've been working hard." He conducted his exam then said he would be back.

I went to put my clothes back on in tha bathroom.

"Lay you gaining weight."

"No I'm not."

"Word you are. Ya ass gettin' fatter."

"Boy shut up."

"I'm serious Baby."

When Dr. Sasillo came back he said, "Everything checked out fine, except one thing." We both had a look of concern on our face.

"No need for tha look of concern."

"Well, what's tha problem?"

"You're 6 weeks pregnant."

"I just told her she was gaining weight, now we know why. I know it's early but do you plan on keeping it?"

"Of course, I am."

"Well, since this is your child you know what you have to do. Stop at tha desk so Londa can give you a date to come back." Me and Keem walked hand in hand happy as can be.

"Congratulations you two," Londa said wit a smile on her face.

"I usually know when I'm knocked up."

"Hey we said we were gonna try to have a son in tha beginning of tha year."

"I know, we're just a little early."

"So now we have two surprises for tha girls. Niya told me about a week ago she wanted a little brother."

"Well, hopefully she'll get that little brother she wants. If I don't have a boy, shit even if I do, I'm getting my tubes tied after this one."

After we ate lunch we decided to go to Best Buy, they had this TV I wanted for tha new house. My phone went off as we walked in tha store.

"I want you to know ya house is ready for you to move in."

"A'ight!" I yelled causing everybody in tha store to look at us, "Scott let me buy this TV and I'll meet you there."

"Was that tha realtor about tha house?"

"Yes, he said it's done."

"Well, you better buy two of those. One for tha bedroom and living room."

"I only need one, I wanted to get tha shit on MTV cribs."

We pulled up to this house that looked like something outta Hollywood.

"Oh My Fuckin' God! Keem this is beautiful."

"You designed it."

"I know, but this is far better than I envisioned."

"You haven't even seen tha inside yet."

"I know."

"Hello Mr. and Mrs. Bell."

"Hello Scott."

"Please come, let me show you your new house."

"Please do," Lay said all excited.

As soon as we walked in, I was amazed. After we looked at tha whole house I couldn't wait to move in.

"So when will you be moving in?"

"We're going to Disney World in two weeks and we'll be gone for two weeks. But when we come back this is where we'll be coming to. My wife will get wit you tomorrow to let you know how she wants to furnish it."

On tha way home Lay couldn't stop talking about tha house.

"Baby I can't wait to have our housewarming. Do you want to bar-b-que and have a pool party?"

"I like that, a house pool warming."

"We might as well pick Niya up unless you plan on comin' back out?"

"No." I stopped by tha daycare to grab Niya.

"Can you go get her please?"

"Yeah, but you ain't gonna play that pregnant card," I said laughing as I got out.

"Niya ya dad here," one of tha kids said.

"Daddy! Daddy!"

"Hey Daddy's Little Diva. What happened to ya shirt?"

"Devon did it."

"Ms. Janice, do you see her shirt?"

"Yes, Keem and I was going to inform you as well Devon's dad."

"This shirt cost too much money for him to be pulling on her clothes tearing them." While we were talking, Devon's dad came in.

"Dad," Devon said running to him.

"Yo your Devon's dad?"

"Yeah, what's up?"

"He tore my daughter's shirt." Devon's dad had on a nice chain, two phones so I knew he was a hustler.

"So what do you want me to do?"

"I know this mafucka didn't just ask me that."

"I don't know if you know it or not but that's a Gucci shirt that cost 200 dollars."

"They kids, shit happens."

"I understand that but when ya son is pulling on her clothes after Ms. Janice told him more than once to stop."

Lay walked in, "What is taking so long?"

"Devon ripped her shirt."

"Well, his parents gon' have to pay for it. That's her first time wearing that."

"Just give me a hundred dollars, I'll take tha lost."

"I'm not giving you no buck for some knock off Shit!" (Ha! Ha! Ha!)

"Knock off, I wouldn't disrespect my daughter let alone myself wit no knock off clothes." He pulled out a knot and passed me a fifty.

"This is all I'm givin' up."

"Let me holla at you outside, no need to cause a scene in here."

"Keem hold on, let me get Ms. Boady to see if we will cover it."

Even if they did, I already had my mind made up I was definitely gonna still holla at him.

"Ms. Boady said they wouldn't pay."

When we got outside, I asked him if I could holla at him.

"What up, I'm done talking; either you want tha fifty or you don't." This nigga got me Fucked up.

"Where you be so I can holla at you wit out tha kids and away from tha

- 165 -

daycare?"

"On tha Hill, 3rd & Clayton."

By now his boy got outta tha Crown Vic they were in.

"Jacob what's tha deal?"

"Nothing I can't handle."

Stacks pulled up wit Layla.

"What's tha deal Playboy?"

"Yo, let Layla go wit Lay; give me a ride on Clayton,"

I looked at dude then said, "I'll be waitin' on you."

"Keem everything ok?" Layla asked.

"Nah but it will be." I got in wit Stacks and pulled off.

"What was that about?" I filled him in and he started laughing.

"Stacks it's tha principle of him disrespect'n Niya." I called Jewlz and told him and Beanz to meet me up there wit their heat.

"Lay what was that about?"

I filled Layla in then headed to tha Hill.

"Oh you know I just found out I'm 6 weeks pregnant today."

"Well, when I went to tha hospital I found out I was knocked up too."

"What, why didn't you tell me?"

"I was going to tell you today."

"How far along are you?"

"11 weeks now. I hope I have a boy."

"Me too but if I don't, I'll try again in 5 years."

"I'm threw no matter what I have."

"So, you gettin' ya tubes tied?"

"You better know it. Ya daughter told me she wanted a little brother."

"I know, Niya told me that too."

"Not Niya Nay. Shit that's probably why I'm pregnant."

"No, you're pregnant because you and Keem didn't wear protection." We both laughed at that.

"Why you parking all tha way up here?"

"I know, he just gon' have to be mad." I pulled down tha street. We both got out tha car and started walking towards Keem.

When we got to tha park Lil Tony and his boys was out there.

"What up Keem, Stacks, Jewlz, and Beanz?"

"What's up," we all said in unison.

"Is everything a'ight?"

"Nah, ya man Jacob suppose to be meet'n me up here."

"That ain't my man, he finally gettin' some chump change and it's going to his head. He lucky I let him pump up here, if he wasn't coppin' off me." I filled Lil Tony in on what happened.

"What really made me mad was not only did he say my daughter's shirt was a knock off but this nigga had tha nerve to pull out his money and handed me a fifty."

"Are you serious?"

"Dead! If we weren't at tha daycare I would have beat tha brakes off him."

Stacks tapped me on my arm. When I looked Lay and Layla were walking towards us.

"What are y'all doing up here and where is Niya?"

"Niya is wit Shy and I'm making sure you're a'ight."

"I'm fine, so you can leave." Jacob pulled up wit two of his boys.

"So, what you want to talk about?"

"I didn't want to cause a scene at tha daycare. So I figured I'd holla at you up here. Look, this ain't gotta turn into nuffin, I just want you to pay for my daughter's shirt."

"I already told you where I stood on it," then he pulled out a bigger knot and asked, "do you want tha fifty or not?"

"Jake is it?"

"Jacob."

"Listen Jacob, I don't really need tha money."

"I can't tell you going through all of this."

"First of all, you disrespect'n me by offering me fifty for a two-hundred-dollar shirt."

"Listen, I don't have time for tha bullshit, I got money to make and he dropped tha money at my feet.

Wit out say'n anything I punched him in tha face knocking him down.

Before I could stomp him, his boys pulled out. Stacks, Beanz, and Jewlz did tha same.

"Get tha Fuck in tha car!" I yelled to Lay and Layla. But to my surprise they both had guns drawn on them too.

Jacob got up and said, "Just give me a one on one."

To make a long story short. I beat tha shit outta him. When it was over I went in his pocket and took my two hundred.

"Jacob don't ever disrespect me again or next time you won't be gettin' up!"

When we got down tha Hill I let Lay and Layla have it.

"Where did y'all get those pistols and why did you come up there after

I told you not to?"

"This," Lay said holding up her Cat 9 is registered and I have a license to carry it."

"Yup and so do I."

"You already know, no matter what I got ya back."

"I know but you're not going to put yaself or tha baby at risk."

"Wow, you pregnant too?"

"Too?" I asked looking at Layla.

"What, it's not like I got 10 kids, this my first one."

"Is.."

"Yes, Stacks is tha father." Shy and Niya came walking up tha street.

"Aunt Lay my mom said call her."

"I did, she had her phone off."

"You know she snapped when she seen Niya's shirt. Oh yeah, I got to get some invitations but I'm having a housewarming in a month when we come back from Disney World."

"When y'all going to Disney World?"

"In two weeks, Keem is going to make reservations tomorrow."

"Well, book us a room and flight," Stacks said.

"No offense but this is a family vacation."

"Well since we are family that counts us in. Do you agree?"

"Anyway, let's get Niya and go home so we can give tha girls tha triple good news."

Later that night after dinner and tha girls had gotton their baths, I called them into tha living room.

"Listen, me and ya mom have some news for you two."

"Uh Oh, is it bad news Daddy?" Nay asked.

"I'll let you be tha judge of that. Well, since school is out in two weeks, I or we thought it would be nice if tha 4 of us and Fiza go to Disney World.

"Yeeeeah, Yeeeeah, Yeees, Yeees!" They were happy to say tha least.

"Next your mom is having a baby."

"Wheew! Yes we gon' get a little brother finally!" they screamed.

"Last but not least, when we come back from Disney World we won't be coming here."

"Where we going Daddy?" Niya asked.

"Me and mommy had a big house-built wit a swimming pool." They really got excited.

"We got our own rooms?"

"Yes you do and you get to tell ya mom how you want your room."

"OOOH me first!" Niya screamed.

After they told Lay exactly what they wanted Lay sent them to bed.

CHAPTER 20

Home Sweet Home

We had a wonderful time in Disney World. All tha girls including Lay and Layla wanted to stay longer, but me and Stacks had to get back. While we were gone, Scott called to say that tha house was completely furnished just tha way Lay wanted it.

When we pulled up to tha driveway Nay asked, "Is this our house Mom?"

"Yes it is."

"Oh snap!" Niya yelled.

We walkd in, "Welcome home ladies." Niya and Nay both took off running through tha house.

"Baby you really did tha damn wit tha house and tha decorating."

"So you like it?"

"Baby I love it."

Tha living room had dark cherry red furniture wit matching coffee and end tables. She had these 2 floor to ceiling dark cherry red and cream lamps. Tha dining room had a cream table set wit designs tha same color as tha furniture wit a beautiful China chest. Tha kitchen was state of tha art, I couldn't wait to cook in there. Oh, did I mention tha 72-inch TV mounted on tha wall. There was a computer room that had 5 computers in it, then there was a game room in tha basement that I thought of. There was a 62-inch flat screen for tha X-box One and PS5, Foo's ball & pool table, pinball machine, Ms. Pacman, Championship Sprint and NBA Jam that was for when tha fellas came over. Tha upstairs were what everybody wanted. Niya had her Gucci room, Nay had her Heaven room, Fiza's room was pink and white, our room was Fendi and tha baby's room Ralph Lauren. Both bathrooms Prada. I really liked tha way she had our bathroom done; his and hers double sinks and toilets, a glass shower that 3 people could fit in and a jacuzzi style tub. In tha backyard was tha pool, bar-b-que pit wit a built-in grill then it was a kettle I wanted for my dogs that I bought. Speaking of which, I need to call Mike to see if they have arrived yet. My dogs were being sent from East Asia; these dogs were very rare. There were only 6 in tha world and I had 2. These dogs cost me a quarter mill; I have never ever seen pure white Rottweilers. Mike has a dog farm so when I told him I wanted something different and he showed me these puppies.

Niya came out back, "Daddy can we go swimming?"

"Did you ask ya mom?"

"She said to ask you."

"Well, I don't care."

Nay he said yeah. Daddy what's that for?" she asked pointing to tha Kettle.

"It's for my dogs."

"We getting dogs?"

"Yeah." I went over to tha lounge area and took a seat.

"It's beautiful ain't it?" LAY asked sitting next to me.

"Yes, I have to commend you again, this house is definitely a dream house."

"Thank you, when are your dog's gon' be here?"

"I'm bout to call Mike now."

"I hope you ain't get no pitbulls."

"Unh, Unh Rottweilers."

"Them big ass dogs?"

"They won't let nobody come in tha house."

"Tha alarm system won't let them come in."

"Look at it as a double alarm." I put a finger up to say hold on.

"Hello Mike, this Keem...

Oh yeah, I'm on my way. Damn he said they came in a few days ago and they're beautiful."

"They all look tha same to me."

"Not these, that's why they cost so much."

"How much did they cost?"

"I knew you was going to ask that. I'll be back in a half."

"You still didn't answer my question."

"You don't want to know tha answer to that question."

"Yes, I do or I would not have asked."

"A quarter mill."

"What 250,000!"

"I'll be back, love ya."

"I can't wait to see these dogs and I love you too."

"GERANIMO!" NAY Yelled, as she cannon balled in tha pool.

"Niya, you stay down in tha shallow end."

"O.K. Mommy," she said diving in. I went in, got my phone, and tha invitations.

"Mommy, I love tha new house," Niya said wit a big smile on her face.

"I love It too."

"Mom, I'm not going to be able to go to tha same school, am I?"

"Yes, they have that choice program. Me or ya dad will have to drive you to tha bus stop. After school, you can go to Candy's house until we pick you up."

"I don't know, I might want to go to school out here."

"Well, you have a little time to decide."

"O.K.," she said, running back to tha pool. I made out my invitations then called Sandy.

"Hey Girl."

"Hey, how you like tha new house?"

"Like it "Bitch" I love it!

"So, when you having ya housewarming?"

"Next Saturday, I just finished my invitations. Make sure you bring y'all swimsuits."

"Bitch" you do not have a pool."

"Yes I do, this house is tha bomb."

"Where is ya husband?"

"He went to pick up his dogs."

"He got dogs?"

"Yeah, Rottweilers that cost 250,000."

"Are you serious?"

"Dead serious."

"Wow, they must be magic dogs."

"Same thing I said. I'll call you tomorrow I'm about to fix dinner."

"O.K, don't forget to bring tha invitations in tomorrow."

"I won't." I was in tha middle of cooking dinner when Keem came in wit a big bags of dog food.

"Where are these expensive dogs?"

"Diamond, Dutch!" he yelled and these two beautiful white puppies came runnin' in.

"OH MY GOD" I have never seen white Rottweilers before in my life."

"That's because they are rare; there's only 6 in tha world and we have 2."

"I see why they cost so much. Where did you get them?"

"East Asia." Nay and Niya came downstairs.

"OOOH, look at my dogs," Niya said wit a big smile on her face.

"They not just ya dogs," Nay said picking Dutch up.

"Yes, they are, ain't they Daddy?"

"No, their all of ours."

"See I told you."

"Keem, you gotta train them I don't want them pissing all over my carpet."

"They're already trained, see," he said pointing to tha back door.

Niya opened door so Diamond can use tha bathroom.

"Daddy, how old are they?"

"3 months. They had their shots, but I'm gonna take them to tha vet to get tags." I went to get tha diamond collars I had made and put them on.

"Daddy, can Diamond and sleep in my room?"

"They're going to sleep in tha Kettle."

"Baby I think you should wait until they get a little bigger to let them sleep outside."

"Yeah, you probably right."

We ate dinner, watched a movie until we fell asleep.

CHAPTER 21

HIT

Biz-ness has been getting better wit each passing month.

"Keem, Keem A lot of people have been try'n to buy heroin."

"No, we will not Fuck wit any heroin and if I find out anybody is messing wit it then they will be dealing wit tha consequences! Listen Jewlz we make more than enough money between tha weed, coke, and e-pills so there's no need to bring tha type of heat that dope brings. Unless you want to go to Jail?"

"I'm good, tha last 10 months have made me a very wealthy man thanks to you; might I add."

"Jewlz, you kept it real tha whole time I was down whether it was magazines, books, pictures, letters, or money orders and I respect that."

"Keem, I didn't do anything any real nigga wouldn't have done."

"That's why I had to put you on; there was no way I could be on top and not have you eatin' too. See, Perk and tha rest of them couldn't even fly me a kite. But yet, they thought I was suppose to come home and put food on their plate, Yeah Fuckin' Right."

"Funny you said that cause Hov, Big Head, and Chulo came to see me yesterday and asked if I could put them on."

"Better you than me cause I would have told them no."

"I did, when they was up and I wasn't they didn't help me out and I reminded them about that."

"Let's take a walk down 5th I'm hungry."

"Come on, I can go for strips and fries myself. Why would a mother let her child come out tha house like that?"

"I know, I'll bust my daughter's ass if she came out tha house wit that little shit on. Jewlz as long as I'm pay'n for their clothes they ain't gotta worry about no little shit like that. Lay told me I'm overprotective but you gotta be tha way niggas be."

"Yo what up Keem, Jewlz?"

"What up Redz?"

"What can I get for you?"

"I'll take tha strip and fries special."

"You can give me tha beef and chicken gyro."

"Did Lil' Tony call you?"

"Nah, why? He ready already?"

"No, he said tha boy Jacob tellin' niggaz you betta watch ya back."

"That nigga see me every day at tha daycare and he don't say shit."

"Well, just be on ya P's and Q's."

"I'm definitely gon' do that; I don't want to get shot tha Fuck up."

"Keem, Jewlz ya food is ready." We paid Redz then headed to tha park; when I saw Niya I knew I would have help eating my food.

"Daddy!' she said running up to me.

"Hey, my Little Diva," I said kissing her forehead.

"What you got to eat in that bag?"

"Damn, can I eat my meal in peace?"

"Now you know you can't," Lay said laughing.

"Why don't you go get her something to eat?"

"I want a chicken and beef gyro."

"Here, you might as well take half of this one."

"Damn Keem she knew what you had." (Ha! Ha! Ha!)

"It ain't about nothing, where is Nay at?"

"Her and Shy went into the center to go swimming."

"She could of did that at home."

"I wanted to come in town for a while."

"If I knew you was comin' in town, I would have told you to bring Diamond and Dutch."

"I started to bring them."

"See Mommy, I told you we should have brought them."

"Well, I can't wait to see these dogs," Blondy said.

"Y'all will see them this weekend at my housewarming."

"Oh Shit, here Jewlz," Lay said handing him an invitation.

"Thank you Lay, I wouldn't have known if you didn't give me this."

"Keem didn't tell you about it?"

"Nope."

"I knew you was givin' those out that's why."

"Jewlz cause you done started something."

"No, he didn't." We walked across tha park headed to 8th when this car pulled up."

"Yo Keem." Neither one of us answered since we didn't know who dude was.

"Yo Keem," he said again. We kept walking.

"You know who that was Keem?"

"Nah, you got ya pistol?"

"No, but let me go get it," he said taking off."

Dude came back around tha block. This time he didn't ask Shit he just started shooting. Pop! Pop! Pop! Pop! Pop! Tha first shot hit me in tha side but I kept moving until tha next shot hit my leg. Boom, Boom, Boom! I looked up to see Jewlz dumping at tha car before he peeled off.

"You a'ight?" I heard Jewlz ask before I blacked out.

"Girl, I can't wait to see what ya house looks like."

"You are to want to leave."

"Y'all got a pool," Maxi asked.

"Yeah, so bring a swimsuit if you're planning on swimming."

Pop Pop Pop Pop Pop! Boom Boom Boom!

"Oh Shit! Somebody shooting across the park!" Then we saw the car come flying past with the black window shot out.

"Shy, Nay, and Niya just went over there to get some money from Keem," Blondy said getting up and taking off across the park. Everybody else did the same.

"AAAAH!" Shy, Nay, and Niya screamed in unison while running into tha store.

After tha shots stopped they came out tha store and looked up tha street.

"NOOOOO DAAADDY!" Niya Screamed running up tha street, "DAAADDY, DAADDY NOOOO! Please don't take my Daddy!"

Nay cried! "Uncle Keem, Uncle Keem, NOOOO GOD NOOOO!" They all ran to Keem's side.

"Y'all back up!" Jewlz said.

"NO, I'M NOT LEAVING, MY DADDY," Niya said holding Keem's head.

"OH MY GOD!" Maxi said when she turned tha corner. As soon as Lay seen tha girls holding Keem she lost it.

"Keem Oh My God! Somebody call tha fuckin ambulance!" Lay yelled at tha top of her lungs.

"What tha Fuck is going on here?!" Stacks asked looking at Layla. When they go closer, he slammed on tha brakes causing Layla to almost hit her head on tha dash board.

"What tha Fuck!" but when she seen Keem laying on tha ground covered wit blood she shut up.

"Yo, what tha Fuck Happen, who did this?"

"I don't know but we gonna take him to tha hospital now! Help me put him in my truck." They lifted him up and put him in.

"I'm riding wit him," Lay said, "Blondy meet us there wit the girls," she said throwing her tha keys.

They were cry'n and wanted to ride wit us. Stacks drove off tuning up 7th Street to ST. Francis Hospital.

"Come on Baby, hold on. You gonna be a'ight. Just Hold on."

"Nigga you can't leave me," Stacks said looking through his rear-view mirror.

We pulled up to tha Emergency door.

"Somebody help! We need a doctor!" Stacks yelled while him and Jewlz pulled Keem out.

They rushed to us putting Keem on a gurney. We all sat in tha waiting room while Keem was in surgery.

2 hours later tha doctor came out wit Keems blood all over him.

"Mrs. Bell."

"Yes, that's me."

"Your husband was shot 3 times. Once in the leg and twice in tha stomach."

"Is he alright?"

"Well, I had to give him a shit bag but he should only need it for a few months."

"Can I see him now?"

"Yes, but he's still out from tha medicine."

Me and tha girls went in to see Keem, just tha sight of him wit those tubes in him made my cry.

"Mommy is Daddy alright?" Niya asked.

"Yes Baby, Daddy gonna be OK.

"DADDY! Nay yelled when she seen him open his eyes.

"WHERE AM I?" he said, try'n to get up?

"Slow down and lay back you're in tha hospital you were shot."

"Did I just hear you right?"

"Yes, you were shot 3 times."

"By who?'

"We don't know and tha police were here."

"I ain't talking to no fuckin' cops."

"I told them you were a innocent by stander, so just stick to that."

"Why do all of U have blood all over you?"

"We were all by your side until Stacks and Jewlz put you in tha truck."

"Daddy who shot you?"

"Yeah, who did this so we can beat 'em up," Niya said. (Ha! Ha! Ha!)

"Damn it hurts to laugh."

I looked under tha cover and was pissed at what I saw. Lay must of known it because she told tha girls to go wait outside.

"How come we gotta leave?"

"Cause I said so, that's why. Now go out there and wait for me." They both looked at Keem.

"Listen, you can come visit me tomorrow; so come give me a hug and kiss." They both kissed and hugged him causing him to wince in pain.

"Love you Daddy," they said walking out.

"Love y'all more."

A few minutes later Stacks, Jewlz, Beanz, Cream and Jungle were walking in.

"Damn, Big Brother what you try'n to go give a mafucka a heart attack?"

"Heart attack, a nigga tried to put me in tha boneyard."

"You have any idea who it was?"

"I do," Lay said.

"Who?"

"That Mafucka Jacob."

"Same thing I've been thinking," I said.

"Everybody just stay calm he'll get what he deserves. Did they give y'all your invites to the housewarming?" Everybody except Jewlz said no.

"Babe why didn't you? Let's see I didn't know if my husband was dying or not and that was the last thing on my mind. Did the doctor say how long I have to be here?"

"Until Friday."

"Baby why don't you go home with the girls."

There should be a law against this food," Lay said walking in.

"Lay call me, me and the girls are leaving Keem I'm going to take a shower and change my clothes then I'll be back."

After she left, I'll talk to the fellas about Jacob. We all agreed that nobody would do anything till I was 100%.

Four days later I was released from the hospital.

Baby you alright?

I'm not feeling this pain or this Shit Bag.

It's only temporary.

I know but you know he's been looking at me all crazy at the daycare. Probably wondering if we know it was him is everything ready for tomorrow?"

"Yes, Sis said he would handle the grill. Rachel and Paris said they would be there too.

She better especially since she didn't come to the hospital.

She didn't want to see you like that."

I know that's what she said when we talked on the phone every day. I can't wait to get in that king size bed. As soon as I got in the house, I went straight to the bedroom to take a nap.

Hello.

Oh, hey Luddy I'm doing fine.

Yup, I'm 9 weeks now.

who told you Layla?

Damn I couldn't believe this nigga was still calling her. I wonder how many times he called since the first night I came home.

"Are you going to stretch just to see what she would do."

"Well, it was nice that you called but I have to go."

I don't believe this shit; here I am being faithful and she still talking to this nigga, you can play that shit. I set up,

"Hey sleepy head I thought you were going to sleep all day."

"Them pills I took, knocked me out."

"I see, what time you going to pick Naya up?"

"In another half hour, why?"

"I need to drop my prescription off."

"I'll drop it off when I go into town; you just get some rest."

CHAPTER 22

Housewarming

When I woke up Lay was already getting things ready.

"Hey Daddy."

"Hey Baby Girl, where's Niya?"

"In the computer room."

"Did anybody let Dutch and Diamond out for their walk?

"Mom took them out." I walked into tha kitchen where Lay was prepping all tha meats.

"Why didn't you wake me up so I could help?"

"I wanted you to get your rest, but since you up now you can make tha seafood salad."

"It's 2 o'clock what time is everybody coming?"

"3 o'clock"

"Well, Imma start tha grill until Stacks get here."

"You sure?"

"Yeah, we gotta have some type of meat done."

I went out back to fire up tha grill. As soon as Diamond and Dutch saw me, they started barking like crazy.

"Aye shut it up and sit down!" I yelled. Tha barking instantly stopped.

I had tha grill designed to hold a lot of meat, so by tha time tha guest started to arrive hot dogs, hot sausage, burgers, chicken, and shish kebab were done. I even had tha grill designed wit a warmer to keep tha meat that was already done so it wouldn't get cold. Lay showed everybody tha house as the came. By tha time she was done she said, "I know what a tour guide feels like now.

By 5 o'clock we were in full swing. All tha food was just about done except my steak and shrimp I wanted. All tha kids and some of tha adults were in tha pool.

"Keem those dogs are something special," Cream said.

"Did he tell y'all how much?" Stacks asked.

"Quarter Mill," Lay responded wit.

"Quarter Mill!" Maxi yelled almost choking on her food.

"I don't care what nobody say, there are only 6 in tha world and guess who got 2?"

"I would've spent that for them too," Jewlz said in my defense.

I took tha last of tha food off tha grill then sat then sat down.

"Nay, Nay."

"Yes Dad."

"Could you get my pills off my dresser please?"

"No, I'll get them; I don't want her tracking water all over my house."

Rach came over and sat next to me.

"Hey Brother, how you feeling?"

"I could be better."

"I love this house it's some cribs shit. Ya nephew said he wants to live wit you."

"He's welcome to stay any time he wants."

"Between tha pool, dogs, and game room you not going to be able to get rid of him. Oh, I know what I had to tell you."

"What?"

"You know Perk called me this morning asking about you."

"About me?"

"Yup, said he heard it through tha grape vine that some dude named Jacob had his young boy Flash shot you."

"Oh yeah."

"Then he asked if you were still in I.C.U; I told him yeah."

"Good, did he tell you where he was at?"

"He said he was in D.C. but I know he was lying. Outta all people I never would have thought he would be on some Bullshit."

"Me either Sis but wit so called friends like that who needs enemies."

"I just can't believe it the way you use to look out for him. Shit, if it wasn't for you, I would have never talked to him."

"All I can say is we learn from mistakes so we don't make them again."

"Excuse me, I'm not interrupting, am I?"

"No, we were done," Rach said getting up.

"Baby did you see all tha gifts we got?"

"Laysha, what could they have bought that we actually need?"

"It's tha thought that counts."

Since I heard her on tha phone wit that Jamaican Mafucka all I see is her hugging him that night in Palmers.

"Keem, Keem"

"Oh huh."

"What you thinking about?"

"Nothing."

"It's Jacob, isn't it?"

"Yeah," I said lying.

"He's gonna get what he deserves; you can count on that."

I had to look at her; she said that like she knew something I didn't.

Everybody had made their way inside. Tha kids went to tha game room while we went into tha computer room to get superman high. After a few hours they all started to leave.

Once everybody left Lay decided to open tha gifts. To our surprise it was a bunch of name brand kitchen and bathroom stuff. Beanz had gotten us his and hers bathrobes wit our initials on them which Lay loved.

"I'm about to take a shower," I said grabbing my cane and heading up tha steps.

As soon as Keem was outta earshot I called tha number I had gotten earlier to set my plan in motion.

CHAPTER 23

Never Seen it Coming

I called Layla to let her know that if Keem called that she hadn't talked to me.

"What are you up to Lay?"

"Nothing, I just need to handle something important and I don't want Keem to know about it yet.

"Oh, you're planning a surprise for him?"

"Yup, so please don't tell him."

"I won't. Oh, did you see that Gucci stroller online?"

"No."

"You'll love it, trust me."

"A'ight, well don't forget; I'll call you later."

"A'ight."

"Hello."

"Hey you."

"I didn't think you was going to call, I hit you wit my number almost 3 weeks ago."

"I know but I am a married woman."

"So, when you gonna let me take you out?"

"Look, let's cut tha bullshit; I'm married so we already know this ain't about nothing but sex."

"Not for me, I've been peeping you for a while; I just didn't want to overstep my boundaries. Especially when I found out you were married. By tha way, how is he doing? Words around town is he got shot a few times."

"Yeah, but he'll be Ok in a few months."

"What are you doing now?"

"Nothing."

"Well, let's get a room."

"We can go to tha Marriot by tha airport; I can't be seen."

"I understand, you can meet me up there; I'll call you back wit tha room number."

"Ok." All I could do was smile knowing I was about to do something forbidden.

An hour later I was pulling into tha parking garage of tha Marriot. Before I got out I made sure my wig and sunglasses were on straight. I took tha elevator to tha 5th Floor; got off then went to tha room that he said he would be in. I knocked on tha door and after a few seconds tha door came open.

"You make sure you're incognito, don't you?

"Sure do, now let's get down to biz-ness."

"I love a woman who takes control."

"Oh, you do," I asked while pulling out a pair of handcuffs.

"Now that's what I'm talkin' about; cuff me Baby cuff me."

I obliged his request by cuffing him to tha bed then I stuffed a pair of dirty panties that I got from this homeless woman for 50 dollars in his mouth.

"Hold up let me change into something more comfortable." I came back wit my Baby 9. He tried to say something but his words were muffled from tha panties I stuffed in his mouth so I took them out.

"Shoot me, Baby shoot me."

"Trust me I plan to," I said as I stuffed them back into his mouth. I pulled the silencer out of my bag, that's when he realized it wasn't a game.

"Did you think I was going to actually Fuck you after you had my husband shot; you piece of SHIT!" He tried to say something. Right when I was about to shoot him my phone rang.

"Hey Baby…Nothing, on my way home…Down Sandy's…Ok I love you."

"Now, where were we? Oh yeah," I said putting my gun in his mouth in place of the panties that were there.

"Hold up, Hold up," he said, sounding like he had a mouth full of food.

"Now didn't ya mom tell ya not to talk wit ya mouth full?" I couldn't help but laugh at that, "now I'm gonna let you give me one good reason why I shouldn't kill you."

"How much money do you want?"

"I don't need ya chump change. I have about 5 stacks in my pants."

"But I can get you plenty more."

"How much is plenty?"

"25,000." (Ha! Ha! Ha!)

"Nigga that's like offering me a 10-dollar bill. I'll do you a favor; I'll let you keep tha money so you can have a decent funeral.

"Fuck You Bitch!"

"No Fuck You!"

SPT, SPT, SPT, SPT, SPT, SPT, SPT, SPT, SPT, SPT, SPT, SPT, SPT, SPT, SPT, SPT was tha sound of tha whole clip being emptied in Jacob's body. I made sure I wiped tha whole room down, uncuffed him then left as quietly as I had come. On my way home I called Sandy to let her know if Keem asked I was at her house. Of course, she wanted to know why so I lied and told her I was out getting him a better ring.

CHAPTER 24

Set Back

I have been on the hunt and I still can't find Perk or Star. I think it's time to ge back on tha grind. So I pulled my phone out to make tha call. As I was about to hang up somebody picked up.

"Yo who this?"

"What's up Keem?"

"Who dis?"

"Damn, I know it's been a minute but damn big Homey."

"Grams."

"Yeah."

"Oh Shit"

"How long you been back?"

"A few months now."

"I heard ya wifey has pulled tha plug."

"Nah, we just put that out there so tha niggaz that did it would think I was dead.

"So you know who did this?"

"Yeah these two niggaz but Imma deal wit them as soon as they surface."

"You need my help just say tha word. I was calling because I need to know if every this is still everything?"

"Yeah, do you need me to front you some shit?"

"Nah but I do need 4 birds."

"No problem, I'll send my folks to tha same spot."

"Cool, I should be there in 30 minutes tops."

"Grams Imma throw one in just on tha strength."

"You don't have to do that Keem."

"I know but I am, call me after you get it."

"Baby, I just seen Star on 53rd Street."

"Hold on I'm on tha phone."

"Yo Grams did she just say Star??

"Yeah."

"Does he be wit a nigga named Perk?"

"Yeah."

"You fuckin' wit them niggaz?"

"Hell Nah, them tha niggaz that shot me and killed Flynn.

"What a small Fuckin' world."

"You know them niggaz Keem?

"Do I know them, I've been looking for them since they robbed my peeps and kidnapped my niece."

"Talk about a small world."

"Listen, we need to work together on this."

"So, what do you think we should do?"

"First, let them know you're not dead. If they ask you why you said it, just tell them you didn't want tha killers to try and finish what they started. They have no idea that you know it was them."

"A'ight, I'm bout to leave now; I'll get on that as soon as I get back." I hung up only to be questioned by wifey.

"Who are you talking to?"

"What did I tell you about being in my biz-ness?"

"Nigga I ain't try'n to hear that. Who was that?"

"Damn it was Keem."

"How is he doing? You know he got shot a few months back."

"How the Hell do you know that?"

"My cousin Maxi told me. You know she messes wit his boy Jewlz."

"I'll talk to you when I get back; I got to handle a few things."

"Grams be careful."

"I will and if you see Star or Perk, let them know I'm still alive," she had this profound look or her face, "trust me," I said while walking out tha front door.

CHAPTER 25

He Don't Want U

"Girl, I wish ya brother wasn't married," Brenda said.

"He ain't," I said talking about Cream.

"Bitch I'm not talkin' about Cream; I'm talkin' about Hakeem." looked at her like she was crazy. Before Keem went to jail he was knocking Paris off.

"You probably already tried to holla at him," Paris said with sarcasm.

"And I did."

"So what happened?" I asked wanting to know. "That's just it, nothing happened." Keem pulled up right when I was about to say something.

"What up Sis? Hey Brenda. Paris you ready."

"Yup."

"You got a wrap."

"Yeah."

"Let me get it to roll this weed up."

"How are you getting it done Keem?" He turned his head around and gave Paris a look that said like you don't know.

"My fault, you ain't gotta look like that."

"Damn that shit smells good as a Mafucka."

"This is tha best shit in tha land."

"Nah, ya brother got tha best shit."

"Same thing."

"Well, pass it then. So Keem how's tha wife and tha kids?"

"Fine."

"Rach and Paris said you got one of those MTV Cribs houses."

"Oh, did they?" I didn't feel like Brenda's bullshit so I cut her off.

"Rach you know my nephew called last night."

"He did, what did he say?"

"He wanted to know if he could stay tha weekend. I told him I didn't care but he had to ask you."

"That's why he said he wasn't going over his grand mom's this weekend."

"Did he ask you?"

"No, more like told me; I swear he thinks he's grown. I'll drop them off later."

"Lay will be there. I'm thinking about hiring a maid."

"For what?"

"Well, since Lay is pregnant, I figured she should have somebody wait on her hand and foot."

"Slow down, did you just say that Sis was pregnant?"

"Yes, she's 13 weeks."

"Imma cuss her out she didn't even call me."

"That's because she's been busy taking care of me."

"I wish I was having ya baby." We all looked at Brenda like she had lost her mind.

Paris finished tha last braid and said, "If you wear a durag you wouldn't have to get it done every week." "As long as you get paid, does it matter?"

"Excuse me, I'm just try'n to save you some money."

"I wasn't try'n to be smart," I told her handing her 15 dollars and some weed.

"Thank you much." I couldn't help but smile at tha two of them secretly flirting.

"Brother what you doing for your birthday?"

"Sis I have tha slightest idea."

"Paris, I am gonna need you to do tha damn thing to my hair for my birthday."

"You know I got you for tha right price."

"A'ight y'all, Rach make sure you drop Nazir off later."

"You don't have to worry about that; he's not going to not let me drop him off."

As he was getting in tha car Brenda walked over to him.

"Keem when you gonna stop playing?"

"I don't play no games; you should know that by now."

"I can't tell."

"Brenda let's stop tha games. What do you want me to do, fuck you?"

"Damn that's how you feel?"

"Let's be real I'm married so, what else could you want?"

"I was hoping to be ya mistress, side jawn something."

I couldn't front Brenda wasn't bad looking; she was 5'7", brownskin, brown eyes, hair cut like Anita Baker with an ass like tha Jamaican chick from back in tha day Patra.

I sat there listening to Keem and Brenda talk.

"UM, UM, UM she playing herself talkin' about being his mistress," I said to Paris, "she think he gonna pass off some money."

We both looked at each other then said "NOT."

"He ain't fuckin' around this time around."

"I know, he told me that a few weeks ago when I was doing his hair plus if he was she don't got a shot over me."

"Bitch I knew y'all was fucking."

"I told you and so did Keem."

"No y'all didn't, y'all kept say'n y'all was just cool."

"Well, I thought I did."

"Bitch you thought tha Fuck wrong!"

"Not that you care or even want to hear it but Girl he got it going on UNH, UNH, UNH,"

"EEEEL, you right I don't want to hear that."

My mom was coming up tha street wit Naz, as soon as he seen Keem's car he took off running.

"Uncle Keem! Uncle Keem! Cuse me Brenda. You came to pick me up?"

"No he didn't."

"Awe man."

"Get in you can go with me I gotta pick Niya up anyway."

'I didn't even pack his clothes yet."

"I packed them last night."

"Well, I'll swing back past before I go home." He pulled off wit out say'n anything to Brenda.

"I think he wants me."

"Why you play yaself with that mistress, side jawn bullshit."

"I know," I said "Stop Hatin' Bitches!"

"If you think so."

"I know so," she said walking off.

"Imma tell him to stop leading her on."

"Rach you heard tha conversation just like I did; now if that was leading her on, WOW."

"You probably right."

"Probably?"

"OK you're right; now walk me to my house so I can get Nazir's bag."

"Come on, I want to get me a wrap anyway.

"I called Keem to let him know to pick Nazir's bag up at Paris house."

"Somebody is bump'n," Brenda said.

"That's Keem," I said.

How do you know?

"Cause all he play is that song by Drake Successful."

Sure enough it was him. Brenda was right about to go to tha car until she seen my niece.

"Aunty Rachel!" Niya yelled jumping out to give me a hug.

"Hi Paris."

"Hey Niya, I like that Prada dress."

"It's not Prada, it's Gucci."

"My bag."

"That's OK. Aunty Rachel Naz is staying tha weekend wit us."

"I know, I'm tha one who said he could stay."

"Well, he'll be home Sunday night cause we going to Dorney park Sunday.

"We are?"

"Yeah."

"Yeah," Naz said all happy.

I could tell Keem didn't know nothing about it so I asked Niya who was taking them?

"My mom, her friends, and their kids."

"Brother you ain't going?"

"Hell No, I ain't going wit a bunch of females."

"You went wit us that year on tha ski trip wit Power 99."

He looked at me smiled and said, "That was different. I'll call you later; get in tha car and buckle up Naz and Niya."

After they left Brenda went back to talking about Keem.

I quickly let her know, "Look we don't wanna hear that Shit."

"I know that's right," Paris said agreeing with me.

"I'm bout to shoot to Lady Blue to get me at outfit for tonight."

"I'm going."

"Me too."

"We out then, and Brenda you driving ya car."

CHAPTER 26

Dorney Park

Wilmington man found shot to death in hotel next to airport.

After I finished reading tha article I called Stacks.

"Yo, did you see today's paper?"

"No, why?" I read him tha article that I had just read.

"Damn, I wonder who did that shit?"

"So, you didn't do this?" I asked.

"Nah, I can't take credit for this."

"A'ight, let me call Jewlz, I'll hit you back."

I wonder who did this? My whole team said they had nuffin to do wit this. Oh well, whoever it was saved me a little time. I was still gonna get tha shooter.

A few days later, Lil' Tony called to give me tha name of tha shooter. Come to find out it was Beanz cousin. It was only right that I give Beanz tha assignment of executing him.

"Yo, do you think he'll be able to do it? They are family."

"Listen Cream, I need to know where his loyalty is."

"Keem let me ask you a question and keep it real. If you had to kill one of ya cousins in a situation like this would you be able to do it?"

"Yes," I answered wit no hesitation. When it comes to tha 5 of y'all; you damn right I will."

"What you gettin' into tonight?"

"Nothing, I got get up early; we going to Dorney Park.

"Stacks did say something about that."

"I don't really want to go but Lay and tha kids want me to go wit them; so, I'm going."

"What time is ery body meeting up?"

"No later than 8:30."

"A'ight, I'll let Jungle know. Oh yeah, before I forget, I need you to up tha order on tha weed for me."

"No problem, I'll do it when I hang up. I'm glad you said something cause tha shipment will be in tomorrow."

"Well, if I don't talk to you, I'll see you in tha a.m."

I hit Stacks so he could call Zoro and get 600 pounds instead of tha usual 400 we normally purchase.

I was on my way home when I remembered Lay asked me to bring home some shrimp and real crab meat so I had to shoot to Pathmark.

"Damn it's crowded in here for a Friday."

I had to call Lay to see if she wanted them to steam tha shrimp for her. She said it was up to me since I was cooking them. I decided to get tha frozen shrimp since they are already peeled.

By tha time I got home, it was 6 o'clock.

"Honey I'm home," I said walking in tha front door.

"Hey Dad!" Nay yelled from tha computer room."

"Hey Sweety."

I could smell tha fish and fried potatoes cooking.

"Baby you got it smelling good up in this mafucka."

"Why thank you, now get started on those crab cakes and shrimp."

"Do you want steam or fried shrimp?"

"Both." I don't even know why I asked.

"Can you put oil in tha deep fryer while I make tha crab cakes?"

"You know I gotcha Baaaby."

As soon as dinner was done told Niya, Nasir, and Nay to wash their hands. They told Lay they wanted everything which consisted of Fish, Fried potatoes, fried & steamed shrimps, crab cakes, corn, and blueberry cornbread.

"Aunty Lay, this food is off tha chain."

"Thank you Naz."

"Yeah, Mommy it's bumpin."

"Yeah Mom, especially these crab cakes wit tha shrimp in them."

"I can't take credit for those."

"They blazin Dad."

"Thanks, Niya."

"Uncle Keem, you know how to cook?"

"Yeah, my dad can cook his butt off," Nay said while licking her fingers.

"What I tell you about that shit!" Lay said snapping, "If you're done go get in tha shower."

"Lay, did you feed Dutch and Diamond?"

"Yes, I did and took them for a walk."

"Nay, before you get in tha shower let tha dogs in."

Later than night after tha kids were in bed 1 decided to ask Lay about tha Jamaican dude.

"Laysha."

"Yes."

"I need to talk to you about something."

"What have you done now?"

"I haven't done shit."

"Well then what is it?"

"Just wanted to know what's going on wit you and that Jamaican nigga?"

"What Jamaican nigga?"

"Don't play wit me, you know exactly who I'm talkin' about."

"Damn. Now what made him ask that shit?" I thought to myself before answering him.

"He called you tha other week." I tried not to show a surprised look on my face.

"Listen, Layla was messing wit him but didn't know how to break it off wit him so she asked me to do it for her."

"I don't believe her; she really expect me to believe this Bullshit she feed me."

"So, there was nuffin going on wit you and him?"

"No nothing like you think and it wasn't we were strictly business associates nothing more."

I didn't want her to continue lying so I dropped tha subject.

"Did you set tha alarm clock for 6:30?"

"No, I set it for 6."

"Good night," I said kissing her.

When tha alarm went off, I shut it off then woke Lay up.

"It's 6 o'clock already?"

"Yeah, so get up."

After I was sure she was up; I laid back down.

"Unh, Unh get up."

"Man chill."

"Nope, if I gotta get up so do you."

"You tha one who wanted to leave all early."

"No, I wasn't, that was Candy and tha rest of them."

"Just wake me up after tha kids get up."

(Knock Knock)

"What?"

"Are y'all up yet?"

"Yes, we are," I said agitated.

"Can I come in?"

"Sure." Nay walked in we already dressed, and before you ask, they're in tha game room."

"This early? It's only 7 o'clock."

"We gonna have to stop at Micky D's to get some breakfast."

"Can we just stops at J. Farmers instead of McDonalds?"

"Sounds like a winner to me."

"Well, why don't you call to place tha order then.

"Dad you know me and Niya always eat from tha buffet."

By the time everyone got there it was after 8:00. Since we were riding wit Stacks, I let him know to stop in town so we could pick up our food.

"Hold up, I left my weed in tha house."

"I know you not going to smoke wit tha kids in here."

"Why not? I do it all tha time."

I knew I wasn't getting on any rides not as long as I had this shit bag. Damn, I can't wait til next week to have this thing removed.

It was 10:30 when we arrived at Dorney Park.

So how we gonna do this? Sandy asked.

"Do what?"

"Are we all hanging out together or are going our separate ways?"

"I can't speak for ery body else but I'm spending tha day wit my wife and kids," I said winking at Lay.

"Yeah," Niya said jumping up and down.

"She loves her dad, Blondy said.

"Fuck it, we gonna hang out together.

"Who's treat is this," I said playing.

"This one is on me," Cream said, pulling his money out, "hey y'all buying ya own food though." We all laughed.

Tha kids got on every ride they could get on.

"Mommy I'm hungry, can we have something to eat?"

What do you want to eat, a cheeseburger or pizza?"

"No, I want to eat chicken and shrimp."

"Hey ya we bout to get something to eat."

"After we finished eating, we want to play some games.

''Baby I'm going to sit down; I'm not feeling to good.

"Did you bring ya pills?"

"Yeah, I just took one." That's probably why you feel like that." While I was sitting in tha crowd a group of guys came by.

"Yo, look at shortly right there, she fat as mafucka. At first I didn't pay any attention until they started talking reckless.

"I know that pussy probably good, look at her and them boy shorts. Yo My Man, who you talking about?

"Shawty in tha red shorts."

"That's my wife."

"Oh yeah lucky you." His boy started laughing.

"Please don't disrepect me."

"Nigga who tha Fuck you talking to?"

"Ain't no need to cause a scene or get put out tha park."

Stacks and Jungle were tha first ones to come over.

"Keem what's up?" I looked at dude then said nothing. Lay seen tha crowd and walked over; this nigga had tha nerve to blow a kiss. I took my cane and smacked him in the face wit it and before I can swing again Cream was pulling me back."

"Nigga you got me Fucked up. You don't ever disrespect me again!"

"What happened?" Lay wanted to know.

"This Nigga talkin' about you; after I stepped to him and let him know you was my wife."

"Excuse me, is there a problem?" tha security guard asked.

"Nah, we straight," dude said wit his fake ass ice grill on.

I knew him and his crew were soft cause had that been us it would have been on no questions asked.

"Daddy you Ok," Niya asked wit her fist balled up.

"Yeah, Uncle Keem we don't wanna have to hurt nobody," Naz said pounding his fist in his hand.

"Come on, let's finish enjoying ourselves."

By 9 o'clock we were all tired and ready to leave.

"Look at all tha glow bugs," I said laughing.

All tha kids had glow in tha dark glasses, necklace, and bracelets along wit all tha stuff animals we won for them.

"Daddy I had a ball today; I wish Fiza could have came."

"You know how her mom is."

"Keem you need to just take that dumb bitch to court."

"I know, I just don't want to go to through that child support bullshit."

"Fuck that! We have enough money to pay that Shit!"

"Layla let me see ya lighter."

No soon as we got on tha road Niya, Nazir, and Nay were sleep.

"They knocked out."

"They should be all tha runnin' around they did today."

"Keem, so what you doin' for ya birthday."

"Stacks I don't even know. I did treat myself to a 76 Brougham."

"Where you got it at?"

"Joe's, he said it'll be done in another week."

"I was think'n about gett'n me a old school."

"No offense Baby, but Imma have tha hottest shit in tha city. I'm telling you; my shit is cranberry wit cream guts piped out in cranberry sittin on 30's.

"Nigga you snapped you riding 30's."

"I had to treat myself; I've been in my 850 for a year, time to step my game up. We got a 5-car garage wit 4 cars in it. Lay, I'm gonna get us a truck as our family car so when we go places as a family, we can be comfortable."

"We can do that Monday morning cause I already know what I want to get."

"Sounds like you were already planning on gett'n a truck."

"Actually, I was gonna suggest that we get tha new Caddy truck."

"Good choice Lay, I was about to upgrade wit one of those myself," Stacks said.

"Boy you do not need no more cars," Layla said.

"I'm gettin' me a old school and a truck then I'm good."

"Mm Hmm you say that now."

"I'm serious and I'm giving this to you so when you have tha baby y'all be straight."

She was all smiles then said, "I'm getting it painted.

"Niya, Nay, Naz wake up," They looked around, "we home, get up cause ain't nobody carrying y'all so get up."

"And get y'all stuff; if you leave it I'm keeping it," Stacks said playing wit them, "Keem you in for tha night or you try'n to get a few drinks?"

"No, he ain't coming back out," Lay said not giving me a chance to respond.

"That's all it is then call me tomorrow."

"A'ight."

I hit tha alarms then headed upstairs to take a shower. Since it was late, Lay told tha kids to just go to bed.

"You didn't have to speak for me; I wasn't going back out anyway, I'm tired."

"Tired from what? You didn't do nothing at all."

"All that Fuckin' walking?"

"Baby you didn't even look like you were enjoying yaself today."

"I enjoyed seeing you and tha kids enjoying yourselves."

"AAAAWE that's so sweet."

"Well, I am a sweet person, ain't I?"

"Of course, you are."

"I can't wait to get this bag off this week."

"I can't wait either," she said wit a devilish grin.

CHAPTER 27

One Down One to Go

"Oh Shit! You really are alive what tha Fuck is up Nigga," Star asked giving Grams a hug. As much as he hated it, he hugged Star back.

"I wanted to reach out but after Flynn got killed, I didn't know who to trust."

"Nigga you know you can trust us."

"I know I can, that's why I told wifey to let y'all know I was alive. How-y'all looking on tha money side of things?"

"I'm not gonna front we Fucked up; we just had a situation that cost us close to 2 mill."

"Shit! What you have to do pay a ransom?" he asked already knowing tha answer.

"Yeah, she good now."

"You don't know who did it?"

"Yeah, some nigga named Keem."

"So, what y'all gon' to do?" "Nothing," they said then broke ery thing down to me, as if I really give a Fuck."

Well, I got about 100 grand and I'm about to take my city back; is y'all with a nigga or what?"

"Come on, you already know tha answer to that."

"A'ight, I'm bout to meet my folk, I hit y'all when I get back." Everything was going according to plan; I knew they would take the bait.

"Aye yo Perk, this shit is going to be easy. We're gonna help him build his empire then destroy it and him."

"I'm wit that, but this time he's not gon' to wake up!

"Keem this Grams what up?"

"Yo, did you put it in motion?"

"Yup and they did exactly what you said they would do."

"I know, them niggaz is hungry and greedy. I need 10 of them things, if you ready?"

"Nigga I'm always ready; you should know that by now."

"I'm just say'n it's still a recession and everybody is Fucked up!"

"I'm not everybody, I'm Keem."

"My fault, I didn't mean no disrespect."

"None taken, just remember even if it's a heatwave outside we still got snow."

"Say no more then; I'm wit you."

"Grams, how much you lettin' ya pies go for?"

"32,000."

"Up ya numbers to 35,000. You just said it's a recession and nobody has shit."

"My peeps will be at tha spot in 45 minutes."

"A'ight."

"Grams keep a close eye on those niggaz."

"Trust me, they not gon' catch me slippin' this time."

"Hit my phone once tha plane has landed."

"Will do."

Once I got to tha spot I phoned Keem to let him know that tha plane landed smoothly.

"Remember what I said, watch those niggaz."

"Gotcha."

For tha next few weeks I went hard getting my money up and securing my spot back in tha city. Within 2 months, I had tha city in a chokehold and my doe was all tha way up, thanks to Keem. I think it was time to put my plan into action. I had Star at one trap house and Perk at another. Perk told me he heard that a few niggaz from tha south side were overheard talking about hitting one of tha houses. As of yet, nothing has went down. I called Star and Perk to make sure they were straight on tha work I told them to hit me in tha a.m. and headed home for tha night.

Boom was tha sound of tha front door coming off tha hinges.

"Don't even think about it. Put ya hands on tha table where I can see them. Tie that Mafucka up." Once he was, I took my mask off.

"What tha Fuck is going on?"

"Did you think I would let you and Star get away wit what you did to me and killing Flynn?"

"What you talking about?" (Smack Smack)

"Nigga don't disrespect me by acting stupid! That night when y'all thought you killed me, you said Stars name. So, I'm here just to return tha favor."

"Fuck you Mafucka! If you gonna kill me then kill me!"

"Only when I'm ready; do I make myself clear?" I asked pointing my .50 cal in his face, "now since you and Star make a habit out of destroying lives, it's time to return tha favor."

Before he could say anything "BOOM" the .50 cal tore half his face off.

"Oh Shit! Grams you didn't say you was going to kill him." I handed my little cousin tha .380.

"What's this for?"

"Empty tha clip in him."

"He's already dead."

"Jusy empty tha clip," once he had done it, I said, "now I don't have to worry about you telling."

"Nigga, you didn't have to worry about that anyway."

"Well, go upstairs, grab tha money, and let's get outta here."

"Tha police are comin' pull ya mask down and let's go out tha back."

"Damn that nigga probably got one of those bitches in there wit him," I thought hanging up tha phone. I tried to call a few more times only to get tha same results tha answering machine.

Tha next morning when BJ came, I shot across town to tha other stash house. When I pulled up there were a few cops out and tha house was taped off. I walked up to tha house but they weren't letting anybody in.

"My brother is in there," I said try'n to get pass.

"Excuse me Sir, but nobody is in tha house."

"What hospital did they take my brother to?"

"Officer Jenkins I got it from here," tha tall guy wit tha suit said.

"Mr. Uh."

"Webster," I said now concerned.

"Mr. Webster, I hate to be tha one to tell you but your brother was killed early this morning."

"Nah, Nah, that can't be right."

"I'm sorry but it is." I dropped to my knees.

"Nooooo God Please Nooo!"

"Do you know who could of done this?"

"No, I don't."

"Well, here's my card; if you think of anybody please don't hesitate to call me."

I just looked at him like he'd lost his mind. I needed to call Grams.

"Yo."

"Yo, what up Grams?"

"Shit, is ery thing Ok? You sound like somethings wrong?"

"They ran up in tha stash house and killed Perk."

"What, when?"

"I don't know, I just got over here and tha police got tha crib all taped off."

"Stay there, I'm on my way."

"Nah, just meet me at tha pool hall."

Tha whole ride all I could think about was revenge. Maybe this was God's way of paying me back for all tha wrong I've done.

I couldn't help but smile at tha sound of Stars voice. I wanted him to suffer just like I have been for tha past few months. I pulled up at tha same time as Star.

"Yo, what up Baby Boy?"

"I'm just hoping that somehow this a big dream."

"I felt tha same way when I came out of my coma so I closed my eyes, but when I opened them, I was still in tha same place. If that wasn't bad enough, wifey told me Flynn was murdered. Star I'm telling you, it felt like somebody had ripped my heart off of my chest. I still feel tha pain; Flynn wasn't just my best friend; he was my brother. So, believe me, I know how you feel."

"I'm going to find out who did this so we can handle this."

"Fuck that! Imma shoot tha whole south side up!"

"We can't do it like that; we don't want that kinda heat. We still gotta get at this money. We gotta be smart about this and not let our emotions override our intellect." I knew he was right but I wasn't try'n to hear that Shit.

"You gonna be alright? I need to meet my folks."

"I'm good."

"You sure?"

"Positive, don't worry I'm not going to do anything yet."

"I'll hit ya phone when I get back."

On my way to meet Hasan I hit Keem to update him.

"Yo, one down, one to go."

"Which one went to tha park first?"

"Perk."

"I don't want you to kill Star; let me handle him."

"You got that I think now is tha best time to handle it since he's so vulnerable right now."

"I'll be down tonight, so here's what I need you to do."

"I can handle that wit no problem. Just hit me when you get down this way."

"Will do."

CHAPTER 28

Who's Laughing Now

"Babe I need to handle some biz-ness I'll be back later on."

"Should I wait up?"

"No, I just got some info on Star."

"Keem please be careful."

"I will." I called Stacks so he could meet me at tha, park.

"Yo, park ya car on Van Buren; we gon' drive down in this hoopty."

"So, Grams sent Perk to tha boneyard, huh?"

"Do dirt, you get dirt."

"It was gonna happen sooner or later; Fuck him!"

"That's exactly how I feel too."

"Keem, I want to be tha one to pull tha plug on that nigga. I swear every time I think about what he did to Layla and tha fact that she could have lost tha baby makes me want to kill that Mafucka!"

"Nah, we not going to kill him, but he will suffer for tha rest of his miserable life; I promise you." I hit Grams to let him know we were in town.

"Do you know where club Images is?"

"Yeah, be there in a few minutes." Stacks wanted to go in and have a few drinks but I thought it was a bad idea.

"Man, I don't give a Fuck if that nigga see us or not."

"Well, I do, we don't want to scare him off before we get a chance to get him."

"Yeah, I guess you're right; I didn't think about that."

"You were just letting your emotions cloud your judgment."

"Lay said you and Layla find a house shopping."

"Actually, I was helping Layla find a house for her and tha baby."

"I thought y'all were together?"

"We decided that we didn't want to complicate things; so, we would just be friends for now." (Ha! Ha! Ha!)

"What's so funny Nigga?"

"Y'all don't want to commit so that's why y'all just friends."

"Don't shit get pass you."

"You already know, so why you always try'n?"

"Just makin' sure you on ya P's and Q's."

"Always."

"Yo, what time this club over?"

"I don't know but I told Grams to make sure he was drunk."

"Are you sure that shit gonna work?"

"You gonna find out firsthand."

"Light this up," he said passing me a Dutch. I looked at tha clock on tha dash it was only 11 o'clock.

"Damn!"

"What up Keem?!" he said yelling over top of tha music.

"I can't hear you go; to tha bathroom."

"A'ight, hold up"

"Yo, can you hear me now?"

"Yeah, I can hear."

"What time is this shit over wit?"

"2 o'clock"

"We bout to hit one of these bars up."

"Nah, just come in here; we in the VIP."

"We not try'n to be spotted."

"Just go to tha far end bar, that way you can watch tha whole club."

Ok and when we see y'all slide we'll be on ya heels like a thong on a stripper." (Ha! Ha! Ha!)

"You crazier than a Mafucka; Imma let tha bartender know drinks is on me."

We parked next to Grams 600 then went to tha line to get in. After about 30 minutes we got in. Well, it wasn't 30 minutes but that's what it felt like.

"What you drinking Keem, the usual?"

"Yeah."

"Can I get a Remy on tha rocks and Bombay straight both double shots."

"Is that all?" she asked after she made our drinks.

"Yes," I said pulling out my money.

"These are already paid for from tha guy up there," she said pointing at Grams.

I still gave her a 10 which she was more than happy to take. For tha next drink I told her to just bring me tha bottle so she wouldn't have to keep running back and forth. She winked and let me know it was no problem and she didn't mind at all.

About an hour later, I spotted Grams in store heading towards tha exit. Star could barely walk; this was gonna be tha sweetest revenge yet.

"Well, Well, Well, if it isn't Mr. Star himself."

I think he's sobered up real quick when he turned around. I could tell he was try'n to make sure it was us.

"Yeah, it's us, did you think you could hide forever? (Smack)

"AAAAGGHH!"

"That's for Layla Mafucka."

We bound his hands and feet then threw him in tha truck.

"Y'all follow me." We followed Grams to this industrial park that was dark and isolated.

"Is this place secure?"

"You think I would come here if it wasn't?"

"A'ight, pop tha trunk Stacks." We yanked him out tha trunk hitting his head on tha bumper.

"Ouch, that's gonna leave a bruise," Grams said laughing. When we got inside Grams hit tha lights and two pit bulls came charging at us.

"Holy Shit!" I yelled but Grams yelled out "cease!" and just as quickly as they ran at us, they stopped.

"Don't worry, these are my babies; they won't bite unless I tell them to."

"Nigga you almost had no dogs," Stacks said holding his .50 Cal straight out.

"Take tha blindfold off his face and put him up there!"

Stacks snatched tha blindfold and tha tape off his mouth.

"OOOOOW SHIIIIIIT!"

"Nigga shut ya bitch ass up."

"Grams what tha Fuck is going on?"

"You should know, you tha same Mafucka that tried to kill me and killed Flynn. Don't try to deny it; I wasn't dead when you niggaz thought I was. On yeah, I'm tha one who killed Perks Bitch Ass."

"You Mafucka, let me down so I can snap ya Fuckin' neck!"

"Nigga you ain't gonna do Shit, you Pussy!" I yelled.

"I know you're wondering how we found you, huh? Well, is quite simple; you see, Grams here buys his shit from us so when he came out his coma and mentioned that he knew who his assailants were and said you and Perk's name; shit fell into place. Don't worry, we not going to kill you; we got something else planned for you," I said pulling out my stun gun.

"Man, what tha Fuck is that gonna do Keem?"

"This," I said hitting tha button and putting in on Stars spinal cord.

"AAAAAAAAHHH, AAAAAAAAHHH!"

"I still don't see what that is gonna do," Grams said.

"Trust me, when we're done, he'll be nothing more than a paraplegic. Killing this nigga would be to easy. So why not make him suffer for tha rest of his life."

After about an hour, our work was done.

"What tha Fuck did you do to me? I can't feel my legs!"

"Put him in tha car, we gon' drop him off at tha hospital."

"I swear you Mafuckas gonna wish you killed me!"

"Just in case you get any thoughts about telling tha police; we do know where your mom is now living." We pulled up in tha front of tha hospital and pushed him out.

"Now remember, we know where ya mom lives."

We went to have a few more drinks then headed home; mission accomplished.

CHAPTER 29

My Day

I was in a deep sleep until Nay, Niya, and Fiza busted and singing Happy Birthday.

"Get up Daddy, it's ya birthday."

"What time is it?"

"10 o'clock, Mommy said to wake you up at 10 o'clock."

"Where is Mommy at?"

"Her and Layla went to tha supermarket to get things for tha bar-b-que."

"She's having a bar-b-que?"

"Yes, for your birthday and everybody is coming."

"Oh really?"

"Yup, it's gon' be tha bomb."

"You sound more excited than me."

"Daddy do you want ya present now?" Fiza asked.

"Sure, why not." They all ran to get their gifts.

"Open mines first Daddy," Nay said wit a big grin.

I opened tha box to find a pair of pink Ralph Lauren khakis and a cream Ralph Lauren shirt wit RL in pink.

"You got good taste."

"I know it's not Gucci but when I saw it I knew you would like it."

"You were so right," I said kissing her on tha forehead.

"Open mines now Daddy," Fiza said handing me her gift.

"Wow, I love these." Fiza had gotten me a pair of cream and pink leather Ralph Lauren tennis shoes that complimented tha outfit Nay got me.

"My turn, My turn!" Niya screamed really excited.

When I opened Niya's gift I was totally blown away.

"You like it? Mommy helped me buy it. I didn't have enough allowance money saved up, but tha initials on tha face was my idea." Nay and Fiza shook their heads in agreement.

Tha watch was a big face wit HB on it iced out.

"Thank you, now come give ya old man a hug." They all gave me a big hug.

"Awe isn't this nice, I wish I had my camera," Lay said wit a big smile.

"Mommy, Daddy loves his gifts."

"I sure do, in fact this is what I'm wearing today. Is Layla still here?"

"Yeah, she downstairs, why?"

"I need to pick my car up."

"Daddy you got a new car?"

"Yes, I got me an old school."

"Why do you need a ride when it's already out front."

"Out front?"

"Yeah, they were pullin' up at tha same time we were."

"Did they leave tha keys?"

"Downstairs on tha key ring. Come on y'all, let's go see Daddy's new car."

"It's only 11 o'clock, I'm bout to go back to sleep."

"Well, everybody will be here by 2 o'clock."

"If I'm up I'm up and if I'm not, don't wake me up!"

"Whatever."

"Daddy, Daddy wake up!"

"Huh."

"Mommy said get up." I sat up and looked at tha clock.

"Damn, it's that late?"

"You up Daddy?"

"Yeah, I'm up. Let me get in tha shower. Niya is it a lot of people downstairs?"

"Yup, a whole lot."

"A'ight, let ya mom know I'll be down after I get dressed."

By the time I got out tha shower and got dressed it was 4:30.

"Damn Nigga, we didn't think you was going to come to your own bar-b- que.

"I was tired as hell." Dutch and Diamond started barking when they saw me.

"Nay let them out of their cage."

"We had them out but Walynn is scared of them so mommy told us to put them back in."

"Where's Walynn at?"

"In tha game room."

"Well, let them out until she comes back outside."

As soon as Nay opened tha gate they came runnin' over. They were only 5 months but they were getting big as shit. After about 15 minutes, I put them back in their cages since Walynn wanted to come back outside. Stacks had tha grill jumpin'.

"Keem you making tha old school game hard on niggaz."

"I know, first Lay shit now that pretty ass mafucka you got sitting on

30s out front."

I know, I had to come at 'em like that I couldn't let tha wife out do me. How would that look?"

"Don't worry my shit will be ready next week," Stacks said wit a big smile.

"Y'all not tha only ones wit old schools," Jewlz said.

"Now y'all gonna have them boys from 20th hot wit y'all."

"Nah, they just gonna have to step they game all tha way up cause we riding 30s or better."

"I like that watch."

"Thanks, Niya got this for me."

"You know Doc B having a party tonight."

"I know, but if I can't get in wit this on I'm not Fuckin' wit it."

"You should be able to get in wit that on wit no problem."

"I hope so cause I don't feel like changing."

"Lay did you give Keem his present yet?"

"No, he'll see it when he goes upstairs."

"Tha girls hooked him up."

"I told you they did."

"We bout to go get dressed, we gon' all meet at my house."

"A'ight."

"Aye, yo Keem we bout to get dressed; meet us at tha park."

After everybody left, I went upstairs to freshen up. I walked into tha bedroom and saw these diamond earrings and necklace to match my watch laying on tha top of this badass Gucci set.

"Oh Shit!"

Lay walked in all smiles, "I take it you like it." All I could do was grab and kiss her.

"I didn't know what to get you since you got everything."

"Thank you, Baby, I love this outfit and jewelry."

"You're welcome, are you driving your old school?"

"I think I'm just gonna drive tha truck."

"Why?"

"Because everybody is getting their cars done; we might as well all debut them at tha Labor Day party."

"Oh, I see."

"Plus, we haven't driven tha truck yet."

"Well, Imma drive ya Beamer, if that's ok wit you?"

"What's mine is yours and vice versa. Why you not going to drive ya Lasabre?"

"I was but I think Imma wait til Labor Day too; besides, I might step my game up wit some 30s." (Ha! Ha! Ha!)

"What's so funny? I can't let y'all shit on me."

"You just like ya husband; can't be out done."

"And you know it."

After we both got dressed, we decided to smoke a blunt.

"I think after I turn 5 months, I'm not going to smoke til after tha baby is born."

My phone rang I knew it was Stacks asking me if I was on my way yet. I let him know I was on my way out tha door.

"Baby you forgot this," she said giving me a long passionate kiss.

"Saved it for tonight."

"Oh, you can count on that Birthday Boy."

I pulled up at tha park; Cream, Jungle, Beanz, Jewlz, and Stacks were all there waiting on me.

"Yo, why you didn't pull up in that old school?"

"I figured since all y'all shit will be ready in tha next week we could just pull them out for Labor Day weekend."

"Well, you know a little birdie told me that tha 20th Street boys stepped their game up to 26s."

"Nigga my wife got 28s which by tha way she said she's getting 30s because she does not want us to outshine her." Everybody started laughing.

"She just like you," Cream said.

"I know, I told her tha same thing; y'all ready."

Cream and Jungle jumped in wit me while Beanz and Jewlz rode wit Stacks.

"Here Brother."

"What's this?"

"Just something me and Jewlz put together for your birthday."

When I stopped at tha next light I looked inside tha envelope.

"50,000. What?"

"It's 50,000 in there and we know you don't need tha money but we didn't know what else to get you."

"Well, let me be tha first to tell you; I know ya birthday is next month so don't expect me to give you 50 stacks."

"Of course not, a 100 would be more like it wit all tha money you got."

"Yeah, you think so?"

We had a ball that night besides tha fact that Shante was being petty. I made sure I stayed away from her because I wasn't for tha dumb shit. Lay must have sensed something was wrong.

"Keem what's tha matter wit you?"

"I'm so sick of that Bitch, I swear if she wasn't Fiza's mom I would send her to the Fuckin' Boneyard!"

"I'll be right back."

"Excuse me can I talk to you for a minute?"

"What?"

"Let me holla at you for a second."

"Go head, I'm listening."

Shante's fat ass sister came over.

"Shante is everything a'ight?" I had to bite my tongue or else it would be on.

"Yeah, Sis I'm cool."

"So, what did you want?"

"Look, I would really appreciate it if you would stop being so petty wit Keem."

"Well, I don't think it's any of ya biz-ness."

"Now see, that's where you're wrong; Keem is my biz-ness." By now, Layla and Blondy had walked over.

"What's tha problem Lay?"

"Ain't no problem."

"Look Lay, when it comes to my daughter, I'm gonna say what I want to him."

"No the Fuck you ain't. For one, Fiza don't need or want for shit, so what could you possibly say to him about her?"

"She said that he always yelling at her."

"Shante stop lying, he lets her and her sisters do what they want to do."

"Shante you don't have to explain shit to her."

"And she don't, you need to mind ya biz-ness."

"She is my biz-ness. Lay come on."

"Nah, Keem this fat bitch always got her mouth in something."

"Fuck you Bitch!"

"Laysha come on," Keem said pulling me away.

"You better pull her away only cause she pregnant."

"If she wasn't I would let her beat ya ass, believe that."

"What ever Mafucka. I'm not going to argue wit you; like I told you before, get ya man."

"You don't want me to do that."

"Nah, you don't wanna do that. You better enjoy this weekend because it'll be tha last time she comes over."

"Oh really? Cause she just told me she wants to live wit me."

"That'll never ever happen Mafucka."

"You know what, I'm tired of ya Shit; I filing for custody she always wit ya mom anyway."

"You go right ahead and Imma file for child support."

"I don't even give a Fuck, I keep all my receipts, so be my guest. Come on, I need a drink this miserable broad is not going to ruin my birthday." For tha rest of tha night I got pissy drunk.

Tha next morning I asked Fiza if she was sure she wanted to live wit me. She couldn't have said yes fast enough so I called Ms. Bunny.

"Hello."

"Hello Ms. Bunny, are you busy?"

"No, is everything a'ight?" I explained to her what happened last night.

"Keem, I'm so sick of both of them, I need a break."

"Well, Fiza asked me if she could move wit me. I called to let you know first thing tomorrow I'm going to file for custody."

"Keem I have custody of Hafiza and if you really want her to live wit you then I'll sign custody over to you tomorrow."

"I do, hold on...Fiza, Fiza."

"Yes Daddy."

"Come here please. I said Fiza, not Fiza, Nay, and Niya. Do you really want to live wit me?"

"Yes Daddy, can I please. All you have to do is ask my nana."

"Your Nana is on tha phone."

"Hello Nana."

"Hey Fiza."

"Nana can I stay wit my Daddy?"

"Is that what you want?"

"Yes, pleeeease Nana, can I pleeeease?"

"Yes, you can."

"Yeah, my nana said I can, here Daddy."

"Hello."

"Just meet me at tha courthouse by 9 o'clock."

"Ok thank you Ms. Bunny."

"No problem, like I said I need a break."

"Wow, that was easier than I thought. Come to find out Ms. Bunny has custody of Fiza and she's going to sign over custody to me tomorrow."

"So, you mean to tell me all this time Shante didn't even have custody?"

"Nope."

"Well, she wouldn't be able to file for child support anyway. I swear if I wasn't pregnant, I would have beat both them bitches up last night."

"Well, unless she files for visitation, we don't have to deal wit her anymore."

"I'm not going to be petty like her. She can see her on tha weekends if she wants."

Tha next few days after I got custody, I did a lot of shopping for Fiza since Shante wouldn't give up her clothes. Tha girls were so happy, Niya and Fiza would be going to tha same school.

"Baby, you want to have a bar-b-que for Labor Day?"

"Why do we have it? Can't somebody else have it at their house?"

"Nobody's house is big enough."

"That's bullshit, we use to have them at tha apartment. We not going to keep playing host to everything Lay."

"I know, it's just that we got tha pool and game room to keep tha kids occupied."

"Did you get something to wear for tonight?"

"Yeah, me, Layla, Blondy, and Whitey went up top yesterday. What about you?"

"Diablo sent tha girls some more things and he sent me this Gucci outfit

Imma put on tonight. Did you put them 30s on ya car?"

"Oh Shit, I got go pick my car up, can you give me a ride?" Tha doorbell rang before I could respond.

"Hey Keem."

"What up Layla? Never mind Honey, I'll get Layla to drop me off."

"You sure?"

"Yeah."

"Well, I'll see you later I'm about to go get my hair braided then hit tha barbershop."

"A'ight love you."

"Love you more."

"You still haven't told him, have you?"

"No, I will eventually."

"I think you need to tell him before he finds out."

"Layla, he's been home for a year and hasn't found out yet so I don't think he will."

"A'ight, I'm just saying, better safe than sorry. Anyway, are you ready?"

"Yeah, come on."

"I JUST WANT THA MONEY, MONEY AND CARS I SUPPOSE I JUST WANNA BE SUCCESSFUL."

"Boy turn that down."

"Sorry Ms. Walker." Rach and Paris started laughing.

"What's so funny?"

"Let me get myhair braided so I can go to tha barbershop."

"You see ya brother and Jungles new whips?"

"Nah."

"They got some pretty old schools."

"We all bringing 'em out tonight."

"Jay and his squad got their cars painted wit different rims."

"See Sis, that's tha difference between them and us."

"What's that?"

"We would never paint our cars; we would just buy new ones. And they only riding 26s. Shit Lay had 28s on hers before she just stepped up to 30s. So, I said all that to say, I'm not impressed at all and they got all this money now."

"Speaking of tha Devil," Rach said as Jay pulled up to let Brenda out.

"Ya girl get around, don't she?"

"You want her?" Paris asked pulling my hair tight.

"Yeah right, she wishes."

"Keem, what tha biz is?"

"I can't call it; I see you got a new whip."

"Nah, same whip just different rims and paint job."

"What are those, 28s?" I asked being petty.

"Nah, they only 26s."

He must of sensed I was being petty because he said, "You know tonight is all about tha old schools."

"Oh yeah?"

"Yeah, you gonna bring ya wife shit through?" he asked smiling.

"Nah, but she probably will; she wants to show off her new 30s."

"Well, I'll get at you tonight; first round on me." I just nodded.

"Hey y'all."

"See you had a hot date last night."

"Sure did," she said looking at me smiling.

"Trifling, " I thought.

But Paris said, "What ever, he paid for my outfit for tonight."

"I bet he did," Rach said.

"Bitch, you just mad cause you don't got no nigga to do that for you."

"She don't need no nigga when she got two brothers wit money."

"I know that's right," she said giving me dap.

"Nazir said you was taking him school shopping this week."

"I am so you can save ya doe. I told Cream he gotta give up 1,500 towards his clothes."

"1,500, Damn how much you spending?"

"Just enough to last him til Christmas."

"Brother, he don't need that much stuff." I gave her that look that said stop playing wit me.

"Hey, do you then, you got it. You just got 50 grand for ya birthday. I'm finished Big Head. Y'all going to tha party tonight?"

"I'm not, why?"

"My money funny, my brother ain't shit so I had to do my daughter's school shopping."

"Here."

"I don't have change for that."

"I didn't ask for none, just make sure you at tha party tonight."

"Well, I had to do my kids shopping."

"Hmm you better call Jay back."

"Let me find out y'all fuckin."

"You just say anything, Paris is like my sister. I don't get down like that, right Sis?" I said winking.

"Brother, you don't have to explain nothing to her," Paris said winking back.

"He sure don't."

"Let me get to tha barbershop, Rach you got some money?"

She hesitated then said, "Yes."

"No you don't, here," I said handing her two 100 dollar bills.

"Brother you do too much for me and Naz as it is."

"Sis, I make more money in a week than most people make in a year; legal or illegal. Oh yeah, that's for my next seven hair do's."

"I figured that."

"See y'all tonight."

When I pulled off I called Craig to let him know I was on my way. Then I hit Paris to let her know that I would still pay her, I just said that for Brenda. After I left tha barbershop I stopped by tha park to holla at Beanz and get me a few epills for tha night.

"Pop, Pop, Pop, Pop" I ducked behind tha wall.

That's up on Jefferson them niggaz been shooting at each other all day. Tha police been riding heavy all day because of that shit. You know that I saw Jay when I was gettin' my hair braided; this nigga gone say that tonight is about tha old schools and would be driving Lay's.

"Nah, did he?"

"Yup, I let him know she would be driving her own shit to show off her 30's."

"I know that busted him."

Tha next few hours flew by and once I was dressed, I was on my way to meet up wit everybody. When I got to tha park it looked like it car show. We all were sittin' on 30's and candy paint. Cream wit his platinum on platinum 67' Skylark, Jungle wit his black/black 72' Impala, Beanz wit his 82' green/white Marque, Jewlz wit his 79' white /white Lemanns and Stacks wit his TI cream/cream LeSabre we all decided to bump that Forever by Drake, Weezy, Kanye, and Eminem. That shit was so loud; when we pulled up wit Lay leading and me driving up tha rear all eyes, I mean all eyes were on us.

We pulled in tha lot wit tha rest of the old schools. I couldn't front there were some nice whips but none couldn't even come close to ours. That 4 inches we had on them made us really sit high when we parked next to them.

"Damn, I guess we gotta really step our game up huh?"

"I guess so," Lay said putting tha top up on her car.

"Damn Brother no wonder you was talking shit earlier today."

"I know y'all snapped, wifey even sittin' pretty."

"Come on y'all let's go inside and have a good time."

When we got to tha line there was some commotion going on.

"Bitch I swear if I wasn't pregnant, I would beat ya Ass!"

"Lay what's up, you Ok," l asked.

"This Bitch gonna say something slick when we walked pass to get in tha V.I.P. line." When I looked to see who it was of course it was Shante and her sister.

"Misery loves company Baby."

"Fuck you!"

"Nah, I'm good Big Girl." Everybody started laughing.

"Mafucka you got it Fucked up," she said pulling out her phone. I wasn't worried Jewlz already had his two Cannon's on deck.

"Hello, where you at? Come to tha front of tha line when you get over here."

I was going in but now I'm going to wait right here. Jay and his boys came up.

"What's up Cuzo?

"This Faggot Ass Nigga right here." I didn't give a Fuck who was her peeps she wasn't going to disrespect me.

"You Fat Nasty Bitch, I will make one phone call and get you Fucked up."

"Hold up Keem," Jay said putting his hand on my chest.

"Nigga don't Fuckin' touch me," I said pushing his hand off me.

"Keem trust me you don't want to go there. I promise you won't like tha end results."

"Is this Nigga serious?" I asked nobody particular.

"Nigga I'm dead serious, believe that." By now security had came over.

"Is everything cool over here?"

"Yeah, we straight."

"Nigga you ain't poppin' that shit now," Lina said, "when I have my baby Imma beat tha brakes off you, I promise you that."

I just kept looking at Jay then said, "I'll see you when this is over."

"Keem, I'm telling you let it go, ya money ain't long enough."

"Money? What money got to do wit it?"

"Man Fuck this Shit I'm tired of hearing his mouth," Beanz said.

Then this nigga talking bout money which he don't have, don't make me pull ya card," Jewlz said.

"I got more money than any of you niggaz."

I didn't say shit because I still didn't want Lay to know I was back in tha game. Since he was try'n to cause a scene, I nodded to Jewlz.

"Nigga you coppin off Young Roco who cops off me."

"So, what that mean?"

"It means I know ya Clown Ass only grab a half bird so next time you wanna talk that money shit do ya homework first."

Ha! Ha! Ha!

"Damn small world, ain't it?"

"He got more money than you," Shante said pointing at me.

"My daughters got more than him. If he had money instead of getting his car painted, he would have just gotton a new one. Shit my wife's car is better than his." (Ha! Ha! Ha!) "matter of fact, you right I don't want no problems, come on y'all we wasted enough time out here; once again I apologized, I don't want no beef wit you especially since I don't have enough money."

When we got inside, I let Jewlz know to hit his yung boys and have them stay on point.

"Damn Brother, y'all made him look like a clown."

"Can't make him look like what he is. I was looking at you; you wanted to say something so bad."

"I did, that's why I told Jewlz to expose him."

"Just watch him."

- 239 -

"I'm already on it; I got people outside."

"You want a drink?"

"Yeah."

We got to tha bar Jay was there.

"First round still on you?" I asked.

"That shit wasn't bout nothing. Listen Jay, I got a daughter by Shante and since her mom gave me custody it's been a lot of shit wit her and Lina."

"See, I didn't know that."

"I know and that's why it's good to know what's going on before you step in unless a nigga putting their hands on them," I pulled him to tha side, "if you really want to get ya money up, I can help you wit that; take my number and holla at me if you wit it," I said giving him my number.

"I'm going to tha VIP, you coming?"

"Nah, you go head Imma shop around. I saw Naz's dad in here; I don't want no shit outta him."

"You ain't gotta worry about that ever since Cream said something to him. He hasn't said Shit."

"Good cause I don't wanna have to bust his ass tonight. I don't like him anyway."

"Bye Brother."

"Nah, that nigga need to start doing shit for Naz for a nigga that ain't never got no doe. He always at tha clubs."

Rach wasn't really try'n to hear it so she said, "We don't need him."

"Exactly, so he has no right to get mad when he see you doing you."

For tha remainder of tha night I kept my eyes on Rach as well as Jay. When tha party was over Jewlz made tha call to make sure it was safe to go outside. All you heard outside were tha different systems coming from all tha cars.

"Yo, this Bitch is not going to be satisfied until I smack tha shit outta her. Yo get tha Fuck off my car!"

"This ain't ya car."

I hit tha automatic start and so did everybody else.

"Look Shante, I don't know what ya beef is wit me; you should be happy I got custody of Fiza; now you can really run tha streets."

"Fuck you Keem."

I could tell she was drunk. This Bitch had tha nerve to stand up on my car.

"You lost ya mind," I said snatching her down making her hit her arm on tha bumper.

"Mafucka!" she screamed and before I knew it, she was on my back clawing my face.

I heard Lay yell, "Bitch you lost ya mind!"

Next thing I knew Lay was dogging Shante and Blondy was doing tha same to Lina.

"Laysha, Laysha," I said pulling her off Shante.

Tha police had came over.

"I want her locked up for assult now."

"Nah, she was defending me, I want you locked up for assault. Look at my fuckin face."

As soon as tha cop saw my face they put her in handcuffs.

"She assaulted me, why am I being locked up officer?"

Tha other cop came over to get my side of tha story and since I didn't

Fuck wit tha cops I let him know I didn't want to press any charges, I just wanted them to detain her so she could sleep off her drunkenness.

"I didn't think you would press charges cause I wouldn't have."

"So, you not mad that I didn't?"

"Hell No I'm not mad. Look at ya face I tried to kill that Bitch!"

"Are you going to tha Guards?

"Nah, we going to tha Gold Club."

"Well, I'll see you at tha house."

"I'll probably be home before you."

"I doubt that."

I ended up not going to tha Gold Club and going home instead.

CHAPTER 30

Paralyzed

It had been 3 months since I was paralyzed and I was in a state of depression. Since I didn't have no money, I had no choice but to move in wit my grandmom in Middletown. I had to settle for tha push wheelchair since my insurance wouldn't pay for a motorized one. Those niggaz are going to pay for this shit no matter how long it takes.

"Star, Star."

"Yes Granny."

"Key is here to see you."

"I don't want no company right now."

"Boy get ya tail out here."

Key was my old girlfriend that I left for Layla but she always had my back no matter what and now is no exception.

"Don't be acting like you don't want to see me."

"Key you already know l don't like you seeing me like this."

"Well, from what I understand that's now a part of your life; so are you saying you never want to see me again?"

"I really don't know."

"Well, to bad cause I ain't going nowhere."

"You really do love me huh, handicap and all?"

"Sure do and always will. I don't care about you being in that chair. Boy you better not let this good thing get away."

"I just don't want you feeling sorry for me, that's all."

"Feel sorry for you? I want to help you get tha Mafuckas back that did this to you. I know you told Granny it was a car accident but I'm not going for that so you might as well tell me tha truth right now!"

I ended up telling her tha whole story from Grams to Flynn and kidnapping Layla.

"Wow, you're lucky to be alive."

"Key I'd rather be Fuckin' Dead!"

"No, you don't, don't say that."

I sat there talkin' to Key when tha perfect plan came to me and if she felt tha way she said she did then she shouldn't have a problem wit it. Once I ran it by her, she was more than willing to be a part of it.

CHAPTER 31

Scheming

Layla had my son 2 weeks ago and Christmas was 4 days away. Me and Layla decided to be friends and nothing more until we were both ready to fully commit.

"Yo."

"What tha biz is Keem?"

"I can't call it; bout to go up top and finish tha rest of my Christmas shoppin."

"Swing by and scoop me up."

"Where you at?"

"Over my Mom's house."

"I'll be there in 20 minutes tops."

"Ok, just hit tha horn."

20 minutes later I was blowing tha horn in front of Ms. Tracy's house. Ms. Tracy stood in tha door and waved. I waved back.

"My mom said don't forget her present."

"I already got her present."

"What you get her?"

"A Tennis bracelet."

"What you going up here for; I thought you were done shopping?"

"I am, I just got to pick up Lay's necklace and her bracelet."

"She already has enough jewelry."

"I know, but I had to get her this made; it's probably tha only kind she doesn't have."

While we were in Ralphies this bad ass chick walked in.

/"Don't just look at her say something to her."

"She looks familiar from somewhere."

"I hope you don't go at her wit that corny ass line."

"Nah, seriously I know her from somewhere, I just can't remember where I know her from." I kept staring at her try'n to remember where I knew her from.

"Are you going to just stare or are you going to speak?"

"You just look familiar that's all and no that's not a pick-up line."

"Geez I hope not," she said wit a smile.

"Stacks."

"Excuse me?"

"My name is Stacks."

"Nice to meet you," she said extending her hand. Wit out giving her name she headed towards tha door.

"I didn't catch your name."

"Because I didn't throw it," she said wit a smile and walked out. (Ha! Ha! Ha!)

"Not use to that, are you?"

"Nah, can't say I am."

"Let me see what you got Lay Now that's unique and different; she's gonna love that."

Keem had gotten her a diamond necklace wit a diamond locket that had a family portrait inside and a matching bracelet with 5 pictures: well 4 since Lil' Keem wasn't born yet.

"How did you come up wit that idea?"

"Came to me in my sleep."

"Let's go in tha mall to tha food court, I'm hungry as hell."

"We can get something to eat on South Street."

"I wanna get something from that Japanese place in tha food court."

"Come on then, cause I need to get Lil' Keem some things from Unica Kids then meet Diablo's cousin. There she is again."

"Who?"

"Her," I said pointing to tha girl from Ralphies.

"Well, it nothing else y'all like tha same food."

"You got jokes, right?"

When she turned around and seen me, she said, "Do I have to get a restraining order?" Keem started laughing like she had just told tha funniest joke.

"I see you do comedy for a living."

"Actually, I am a nurse."

After we got our food, I asked her if we could join her.

"Sure, why not."

"Hi my name is Keem."

"Hello Keem, I'm Takeysha but everybody calls me Key. Is that all I had to do to get a name?"

"Sometimes it's tha simple things," Keem said laughing.

Key was 5'6, brown skin, brown eyes, short haircut, and a nice butt like Eva Mendez.

"I normally don't go to at broads but it's something about you and I don't know what it is."

"Well, I believe in keeping it real; so, here's my number, call me later I have to go."

"Nah, you take my number and if you want to talk call me."

"Fair enough."

"Damn, she wanted to get at me tha whole time; she was just frontin'."

"Ain't that what they do?"

"Yeah, come on let's get outta here."

After Keem dropped me off I kept try'n to remember where I seen Key at before. I kept drawing a blank but I knew eventually it will come back to me. Christmas came and went Layla was happy wit tha things I had gotten her and tha baby.

Five days had passed and Key still hadn't called as of yet. I knew she would, she just didn't want to seem pressed. I was on my way out tha door when my cell phone went off.

"Hello."

"Hey, how you doing?"

"Who's this?"

"You gave ya number out that much?"

"Nah, but when only a number and no name shows up I gotta ask who it is."

"I see, this is Key are you busy?"

"Nah."

"So what are you up to?"

"Nothing just came from seeing my son. Would you like to go to dinner later if you don't have plans?"

"No, I don't have plans and I would love to go to dinner. What part of

Philly do you live in?"

"Who said I live in Philly?" "Don't you?"

"No, I live in Wilmington; do you know where that is?"

"I sure do, that's where I live. Maybe that's why I look so familiar to you?"

"Maybe. Well, what time would you be ready and where did you live?"

"How about 8 and I live in Claymont." I got tha directions then hung up wit plans on picking her up at 8."

"Damn this was going to be easier than we thought."

"Hello."

"Hey Baby."

"Hey what's up?"

"I got a dinner date tonight wit Stacks."

"Listen, Key he's a lot smarter than you think."

"No he's not, he's going to take me to dinner then want some pussy which he's not going to get."

"I'm telling you; he's not going to want to have sex with you."

"So, what do you want me to do?"

"You're going to have to make him believe you want a relationship."

"Star, this is going to take some time."

"We not in no rush; if this shit takes a year or two so be it."

"Are you sure this is tha way you want me to do this?"

"Yes, we have to get him to put his guard down. If not, you could end up dead."

"A'ight, I'll call you after my date, I gotta get ready."

"A'ight, remember tha plan."

"I might have to actually give him some pussy."

I punched Key's address in tha Navi and within 15 minutes I was pulling up in front of her building. I called to let her know I was out front. She came looking good as a Mafucka.

"This is a nice car."

"Thank you, it's one of my toys." Since I made reservations at tha Hotel DuPont I decided to bring out my 600.

"So, where we going to eat?"

"Do you like Burger King? Cause I figured we could go there and grab a bite and head to my spot." She looked at me like I was crazy. When I didn't smile or say sike she asked me if I was serious. (Ha! Ha! Ha!)

"Nah, but what if I was?"

"Then I would have said I was overdressed for Burger King." That made me smile.

When we pulled up to tha Hotel DuPont she said...

"Do you treat all your friends like this?"

"Only tha ones I really like."

"Now I really feel special." Tha valet opened tha door while tha other valet showed us inside.

"Yes, reservations for Jenkins." Tha hostess looked on her sheet until she found what she was looking for.

"Come wit me please," she said showing us to our table, "your waiter will be wit you shortly, please enjoy your evening." After the waiter took her order we made small talk.

"Where did you graduate?"

"Del Castle." Tha more I looked at her tha more she looks familiar.

"Why are you looking at me like that?"

"No reason, just admiring your beauty."

"Now you really pour it on."

"Check this out Key let me lay my cards on tha table so you know where I stand."

"I'm listening."

"Like I told you before, I rarely holla at broads they holla at me."

"Oh no, don't tell me you one of those conceited guys."

"Not conceited, just confident and no I'm not try'n to have sex wit you."

"That's a first, a guy that's not trying to just get some ass."

"Damn Star was right; this is going to take some time."

"Are you okay?"

"Huh? Oh yeah, I was just thinking you might be a good catch after all."

"What that's supposed to mean?"

"I'm just saying, I thought that all you wanted was sex but now I see that there's more to you and I like it." We finished dinner then I suggested we go see Tyler Perry's movie "I Can Do Bad All By Myself."

"And you have a soft side; wow now I'm really impressed."

"So, I'll take that as a yes."

"That was a really good movie."

"Yeah, all his plays and movies are good. Well, I'm glad you enjoyed the movie and hopefully I'll be seeing you again," I said as I came to a stop in front of her house.

"The whole evening was lovely. You better be careful; a girl could get used to this."

"So, that means you plan to stick around for a minute?"

"We'll see," she said kissing me on my cheek before getting out.

"Call me!" I yelled while pulling off."

CHAPTER 32

Lil' Keem

"AAAAAHH, AAAAAHH!"

"Push Baby Push."

"I am pushing!" she yelled.

"Breathe Lay Breathe."

"Shut up!"

"Push hard for me, I can see his head."

"AAAAAHH, AAAAAHH!"

"Here he comes."

"Waah, Waah."

"Would you like to cut tha cord Hakeem?"

"Yes."

When that was done, they cleaned my son up then gave him to Lay. 7 lb. 8 oz is what Lil' Keem weighed. Jonda and Blondy came into tha room.

"Oh My God! Look at him he looks like Keem and Niya. Look at all that curly hair and those hazel eyes."

"I know, I said, "I wasn't messin' wit Lil' Keem but he is so adorable." Niya, Nay, and Fiza walked in.

"Hey Little Brother," Niya said smiling.

"Oooooh he look just like Niya and daddy. My little brother going to have all the girls," Fiza said high fiving Nay.

"Y'all are crazy."

"Where did ya dad go?"

"I don't know."

few minutes later, Keem came walking in wit a handful of balloons that said, "It's a Boy" and a big white teddy bear.

"Can I hold my son? Hey Lil' Man it's ya Daddy. You gon' be a ladies man ain't you?" Everybody started laughing.

"Did I miss tha joke?"

"Fiza said tha same thing. He gonna have all tha girls fighting over him."

"But y'all better not be out there fighting over no boys."

"Daddy we too young for boyfriends," Niya said.

"I know you are I'm talking about when y'all get older. I'm ya boyfriend, Imma be all tha man and boyfriend y'all need."

"You can't be our boyfriend you're our Dad," Nay said wit a puzzled look on her face.

"When you get older, you're understand what I mean." "He going to scare all tha boyfriends off."

"Oh well, these are my baby girls and they will have tha best of everything. I just signed them up for karate too." Yeah! Yeah! they all shouted because they've been asking me for tha last two months to put them in karate.

"I knew you were going to give in."

"No, I'm doing it so they can protect themselves."

"When you we start Dad?"

"Monday but know if y'all don't do what you're suppose to as far as school and home; as fast as you got in I'll take you out, understood?"

"Yes," they all said in unison.

"Daddy, when Lil' Keem get big can he come to karate?" Niya asked.

"If he wants but I think he's gonna box."

"Can't be a pretty boy who can't fight," Jonda said.

"Nah, being able to fight is in his blood. Me and his Dad can fight," I said in my sons defense.

"Well, we're about to leave but we'll be back tomorrow."

Once everybody left tha nurse came back for us to put Lil' Keem's name on the birth certificate as well as sign it.

"I need to go to tha house so I can get him an outfit to get his pictures taken in."

"Make sure you bring back his car seat and me some clothes to go home in too please."

"A'ight but here is something to think about while I'm gone. Since we got married at tha Justice of tha Peace, why don't we renew our wedding vows next month on our anniversary? It doesn't have to be a big wedding just our close friends and family. Well, I'll be back in about an hour so think about what I just said."

I think I wanted to wait until tha Spring to have our wedding. Despite what Keem said, I did want a big wedding. We do everything big so why should this be any different. By tha time Keem got back it was time to feed Lil' Keem so I let him do it.

"So, did you think about what I said?"

"Yes, I did and I think I want to wait until May."

"Uh oh."

"What?"

"You want a big wedding."

"How'd you guess?"

"I just know my wife, that's all."

"Yes you do Baby," I said kissing him.

"I just want you to know everything is on you."

"What?"

"You heard me, you'll be handling tha catering, reception, photographer, and anything else that needs to be done."

"No problem, do you want to at least pick tha colors?"

"Nah, you got all that."

"Good because I was thinking about a pastel wedding."

"You sure about that?"

"Yes, it's different, all tha bridesmaids will have on a different color pastel dress and each groomsmen will have on a color to match whoever they walk wit."

"I'll wear a ivory dress while you'll wear a ivory suit wit pink because I know that's ya color."

"You got this all figured out."

"Sure do, had this figured out for years."

(Ha! Ha! Ha!) "You crazy Baby."

"No I'm not, I knew we would do this, I just didn't know when."

Tha doctor signed tha release papers and I was more than ready to go home. When we got downstairs Keem was already out front.

"Make sure you strap him in good."

"This ain't my first time doing this Lay."

"I know, I was just sayin'. Are tha girls still going over my sisters house?"

"Nah, I got to stop by Blondy's and pick them up." (Beep, Beep)

Tha girls came running out along with Blondy and Shy. "Let me see my little cousin. OOOOH he's a dime mom. Lil' Keem, Lil' Keem, look at all that hair; Uncle Keem he looks just like you even wit his eyes closed." As if on cue he opened his eyes.

"Oh my god he has hazel eyes."

"I told you," Nay said.

"When he gets older all tha girls gonna beat your door down."

"Nothing his sisters can't handle."

"Unh, Unh Dad."

"Well, you better remember that when you want him to beat up one of your boyfriend's."

"Mom."

"Don't Mom me; I'm wit ya Dad on this one."

"Lay call me when you get home; I got some dirt for you."

"Don't you always?"

"Shut up Keem; Lay don't forget to call me."

"Oh, she won't."

"Lay said she wanted Keem to sleep in our room until he got a little older."

"It's fine by me."

"I have to wait six weeks before I can get myself some."

"Look at you, that's what sent you into labor or did you forget?"

"How could I forget about that I'm almost tempted to say Fuck these stitches and get me some more of that good stuff."

"What good stuff Mommy?"

"None of ya biz-ness. Didn't I tell you about walking in my room?"

"Yes, but tha door was open, I didn't open it."

"You still should have knocked to make your presence known."

"I'm sorry, can Nay make us some grill cheese, please?"

"Y'all didn't eat lunch?"

"No."

"Well, I'll be down to make some fingers and curly fries."

"Daddy, I rather have grill cheese and curly fries."

"Ok. I'll be down in 10 minutes." She skipped out tha room calling her sister's name. As soon as tha door closed Lay started grabbing my pants

"Stop, you got six weeks."

"Yeah, six weeks for this hole, not this one," she said opening her mouth. (Ha! Ha! Ha!)

"You crazy as shit," I said pulling away, "I'm going to make tha girls lunch."

"Can you put enough on for me; I want fingers."

"Me too."

"Let me put this stuff away then I'll be down."

On my way down tha steps I thought I should have had that elevator put in.

"Mom you Ok?"

"Yeah, just a little sore."

"Let me put Lil' Keem in his bassinet for you."

"Here but be careful wit him."

"Mom you forgot I helped wit Niya."

"No, I didn't and that was six years ago."

"Lunch is done!" Keem yelled from tha kitchen.

"Good cause I'm starving," Nay said.

"Daddy, did you make me one of those specials?" Fiza asked.

"Sure did."

"What's a special?"

"Grilled turkey and cheese."

"If I knew you was making those, I would have told you to fix me one."

"I did, I made everybody one and two chicken fingers and fries." I made everybody's plate and set them on tha table.

"These some big fingers."

"Yeah, they tha best in tha land by far."

"Baby, how did you find these?"

"Eatmores."

"So that's where Lacy use to get them?"

"I guess? Nay you gonna clean tha grill for me?"

"Yes, after this good lunch it's tha least I can do."

"Since I'm something like a chef I had tha kitchen designed wit a grill like they have in a sub shop, but clearly Keem is tha better cook. Now tha average woman would not admit that her husband is a better cook but I have no problem wit it."

"Mom, Lil' Keem is up." I looked at Keem who got up to warm his bottle up and get a diaper.

"You missed out on Niya but you will have ya hands full this go around."

"Nay, Nay."

"Yes Dad."

"Let Diamond and Dutch in tha house, please."

"Ok."

Two minutes later they came in and went straight to Lay.

"They think you're still pregnant."

Tha whole time she was pregnant Dutch and Diamond stayed underneath her. Dogs are very smart once they sensed she wasn't pregnant they walked over and sat down on both sides of Lil' Keem's bassinet

"Did you see that Keem?"

"How am I going to see anything when I'm in tha kitchen?"

I walked out wit tha bottle in hand and tha first thing I saw was Diamond and Dutch sitting on both sides of my son.

"I guess they knew you were carrying my legacy." "Boy please."

"Seriously, how else would you explain it?"

I don't know and I didn't, what I do know is when Keem picked him up Dutch and Diamond follow him. When Keem came back tha dogs or Lil' Keem were wit him. He left and came back this time wit Lil' Keem and tha dogs.

"Point proven," I said before he could utter a word.

"Wow, we don't have to worry about him as long as Diamond and Dutch is around."

Once Lil' Keem was fed and burped he went right back to sleep.

"Oh Shit, let me call Blondy and tell her about tha wedding in 4 months."

CHAPTER 33

I Do

Tha wedding was in 1 month and I had everything done. We decided to have tha wedding and reception at tha Chase Center.

"So, did they call you back about tha Chase?"

"Yeah, they said for both rooms they needed 50 Grand."

"Hold up, that's for tha room to have tha wedding and tha ballroom?"

"Yeah."

That's expensive just for that," Whitey said.

"Not really, because it's just like having a party so we get it til 3:00 in the morning."

"Yeah, but 50 Grand?"

"Plus, we get whatever we make from tha door."

"Oh, so whoever didn't get an invite can pay to get in tha party?"

"Yeah, Doc B said he posted it on his page.

Tha After Party of tha Wedding of tha Decade featuring Jay Z, Kanye, and Jeezy.)"

"Doc B. Paid for them?"

"No, we did."

"Bitch y'all spent a lot on this wedding."

"I know 120 grand."

"SHIIIIIIT! This is tha wedding of tha decade."

"Actually, it was 150; I forgot about Jesse Powell singing when I walk down tha aisle."

"Y'all went all out."

"I deserve it since I didn't have a real wedding tha first time. You have to see Lil' Keem's suit."

"Y'all found him a suit?"

"We got it made where we got our stuff made at."

"I know, Keem got Gucci tuxes made."

"You know he did but he didn't get tuxes he got suits and of course his sons is matching his."

"I can't wait to see your dress."

"I'm excited and nervous."

"I would be too. Nobody has ever had a pastel wedding."

"I know, that's why I did it. All tha guys will have on ivory suits wit shirt and shoes to match y'all dresses."

For tha next 2 weeks I made sure everything was in order. I didn't want no shit at tha last minute.

"Baby his suit looks real cute on him, especially wit his pink shirt and shoes. He gon' be stunning like his Daddy," I said puttin' on his Gucci frames wit tha pink tint I had made for both of us, "I'm going to cry, look at my Little Man." I had to admit, Lil' Keem looked fly as Shit.

"Baby, I'm nervous."

"Me too and I don't know why we already married."

"Maybe it's because of all tha people that will be there."

"I want to write my own vows."

"Boy get out of my head, I was about to say tha same thing."

"I know what you need."

"What's that?"

"A nice back rub and a warm bath. You been so busy planning this wedding tha past few months."

"That sounds like a winner; Imma hold you to that tonight. Before I forget, would you be mad if I gave Blondy my Audi?"

"Give or sell it to her?"

"Give, she needs a car."

"Why don't you just sell it to her for tha low?"

"This her calling now, hold up. Hello."

"Hey Lay, I need a favor."

"What's that?"

"If you not busy tomorrow can you take me to a couple used car lots? My friend hit me wit some money."

"How much you try'n to spend?"

"He gave me 4,000 but if I can find something for cheaper."

"Where you at now?"

"Sittin' in tha park."

"I know where you can get a nice reliable car for 4,000 right now but you need insurance on it now and you gonna have to go to Motor Vehicle and put it in ya name."

"Come pick me up then."

"Ok, give me 30 minutes."

"See that worked out perfect; now didn't it."

"Yup, now you can put a stack in all tha kids bank accounts."

"You said that like it was a problem."

Blondy was in tha park wit Candy.

"You ready?"

"Yeah, just run me home so I can get tha money."

"Candy did you pick ya dress up yet?"

"No, Imma pick it up tomorrow."

"You better, tha wedding is in 3 days."

"I am, call me when y'all get done."

"Imma call my mom so she can add me on her insurance cause it'll be cheaper."

I drove straight to DMV.

"Why you come here first?"

"Just come on," I said getting out.

When they finally called our number Keem had to get Blondy from outside.

"May I help you?"

"Yes, we would like to get this transferred into her name." We went to all tha steps and 20 minutes later the Audi was hers.

"I'm taking your word; I hope this car is worth it."

"Blondy."

"What Keem?"

"Look at tha title."

"Oh My God! You sold me ya Audi for $4,000? Shit ya system cost more than that."

"Tha system don't come with it."

"Shut up Keem, yes it does."

"I wouldn't care if it didn't thank you so much Lay."

"Your welcome, I knew you needed a car and I was tired of this one."

"Layla told you I bought you a Maybach for a wedding present, didn't she?"

"No! Oh My God you got me a Maybach?"

"Yeah, a white/white wit some dub dueces."

"Where is it at?"

"Joe's, after he finished tha system I told him I would be to pick it up Friday."

"Nope, we're going to get that right now; so, call him and let him know we're on our way."

"I wish I had what y'all got."

"What money?"

"No smart ass, love."

"Blondy you know you my dog that's why I'm always fuckin' wit you."

"I know Keem."

"Damn that mafucka is nice."

"Baby you deserve tha best of everything."

"Keem you spent out for this wedding,"

"Blondy this wedding for everything cost me close to 1.6."

"1.6 what?"

"Million."

"WOOOOOOOOW!" Even Lay Eyes got big.

"Lay ya ring cost a mill, I had it specially made there's no other ring like it and you won't have to worry about seeing anybody else with it on."

"I know you won't for a mill," Blondy said with a smile.

"Does Candy have money to get her dress?"

"I don't know, probably not." '

"A'ight, I'll call her and I'll hit you later tha girls about to come home."

"Ok and Lay thanks again," she said hugging me.

"Just make sure you take care of it."

"Baby I love tha license plate (WHICH READ MRS. BELL)."

On tha way home I called Candy.

"What's up Lay?"

"Do you have tha money for ya dress and shoes?"

"No but Paul said he would give it to me tomorrow."

"Come by the house right now and get tha money cause you know he be bullshit'n."

"Let me pick tha kids up and I'll be there."

An hour later, Candy was at my door.

"Damn Mrs. Bell a Maybach?"

"My husband got me that for a wedding gift."

"Most people get dishes you get a $300,000 car. Where's Keem at anyway?"

"He took tha girls to Karate class."

"They really into that, huh?"

"Yeah, and they good, they all won trophies last month at that ornament.

"Blondy told me about ya ring."

"That Bitch couldn't wait to tell somebody."

"Keem really loves you,"

"He better, we been together for almost 15 years."

"It's been that long?"

"Yeah, I can't believe it myself."

"This is definitely gonna be tha wedding of tha decade."

"It's for all tha haters who thought we wouldn't make it this long."

"Proved them wrong."

"Sure, did and we still got eternity left."

"If Paul gives me money, I'll give you tha money back."

"If he does, get ya hair, feet, and nails done. I'll call you later or first thing tomorrow."

Candy was my girl, but her sense of style was bland that's why I had Blondy go wit her to pick her dress and shoes. We were all going to tha salon together so I would tell her how to get her hair done. Keem wants to wear his hair in a ponytail but I think he should go with braids. Neither of us wanted Bachelor or Bachelorette parties so we didn't. Since its tradition not to see each other before tha wedding I stayed over Layla's and he stayed over Rachel's.

"Brother are ready to do this tomorrow?"

"I'm a little nervous but I'm ready."

"You know ya nephew is siked for his suit and shoes. I know you gettin' ya hair done."

"I wanted to rock a ponytail."

"Paris is on her way down here so you might as well let her hook you up."

"A'ight, cause I ain't going to tha barber shop til tha morning."

When Paris saw my hair she said, "I know you gettin' that done."

"Girl, he said that's how he wearing it."

"Boy sit down and let me hook you up."

"Uncle Keem I like my suit."

"That's what's up."

"You need a shape up."

"No he don't."

"Yes he do, Imma take him wit me in tha morning."

"Told you Mom."

"Told her what?"

"He told me you was gonna say he needs a shape up."

"Did you get Mom something to wear for tha wedding?"

"Boy I been did that."

"Brother you hanging out wit us tonight?"

"Where y'all going?"

"Plush."

"Count me in then."

"Brenda gon' have to drive her car."

"She was driving anyway."

"Who's riding wit you?"

"Me, Paris, Kelly and you."

"Nah, I'll pass on that one.

"Hey, I thought I heard you down here."

"Hey Mom, you ready for tomorrow?"

"I should be asking you that you're tha one getting married."

"He's nervous."

"I would be nervous if I was getting married," Paris said.

"Mom-Mom, Uncle Keem staying tha night wit us cause him and Aunty Lay can't be around each other."

"He love his uncle."

"He better," I said punching him in tha arm.

"Be still, I only got 3 left."

"Oh Snap! That's hot Uncle Keem."

"Tha flyest niggaz in tomorrow," I said holding my hand out for a ɔound.

"That's why he acts tha way he does between you and Cream."

"Cream what?" he said walking in tha front door.

"I said between y'all two that's why Naz is tha way he is."

"Oh cool, sharp and tha shit!"

"You better watch ya mouth."

"My bag Mom I didn't know you were in there."

"Keem what you can't speak?" Brenda asked.

"I didn't know I had to give you a shout out."

"Keem what you doin tonight since you didn't want no bachelor party?"

"I'm hangin' wit Rach tonight up top."

"So are we, You know Meek Millz is at Pinnacle tonight?"

"Sis that's where we at then."

"Ain't no dress code is it?"

"No, I'm going with this on."

"You said that like it's something wrong wit what you have on." I had on a pair of Gucci jeans with a Gucci V-neck and sneaks.

"I'm talkin' about jeans and sneakers."

That night I had a good time and I was pissy drunk. As soon as I got in tha house I went straight to sleep; I had a long day in front of me.

"Uncle Keem, Uncle Keem! Wake up! Wake up!"

"Huh?"

"Get up, time to go get fresh for today."

"What time is it?"

"Mom!" he yelled up tha steps.

"What Boy and stop yelling."

"Uncle Keem said what time is it?"

"Tell him it's 9 o'clock."

"I heard her, let me get myself together and we out."

After I brushed my teeth I called Craig.

"Yo you in tha shop yet?"

"I'm on my way there now."

"Can my nephew get a shape up?"

"Yeah, bring him wit you."

"A'ight will be there in 10 minutes."

"Make sure you get the dye."

"Already got it."

"Cool see you at tha shop."

"Naz."

"Huh?"

"Let's go nephew."

"I'm coming," he said putting tha icing on his Toaster Strudel.

"Where is mine at?"

"I didn't know you wanted one you can have half of mines."

"Nah, that's a'ight I'll get something when we leave tha barbershop. Put ya seatbelt on."

"Uncle Keem can I ride upfront wit you?"

"Yeah, come on."

"Can we listen to Meek Millz?"

"What you know about Meek Millz little nigga?" He started rapping a Meek Millz son.

"HA! HA! HA! You funny" We listened to Meek all tha way to tha shop.

"Keem, Naz what up?"

"I can't call it," Naz said causing tha whole shop to laugh.

"Hop up here Naz, you first."

"Craig I need my thing extra tight today for my uncle's wedding."

"Gotcha Baby Boy."

"Keem I'm bringing my Italian shorty wit me. I heard you spent a nice penny for this big event."

"1.6 mill, that's including tha ring, car, and wedding."

"Damn Baby Boy, this is the wedding of the decade."

"Actually, I only spent 300 grand on tha wedding and after party; Lay's ring cost a mill."

"God Damn I can't wait to see that rock."

When Craig finished me and Naz were both sharp. I even let him get his outline dyed since he asked even though Rach might kill me. When we got in tha car Naz couldn't stay out tha mirror.

"Imma tell ya Mom when I went to tha bathroom you told Craig to dye that."

"Awe Uncle Keem you scared of my mom, you tha big brother.) Ha! Ha! Ha!)

"Boy you wild; you hungry?"

"Yeah."

We were all at tha salon getting our hair done.

"Mommy can I get tha style Daddy loves on me?"

"Yes, all 3 of y'all can get tha styles he likes. Which was their real hair bumped and curled on tha ends. Everybody brought their shoes so they could get tha exact fingernail polish to match. Fiza, Nay, and Niya looked so pretty when they were done.

"Daddy gonna be siked when he see us looking all good." It was 11 o'clock by tha time we were all done.

"So, are you nervous?"

"Girl yes and I got 4 hours before show time."

"Mom what time did you tell Pop-Pop- to be there?"

"He knows what time to be there."

"We might as well go get something to eat, I'm so hungry."

"Whitey you always hungry. If we didn't know any better we would think you was pregnant."

"PHHH Yeah Right, ain't no more kids coming out of here," she said, pointing at her as she calls it prize possession.

"So where are we going to eat?"

"Hometown!" everybody yelled in unison.

"Mom can I see your phone."

"For what?"

"I want to call my dad."

"Where is your phone at?"

"I left it home."

"Here."

"Imma ask my dad if I can get one of these iPhones.

"Hey, I see you couldn't go wit out talkin' to me."

"Sorry Dad, this isn't Mom."

"Oh, Hey Baby Girl is ery thing Ok?"

"Yes, I just wanted to check up on you."

"Me and Naz just left tha barbershop; on our way to J. Farmers for some breakfast." We just pulled up at Hometown.

"Hold on Dad, Fiza wants you."

"Hey Daddy."

"Hey Princess."

"I just wanted to say I love you."

"I love you more."

"Here's Niya."

"Hey Daddy."

"Hey daddy's Diva."

"Daddy you crazy, I love you."

"And I you more. Tell Mommy I love her too and I'll see her at tha alter."

"Here Mommy and Daddy said he loves you and can't wait to see you at tha alter."

"OOOOH y'all look at her blushing."

"Now that's love after 15 years if he still has her blushing," Jonda said.

"Sooo what that's my husband, he suppose to make me blush."

"Lay how do y'all keep tha fire burning after so many years?"

"I don't know, love and other things," I said winking, "we better get going it's after 1 o'clock.

"I'm going home to take a nap; I need to be well rested," Maxi said. I shook my head in agreement.

"We'll at meet up at Layla's at 3:30."

"No let's just meet at tha Chase Center at 3:30."

"Lay! Lay! Lay!"

"Huh?"

"It's 3:15 get up."

"Damn I was sleeping good."

"I know, that's why I let you sleep til now. We better get going."

"Don't forget your outfit for tha party."

"Shit I would have if you didn't just say something."

"I already called everybody else to make sure they were up."

Tha trunk of my Maybach had a lot of room so we were able to put our dresses in there wit out them getting wrinkled. We pulled up tha same time as Jonda and tha girls.

"Laysha is that a Maybach?"

"Yeah, it was a wedding gift from my husband."

"Yeah, he definitely loves you; those are tha new ones, they just came out."

"This is a dream car," Layla said still in tha back wit her feet up on tha recliner, "I've never been in a car that feels like you in ya living room. Did you see tha plate Aunt Jonda?"

"No," she said walking to tha back of tha car, "that's right let 'em know who's car it is. I didn't tell you Cream tried to holla at me."

"OOOOH did he?"

"He said he know I'm a lot older but age ain't nothing but a number.

What am I gon' do wit him?"

"You never know unless you give him a chance. A few months ago, he told me and Keem he thought you look good but we didn't pay it no mind."

"Where's Lil' Keem?"

"Keem mom came in town last night so he's wit her."

"I thought she was doing tha service?"

"She is, she said they'll be here by quarter after 4."

"WOW they did a nice job."

"For what we paying they better had."

"I like this layout wit tha pastel tablecloths."

By tha time we all got dressed it was 5 on tha nose. Rach has Lil' Keem everybody was commenting on his Gucci suit and shoes but tha frames really set it off. Wit all tha camera's snapping it was like tha paparazzi. Ms. Felisha came to see if I had talk to Keem because he wasn't here yet.

"Let's get this show on tha road Keem's here."

"I'll see you at tha alter and you look beautiful Laysha."

"Thank you," I said holding back my tears.

I was running late as Shit. When I got to tha Chase everybody was waitin' on me.

"ALWAYS AND FOREVER, EACH MOMENT WITH YOU. IT'S JUST LIKE A DREAM TO ME THAT SOMEHOW CAME TRUE. AND I KNOW TOMORROW WILL STILL BE THA SAME. WE GOT A LOT OF LOVE THAT WON'T EVER CHANGE."

All tha bridesmaids and grooms' men came in to that. Next, I came in to Case's Happily Ever After; I felt like a superstar tha way people stood up and took pictures. When I got to the alter, I walked up tha steps and took my spot. When tha music stopped you could hear a pin drop.

Jesse Powell came from tha side, *"YOOOU, YOU, YOU, YOU, I FINALLY FOUND THAN NERVE TO SAY, I'M GONNA MAKE A CHANGE IN MY LIFE STARTING HERE TODAY. I SURRENDER ALL MY LOVE, I THOUGHT I COULD."* Mr. James came walking down tha aisle wit Lay as Jesse continue to sing. Damn she looks so beautiful; I have to be tha luckiest man alive. Tha whole place was on their feet taking pictures. When Lay finally reached tha alter Mr. James helped her up tha steps to tha platform where I was. We both stood ther gazing into each other's eyes while Jesse finished his song. At that point, no one else was in that room and all tha nervousness I felt was completely gone.

Oh My God look at my husband; he looks so handsome. I didn't realize I sent out so many invites. So, this is what a celebrity feels like on tha red carpet wit everybody snappin' pictures. That's right haters, SNAP, SNAP. I was no longer nervous when I got to tha alter. I looked at my son and smiled; he look just as handsome as his dad. When Jesse stopped singing Ms. Felisha started tha ceremony.

"Laysha and Hakeem have made their own vows, Laysha."

I took Keem's hands then said, "Hakeem I have loved you since tha first day I laid eyes on you. These last 15 years have been filled wit pain and joy but what relationship isn't. My love for you grows stronger and stronger wit every day that passes. I don't know what's in my future but I do know I don't have one wit out you in it!" All tha bridesmaids had tears in their eyes.

"Hakeem"

"Laysha you have stuck by my side through tha ups and downs, and to ne that means a lot. You could have bailed out but you didn't. My love for you is like tha ocean, endless or a Picasso painting, priceless. You have also given me 3 beautiful children and believe me when I say there's no one who can or will ever take your place. I love you Laysha."

"Could we have tha rings?" Naz came up tha aisle looking like a million dollars.

"Here Uncle Keem that's a biiiig diamond you got Aunty Lay." Everybody started laughing including me and Lay. I gave him dap then he sat next to Rach

"That's a big diamond," I heard someone say.

"Hakeem do you take Laysha to be your wife through sickness and health, for richer or poorer as long as you both shall live til death do you part?"

"I do."

"Laysha do you take Hakeem to be ya husband through sickness and health, righer or poorer as long as you both shall live til death do you part?"

"I do."

"Place tha ring on her finger. Now place tha ring on his. I now pronounce you husband and wife." The whole place went crazy.

"Y'all can make y'all way to tha ballroom to eat some good soul food. We'll join you after we finish."

Told Mom and Rach to stay so they could take some pics wit us. My mom and Rach's mom were good friends. Lil' Keem smiled every time they took his picture. We got tha whole wedding parties' pictures; I knew they were going to come out nice.

"That's a shame this little boy look just like you," Sandy said.

"I know especially wit that fly ass suit on," Jewlz said.

We took way more pictures than we were suppose to but I told him to keep flicking and let me know how much more I owed him.

"Do you want me to take pictures of the dining area too?"

"Yeah, but I also want you to eat and enjoy yourself as well."

"Wow thanks, I've never been offered that before."

"You dealing wit a real Mafucka," I said forgetting my mothers were in tha room.

"You better watch ya mouth," they both said.

"Are you guys ready to be announced?"

"Yes we are." Of course, we were tha last to be announced.

"I give you Mr. and Mrs. Hakeem Bell." They all stood and clapped. I had Lay's hand in one hand and Lil' Keem in my other arm. Since he didn't want to go to anybody else. We had a table on this stage while tha rest were on tha floor. As we sat and ate people were coming up wit cards and envelopes that I'm sure held money.

"Put him in his car seat Baby he's sleep." I motioned for Rach to come get him.

"That's a shame you got him spoiled like that."

"Same thing Naz use to do. Mom said she's going to take him and tha girls wit her when she leaves.

"Keem it feels like we're newlyweds instead of renewing our vows."

"That's because we had a real wedding this time."

"Baby this is a big ass diamond."

"I think its a lil over 10 karats; I don't remember."

"Naz had me baggin up he said that."

"I know he say anything out his mouth."

"HMM, I wonder where he gets if from."

"His mother."

"Mom, Jonda and Layla are going to take turns wit tha kids while we're on our honeymoon."

"Blondy too."

"Oh that's what's up; tha more tha merrier."

We were going to Paris for 2 weeks since we have never been, I didn't want to go at first but I let Lay talk me into it.

It was 9 o'clock when everybody started to make their way to tha party room. Tha older people made their way home because they weren't down with tha hip hop as they call it.

"I'm bout to change out of this dress, you wanna help me," she said wit a very seductive smile.

"Here, now?"

"Why not? Come on," she said grabbing my hand leading me towards tha bathroom. When we got there Blondy, Whitey, Sandy, and Layla were already there.

"What are y'all up to?"

"Nothing, about to change our clothes."

"This is tha ladies' room."

"I was going to need help getting my dress off."

"I bet you was," Layla said tapping Blondy.

"I don't know why you tapped her."

"Y'all think y'all so slick; we can help you since we in here."

"Well, Imma go change and I'll wait for you out front if I'm done first."

"Ok and vice versa, love you."

"And I you but more."

"If y'all don't stop, you only going to change your clothes."

"Whitey stop hating, it doesn't look good on you," Keem said walking out.

"Fuck you Keem!"

"Watch ya mouth."

"Somebody unzip me please."

20 minutes later, I was standing in front of tha bathroom waiting for Keem. I swear he's like a woman when it comes to getting dressed.

"Keem Come On!" When he did come out he was looking goooood wit his ivory linen Capris and his pink V-neck wit matching pink slip ons.

"Where ya glasses?"

"Oh Shit," he said going back in tha bathroom."

"Now what would you do wit out me?"

"If you wasn't rushing me I even left my necklace." He turned around so I could put his diamond necklace on for him.

"That shirt is Gucci," Whitey asked?

"Everything I got on is Gucci."

"I didn't know Gucci came in pink that's why I asked."

"Gucci comes in any color but I had this made just like Lay had that made," I said referring to tha pink and ivory Gucci dress and matching shoes Lay had on.

"Whitey I never knew you was a hater like that."

"I'm far from a hater."

I knew that Whitey didn't care for me she just delt wit me on tha strength of Laysha. I put my Frames on grabbed Lay by the arm and headed to tha party.

"Listen Lay I'm tired of frontin' and playin' this role wit Whitey for you. I don't Fuckin' like her!"

"I know and I'm going to tell her not to say shit to you."

What I don't understand is why she always hatin' like she tha shit or something. I never told Lay but I think Whitey was tha anonymous person that was writing me when I was down.

"Whitey, why you always being petty to Keem?"

"Sandy you know I don't like him, I only deal wit him because of Lay."

"Well, if you ask me I think you should just not say anything at all to him to avoid a potential fall out between you and Lay."

"Sandy, I swear she better not pick him over me."

"Do you hear what you just said, that's her husband."

"And I'm her Fuckin' friend!"

"Exactly, her friend and a real friend wouldn't put a friend in a position to have to choose because if you do I hate to tell you; you're not going to win."

"So you telling me you would put Sean before one of us?"

"Yes I would, y'all bitches ain't got no loyalty," she said walking away mad.

"What was that all about?"

"Lay we need to talk but not tonight; this is your day and you should enjoy it."

"Sandy out of all of them you are my best friend; so if there's something I should know just tell me."

"I will but not tonight Lay."

"Sandy you know I'm not going to let it go so you might as well start talking."

"Can't you just wait until tomorrow?"

"No I Can't!"

"Well, if you insist. Whitey said she doesn't like Keem and she seems to think if it came down to it you would side wit her over him."

"What would make her think that?"

"Same thing I told her then she had tha gull to ask if I would side wit Sean over y'all."

"I know you told her yeah."

"Of course, and I also told her a real friend wouldn't put a friend in that position."

"I know that's right but Sandy she's tha one that's always being petty to him; she knew that was Gucci."

"Lay I know and I might be out of line but to me she acts like she likes him. Do you remember when Keem was locked up and somebody was writing him."

"Oh yeah and you did say you thought it was her; now that I remember. Sandy, I swear on my mom if that bitch is tha one that was writing Keem its on."

"Come on, let's get back to tha party."

"I don't know what's up wit Whitey but she just cussed Beanz out."

"Why?"

"Cause she said something slick to Keem and Beanz snapped on her."

"Where is she? I'm tired of her bullshit."

"I think she left."

"Lay let me holla at you please."

"What's up Baby?"

"Tha next time that bitch says something to me Imma get Rach to Fuck her up."

"What happened?"

"She got in my face talkin' bout I'm try'n to turn you against her and I ain't shit. Beanz snapped on her before I could say something and made her go home. Lay I don't Know what I ever did to her for her not to like me."

"That's just it; me and Sandy thinks she likes you."

"It's funny you say that because I think she was tha one sending me those letters."

"We are one cause I told Sandy tha same thing when you was locked up. Remember they said they would try to break us up so they could have you for themselves."

"Lay, I hope you know I would never ever mess wit any of your friends."

She frowned her face and said, "I would hope not. Don't get me wrong, those are my girls but none of them have anything on me."

"We don't keep secrets so let me say this, since Whitey doesn't like me then please don't have her over tha house."

"If there's any of my friends you don't like just tell me and I won't have them over anymore."

"I'm not telling you not to be her friend or hang out wit her. Matter of fact, I don't care if she comes over if I'm home I'll leave. If I'm not, call me all I'll come when she leaves."

"Baby I'm not going to have you inconvenience yourself on tha count of her."

All in all, tha party was tha bomb Kanye, Jeezy, and especially Hov snapped; they sent tha crowd into a frenzy. Since we weren't leaving until Monday, we decided to stay at tha Hotel DuPont for tha night.

CHAPTER 34

Exposed

It had been 5 months since I met Key and today I made tha mistake of having her in tha car when I dropped my son off to Layla. I walked up to tha door and rang tha doorbell.

"Why don't you just use ya key?"

"I didn't know if you had company or not."

"I don't bring anybody to my house," she said, looking over my shoulder, "I know that ain't that bitch Key?"

"How do you know Key?"

"That's Stars girl." I walked in tha house.

"Oh Shit!"

"What?"

"I knew I knew that Bitch from somewhere."

"She's probably setting you up."

"I got a surprise for her ass. I need to settle down these bitches are going to be tha death of me yet."

"Funny you said that cause I was thinking tha same thing."

"What, that these broads are going to be tha death of me?"

"No, that I need to settle down too."

"Let me handle my biz-ness wit this whore and we'll talk."

"A'ight but don't take too long, somebody else might snatch me up."

"Yeah right, you gonna get a nigga bodied."

"Boy go head talkin' all crazy Mom is keeping Stacks tonight so if you're not doing anything, we can grab some dinner."

"A'ight, I'll call you about 8 o'clock."

When I got back to tha truck Key was visibly mad.

"What tha Fuck was you doing, Damn?"

"Talkin' to my son mom."

"Next time do that shit on your time."

"Excuse me."

"You heard me, take me home!" I had to play this right so she wouldn't suspect nothing.

"You be buggin', next time you can come in wit me."

I pulled up to her crib and she jumped out like her clothes were on fire, so I pulled off. I had to think of a way to find out if she really is working with Star.

As I was getting out of my truck, I noticed Key had left her phone. She had it locked so I couldn't get in it then it started to ring. Tha name that flashed across tha screen brought an instant smile to my face. I made a phone call to tha Wiz Kid and within an hour my mission was accomplished.

"Hello."

"I think I left my phone in ya truck; can you check please?"

"Hold up," I said acting like I was checking, "yeah, you left it."

"Can you bring it to me?"

"Give me 15 minutes."

15 minutes later I was pulling back up to her house. (Beep-Beep). She came out, got her phone, and went back in wit out say'n thank you.

I had 3 missed calls and they were all from my baby. I called him back.

"Damn, took you long enough."

"I left my phone in Stacks truck."

"You gotta be more careful."

"He couldn't get in it if he wanted to. How much longer do we have to do this; can't I just kill him?"

"Not yet, in another month or two."

"You know he has a baby by that bitch you was messing wit?"

"Who Layla?"

"Ain't that tha bitch you was Fuckin' wit?"

"Fuck that bitch, I might kill her baby just so she can suffer for tha rest of her life like I am."

"I'll be down there to stay wit you tonight if you want me to."

"You don't have anything set up wit Stacks?"

"Nope, I'm letting him think I'm mad at him so I'm all yours. Well, I'll see you when you get here in a few hours."

"You're only down Middletown, it's not going to take that long to get there."

Dirty Bitch tha next time she sees me will be her last. I had tha Wiz Kid install a bug in her phone. There is no way Imma let her live. I had to call Keem to tell him what I just found out.

"What tha biz-ness Big Homey?"

"Yo, you not going to believe this shit."

"Where you at because this sounds like something serious?"

"On my way to tha park to play some ball."

"I'll meet you there since I'm right around tha corner."

"Is Lay wit you?"

"Yeah, is that a problem?"

"No, I'll be waiting on you." When I pulled up Stacks was in tha par shooting jumpers.

"So, what is up?

"Hold up," he said walking tohis car and coming back wit a mini tape recorder.

When I heard what was on there, I couldn't believe it.

"How did you put it together?"

"Layla."

"Layla?"

"Yeah, I had her key in tha car when I took Stacks home and she asked me why I had her in tha car. Once she told me who she was I called the Wiz Kid so he could bug her phone."

"How did you get her phone to do that?"

"She left it in my truck rushing to get out."

"Damn, so she been try'n to play you these past few months?"

"Yeah, and she probably followed us up Philly that day."

"You know what needs to be done."

"Don't worry by tha time you come back from Paris she'll be no more."

"I told you we should have killed him now he's talkin about killing my son."

"That'll never happen you can always kill two birds wit one stone."

"Nah, I have a better plan."

It had been a week and just as I thought Key led me right to Star. Key had called me a few times but I didn't answer until I had my plan in order."

"Damn what you ain't Fuckin wit me no more?"

"I was outta town for a few days."

"Well, can I see you tonight or are you busy?"

"I'm not busy, I'll swing by and pick you up in about an hour."

Key came out wit her overnight bag as if she knew we would be spending tha night together.

"I see you got my favorite bag wit you."

"I can't speak for you but I'm overdue."

I took her to tha Outback Steak House for dinner than we got a room. We had sex until tha wee hours of tha morning.

"Key what's Stars address in Middletown?"

"Huh?"

"Bitch you heard what I said."

"Who is Star?"

"Please don't insult my intelligence."

"I don't know what you talkin' bout." (SMACK) She tried to get up but I pulled my .40 cal out stopping her in her tracks.

"What's going on?"

"You tell me," I said pushing play on tha tape recorder. Her eyes got big as golf balls.

"I-I-I can explain." (SMACK)

"I knew I knew you when we first met, I just couldn't put my finger on it until that day over Layla's house. So, this was all a game to you huh. Well, Bithch you should have killed me when you had tha chance."

"It's not what you think; it started out like that but now I'm falling in love wit you." (SMACK)

"Bitch spare me, I don't believe anything you say. Don't worry Star won't have to suffer for too much longer." She opened her mouth to say something and "SPT" tha bullet went straight to her forehead. I put her in tha body bag then wiped tha entire room down and left first checking to make sure no one was out there.

This broad is not picking up her phone.

"Star."

"Yes Granny."

"There's a package for you."

"Just sit it on tha table, I'll get it." I tried Key's phone one more time before heading to tha living room to see who could have left me a package.

"Star I'm going to church, if you need anything call my cell phone."

"Ok Granny," I picked tha box up off tha table tha return address had Key's address, "now what could you be sending me?" I wondered opening tha box. "Oh Shit! What tha Fuck Happened?"

There was a letter inside that said, "IF SHE USED HER HEAD MAYBE SHE WOULDN'T BE IN THIS PREDICAMENT!" I made it to tha bathroom in time "UUUGH, UUUUGH" all my lunch came out.

"What kind of person would decapitate another human being wit no remorse? How did he find out? I need to call tha police. I can't call tha cops it goes against tha code of tha street."

There was a knock on tha door. I closed tha box before I answered it. When I opened it, I felt sick to my stomach all over again. I tried to shut tha door.

"Now, Now is that anyway to greet old friends? I thought I was doing you a favor by letting you live but I see you're not going to stop until one of us are dead so I think there's only one thing to do," I said pulling out my 9 mm wit tha silencer.

"W-W-What are you doing?"

"Something that I should've been done and by tha way you'll never get tha chance to kill my son! SPT, SPT, SPT, SPT, SPT, SPT, SPT, SPT, SPT, SPT, SPT, SPT SPT, SPT, SPT, SPT, SPT, SPT, SPT! I emptied tha whole clip in his face and chest.

"Jewlz grab tha box and let's get outta here."

CHAPTER 35

Betrayed

We had just gotten back from our honeymoon and already I had to deal wit tha bullshit.

"What tha Fuck he mean he doesn't have the money? Meet me at tha park in 30 minutes." (CLICK)

"Baby is everything OK?"

"I let Cheeze borrow some money and told Jewlz to collect it while we were in Paris."

"So, what's tha problem then?"

"Tha problem is he said he didn't have it."

"I told you about that loan shark shit."

"I know, I know but he gonna pay me my money. I'll be back, I have to meet Jewlz in tha park."

"I'll be over Layla's once I pick tha kids up. I just want you to be careful."

"I will."

"Is that your phone or mines?"

"Yours."

"Holla at ya girl," she said picking up her phone, "OK I'm on my way. Baby is it a'ight if I ride with you? That was Layla she got tha kids and they at tha park."

"Yeah, I'm leaving soon as I roll up this dutch."

"Come on I'm ready, Damn that means we gotta take tha truck. I was try'n to drive my Brougham since you said I never drive it."

"You still can, I'll just drive mines."

"Yeah, cause I don't know when I'll be home plus Inma take Diamond and Dutch in town; I know they wanna get out for a while."

"Well, I'm leaving."

"I'm right behind you."

I walked out back, as soon as they seen me, they went crazy. I opened ha gate and they wasted no time jumping on me.

"Down," I said, "sit."

I walked to tha garage, got in my car, dropped tha top then whistled. They both came running full speed. As soon as they seen me in tha car they stopped and waited for me to open tha door."

I pulled up to tha park it was packed, and Stacks was runnin full court.

"Daddy, Daddy, Dad!" Niya, Fiza, and Nay yelled runnin towards me.

"Y'all didn't act like that when I pulled up," Lay said sounding like a spoil brat.

"Diamond, Dutch get over here and bring ya leashes." A couple of kids took off when they came in tha park.

"Y'all Ok, they not going to bother you."

"Dad can I walk them?"

"No, they gonna stay right here."

"Well, can we have a dollar to go to tha store?"

"Here, you take 4 and give them 3 a piece," I said handing her a ten-dollar bill.

"Thank you, Dad."

"You welcome."

"Don't spend it all in one place!" Lay yelled to them as they were walking down tha street.

"If they want to spend it all, let them."

"Keem you got them so spoiled. Tha whole time they were wit me al they said was my Daddy let me do this or my Daddy let me do that."

"It's not funny, I told you to stop catering to them."

"I do tha same thing for you."

"I'm grown."

"They will be too one day."

Blondy and Layla started laughing, "Boy you stupid." Diamond and Dutch looked but didn't move; they knew better.

"You got them trained."

"Layla where is my son at?"

"Whitey took him to tha store wit her. Here they come now."

"Keem, I just talk to Cheeze he's on his way over wit that change." Diamond and Dutch started barking when they saw Lil' Keem.

"Quiet!" and they stopped just as fast as they started.

"They do not play when it comes to Lil' Keem."

"I know and I don't know why they act like that."

"Hey Lil' Homey," I said holding my arms out to him of course Whitey being tha petty person she is handing him to Lay which cause tha dogs to growl.

"Shut up," Lay said to them, "hey mommy Little Man, Mommy missed you, yes her did."

"Babe let me holla at Stacks be right back." I could tell Keem was mad.

"Whitey what's ya problem wit Keem?"

"I don't like him."

"Why, what did he do to you?"

"It's not what he did to me but what he hasn't done to you. Lay you deserve better than him."

"What ever he did, she forgave him and chose to stay wit him."

"Oh, Blondy shut up and mind ya biz-ness; you need to decide whether you want men or women."

"You know what, I'm not going to respond to that because what ever sex, I like it's no secret, you act like you like him if you ask me."

"What? Yeah, right if I liked him I could have had him before they started messing."

"What?"

"He tried to holla at me before y'all met."

"Hakeem, Hakeem come here!"

"Why you calling my government out like?"

"Boy please, you never told me you tried to holla at Whitey before we started messing."

"Yeah Fuckin Right. Who said that?"

"She did."

"If you gonna tell something at least keep it 100. Lay she came at me but I declined on more than one occasion."

"Keem you wish," Whitey said.

"So, you telling me you didn't try to holla at me and even after I was starting to mess wit Lay you didn't still try to come at me?"

"No I did not."

"I said I would never say anything only cause I didn't want to break up your friendship wit Lay but since you insist on lying just know it's all on you."

"Lay he's lying but I know you're going to believe him; you always do."

"Well, why didn't you tell me?

"Because it was before your time."

"So why you say'n something now, then?"

"That was to let Blondy know I could have had him if I wanted him."

"Bitch you could never have had me you was throwing tha pussy at me and I put that on my kids. You even told me that Lay was cheating on me so I might as well cheat too."

"This Sneaky Ass Bitch I'm tha only one who had her back when she was Fuckin out of every hole."

"Whitey if I ever even thought it would turn out like this I would have told Lay from tha jump."

"You should have told me."

"I didn't only because I knew she was a SMUT and was probably just drunk."

"Mafucka ya Mom is a SMUT!" Before I could say anything Lay was on her ass.

Stacks, Jewlz, and Beanz ran over, "YO BREAK THAT SHIT UP!"

"Don't nobody Fuckin' touch her." Diamond and Dutch stood there growling.

"What tha Fuck is going on?" Beanz asked.

"Ya Bitch disrespected me and my mom for tha last time." When I spotted tha girls coming up tha street, I pulled Lay off her.

"Laysha you gon' jump on me over this Clown Ass Nigga," Whitey said crying.

"No Bitch, you 'pose to be my girl and you gon' do some shit like that."

"All I did was try to save you from heartache." Sandy have pulled up.

"You probably tha one that was writing him when he was locked up." Beanz looked at Keem then asked, "Is ya inmate number 267826?"

"Yeah, this his number. (SMACK)

"You Sneaky Ass Bitch," Beanz said, "all that time you were writing him and not ya cousin." Everybody had their mouths open except Lay; she went at her again.

"Bitch all this time you smiling in my face you been try'n to steal my husband." Fiza, Niya, and Nay was about to get in it.

"Y'all better not," I said.

Cheeze walked over and was about to grab Lay when Diamond lunged at him just missing his face.

"Nigga don't touch her!"

"That's my cousin."

"I don't give a Fuck; you heard what I said!

"Ain't they girls?"

"This Bitch is dead to me," Lay said getting off her.

Cheeze helped her up, her face was swollen and bloody.

"Nigga what kind of man are you to let this shit go down," Cheeze said to Beanz.

"Mafucka Fuck you and that Bitch you call ya cousin."

"Don't get ya self in no shit," Jewlz said.

"Matter of fact you go my money since you got so much to say?"

"In my car. Come on Whitey."

"Jewlz grab that for me please."

"You better than me cause I would still be kicking her ass," Sandy said.

"I know that's right, now it all makes sense."

"What?"

"How she was always try'n to put focus on somebody else I just never paid her or it any mind. Wit friend like that who needs any enemies."

Diamond and Dutch came and stood by me. When Cheeze was about to break it up Diamond tried to take his face off.

"Bitch them dogs don't play when it comes to y'all."

"Well, now I know who was tha secret admirer."

"You said you had a feeling it was her."

"I just can't believer after all I did for her and her kids, I even let her move in wit me when she got evicted."

"Oh, you did?"

"It wasn't for that long that's why I didn't tell you."

"Well, that explains why she was always there when ever I called."

"We'll talk at tha house," he said wit an attitude.

"OOOOH Mommy you in trouble," Niya said holding her mouth.

"Girl be quiet, Mommy is not in trouble."

"Nay shut up and mind ya biz-ness."

"Both y'all shut up."

"Take this home wit you," he said handing me tha bag of money.

Before I could ask how much it was," he said 100 grand all I could do was smile.

"Why you smiling?"

"I wasn't."

"Yes you was."

"Boy don't make me hurt you."

"I'm not Whitey I can fight."

"Why don't you come home you haven't seen tha kids in two weeks."

"Yeah, Daddy come on; we going home and I'm riding wit you." Keem started laughing then told Stacks he would call him later.

"Mom, I'm hungry."

"Me too Mommy."

"Damn Layla did you feed my kids?"

"Not since lunch."

"Lay we might as well go to T.G.I. Friday."

"Yeah!" they all yelled.

"Daddy you know that my favorite place to eat," Fiza said smiling.

"I'll meet you at tha house Diamond, Dutch lets go."

When we pulled up at tha restaurant, I knew it was going to be at least a half hour wait.

"Imma tell y'all now; don't get in her and act up. Do y'all understand?"

"Yes."

"5 please."

"It's a 30-minute wait.

"We're fine with that. Fiza there goes your mom."

"Where?"

"Over there."

"Oh."

"Are you going to speak to her?" Lay asked.

She looked at me all I did was nod my head and she walked over there.

Since I got custody Shante hasn't been involved according to Ms. Bunny this is nothing new. Fiza goes wit Ms. Bunny every other weekend unless she's busy.

"Hey Mom." Shante and her friend just looked at her. When they didn't say anything Fiza it came back over.

"Mom why is Fiza crying?

"Baby what's wrong?" Lay asked.

"She didn't even speak to me; she acted like she didn't know me."

Keem came out of the rest room, "What's wrong wit her?"

"She said Shante acted like she didn't know her."

"What?" I walked over to Shante's table.

"Look, I don't give two shits if you like me or not but you will acknowledge Hafiza."

"Shan do you know this nigga?" her friend asked standing up.

"This ain't got nothing to do with you so stay out of this."

"Nigga do you know who I am?"

"It really doesn't matter to me who tha fuck you are; I'm talking to my daughter's mother."

"Listen, she's not wit you anymore so she's not obligated to play mommy to your kid."

(Ha! Ha! Ha!) "Is that what she told you?"

"Yup."

"You know what you're right, what we had is over and Fiza will not bother you anymore. Sorry for the interruption; please enjoy ya dinner."

"I thought you were going to snap."

"I was but then I thought about it; Fiza fuck that Bitch, you don't need her."

"You got my mommy," Niya said, "Dad can she call Mom, Mom?"

"That's up to her and Lay."

"It's not up to me, that's Fiza's decision."

"Your table is ready, follow me please."

When we walked past Shante's table, Fiza stopped and said, "You're dead to me Bitch!"

I could tell Shante wanted to say something, but she didn't. I didn't even say anything to Fiza for cursing.

"Daddy why are you crying?"

"Niya, these are tears of anger."

"You mad at Fiza's mom?"

"Niya stop asking so many questions."

"No, she's Ok. Yes, I'm mad at Fiza's mom. How can a mother deny her own flesh and blood? That's something a dead-beat dad does, not a mother."

"Baby there are dead beat moms as well." I looked at Fiza who looked hurt which brought more tears to my eyes.

"It's Ok Daddy, we don't need her," Fiza said getting up giving me a big hug.

Lay wiped my eyes then said, "Who wants to go to Toys R Us after dinner?" They all started yelling causing everybody in tha restaurant to look at us.

"SSH, SSH Keep down."

The waiter came wit our food while I was outside on tha phone wit Ms. Bunny.

"That must have been an important call."

"It was Fiza's grandmom, she said it doesn't surprise her that she acted like that."

"I could never ever do that to my children that I hauled around for 9 months."

"I feel tha same way about niggaz that don't man up. Girls let me ask you a question."

"What Dad?"

"If I wasn't rich and couldn't buy y'all all tha things you wanted would y'all still love me?"

"I would, me too, I need some time to think about that."

"What?"

"Sike, of course I would Dad."

"Dad you rich?"

"Yeah."

"Millionaire rich?"

"No billionaire rich."

"Mommy what's millionaire or billionaire rich?"

"A lot of money," Nay said rubbing her thumb and index fingers together."

"Y'all ready?"

"Yes, let's go before tha toy store close."

"We got plenty of time," I said looking at my watch.

Lay came back from changing Lil' Keem, "Let's go, did you pay tha check?"

"Yeah, we was waiting on you."

When we were me you tha waiter came up to me, "You forgot your change."

"That's for you and tha good service you gave us tonight."

"Good lookin' Man."

"No Problem."

It was 9 o'clock when we pulled up at Toys R Us.

"Mommy, Daddy can we get anything we want?" I looked at Keem who shrugged his shoulders.

"Yes."

"OK remember you said that I already know what I want." We walked over to where tha bikes were at.

"Can I help you wit something?" tha sales lady asked.

"By chance do you guys have those bike racks?"

"Yes, we do, what size?"

"The biggest one you got."

"Well, this is tha best one and all you do is clamp it to tha roof of your car."

"Thank you."

"Is there anything else I can help you wit?"

"No, that's it."

"Daddy, can me and Niya get a new bike too?"

"Yeah, ya mom said y'all can get what ever y'all wanted."

"OOOH I want this one."

"Take those up to tha counter while we go get this Scrabble game."

"If I knew they were going to want bikes I would have rather them get 'em from Dunbars."

"Well, tell 'em to put them back; they can't ride them until tomorrow anyway."

"I guess you right." They came riding pass us.

"Come here!" Lay yelled, "what did ya Dad tell y'all to do?"

"Take the bikes to tha counter."

"Then why are y'all riding them around tha store?"

"We don't know."

"Well, since y'all don't know put them back." They looked at me.

"You heard what she said, put them back."

"Awe man, see I told y'all we was going to get in trouble," Niya said starting to cry.

"Don't start that crying cause we don't want to hear it!"

"Damn, I feel bad."

"Why, they'll be getting bikes tomorrow."

On tha way home nobody said a word.

"When y'all get in tha house take y'all bath and go to bed."

"Mom can we stay up for a little while?"

"No, ya Dad is taking y'all somewhere in tha morning."

"Where we going Daddy?"

"It's a surprise."

"OOOOH Yeah, I like surprises."

"OOH me too."

Tha next morning, Niya made sure she woke me up.

"Niya it's only 9 o'clock; come back at 11 o'clock."

"Ok Daddy."

I was tired I had just put Lil' Keem back to sleep after feeding and changing him. As soon as the clock struck 11 Fiza was knocking on tha door.

"I'm up! Damn I'm tired and since you told them I will be taking them somewhere you might as well get ya ass up too."

"I'm not sleep, I was just laying here thinking how lucky I am to have you in my life."

"Laysha I didn't want to come between you and Whitey but I couldn't let her lie on me like that."

"Why didn't you tell me she was living wit you?"

"I knew you would tell me to put her out."

"Not if she didn't have anywhere else to go and she must didn't or she would have went there, right?"

"Yeah, but I ended up telling her to leave because she's trifling, and I don't live like that. I know I should of told you and I'm sorry."

"Lay you know you can tell me anything."

"I know I can."

"I need to tell him about Luddy but I don't know how," I thought to myself.

"I need to be honest and tell her I'm hustling but I think she might flip out."

After I got dressed, I took tha girls to get their bikes.

"Dad we getting bikes?"

"Yes Nay."

"So, this is why we didn't get them last night?"

"Yup, these bikes here are a lot better than tha ones at Toys R Us." I ended up spending close to 3 stacks on bikes and accessories.

"I can't wait to ride my bike."

"If y'all tear them up you won't get another one, understood?"

"Yes."

"Hello."

"How you doing?"

"I'm good and yourself?"

"You know me, Diablo makin' sure this money is right. Why don't you and Lay bring tha kids down for tha summer; give yourself some time to be alone."

"I don't know if Lay will let Lil Keem come down for that long of time."

"Well, talk to her and call me back."

"I'm on my way home now, I just bought tha girls some new bikes."

"Tell them I said ola (hello)."

"Girls Diablo says hi."

"Ola tio (hello uncle)! they all screamed.

"I'll hit you in a couple hours."

As soon as we got to tha house they jumped on their bikes and were out.

"Honey I'm home," I said walking in tha house.

"Where they at on their bikes?"

"You already know. Diablo called."

"What he want?"

"He wants tha kids to come down for tha summer."

"The girls can go, but Lil' Keem staying wit us."

"I already told him that."

"When are they leaving so, I can pack their bags?"

"I told him I will call him back once I talked to you."

"Did you tell tha girls?"

"No, I wanted to talk to you before I asked them if they wanted to go."

"Ask them? They don't have a choice in tha matter."

"Yes they do, I'm not going to send my daughters anywhere they don't want to be."

"Mommy come look at my new bike," Niya said runnin' to tha refrigerator slinging it open.

"Water!" I yelled to her.

"DAAADDY."

"Don't Daddy me, it's hot and you need to drink some water. When you get done, go get ya sister and come here.

"Dad you wanted us?"

"Yes, how would y'all like to stay the summer in Miami with Diablo?"

"I don't know about Niya and Fiza, but I do."

"Me too Daddy."

"I'm going wit y'all," Niya said wit her hands on her hips."

"A'ight, let me call Diablo and let him know...Hey Diablo tha girls are coming but not Keem. Yeah, me an Lay will fly down wit them next week."

"OK see you then."

CHAPTER 36

Tha Ending

POP, POP, POP, POP, POP!

"Nigga you think this Shit a game? I told you not to play wit my money, didn't I?

"AAAAH SHIIIT! You shot me."

"Nigga I only hit you in tha legs, stop ya crying; you got two days to get my money or tha next shots will be fatal."

As I was about to walk away, I heard him say, "Imma kill you."

"Not if I kill you first." POP!

Just to make sure he was dead I put one in his forehead like a prostration mark.

"Yo Jewlz you local?"

"Yeah, I'm in tha park."

"I'll be thru in 15 minutes."

My phone kept ringing but since I knew it was Whitey I didn't answer. Ever since Lay kicked her ass and I found out she was writing Keem and not a cousin like she claimed, I cut her off.

"Damn," I said pulling up and seeing her in tha park.

"So that's how you doing it now?" I didn't say shit, just kept it moving.

"What up y'all?"

"I can't call it."

"Me either. I just had to off Cheeze's boy bout that paper he owed me."

"Oh Well, Fuck 'em."

"When is Keem coming back?"

"Next week, he said he was going to chill wit Diablo for a while and catch up. Here comes ya wifey."

"She just don't get it."

"Beanz can I talk to you for a minute please?"

"I'm listening."

"Alone."

"Whatever, you need to say you can say it."

"I just need to talk to you in private; it will only take one minute."

"Nigga just see what she want."

"Nah, I'm good. I ain't got shit to say to her."

"Well, you need to know I just found out I'm pregnant."

"It ain't mines!"

"What Mafucka don't disrespect me!"

"Once a whore always a whore."

"I've been dealing wit you for 2 years."

"Yeah, me and who ever else; but that's my fault for try'n to turn a hoe into a house wife." She went to slap Beanz but he caught her hand.

"Don't get hurt and how much do you need for an abortion?"

"I'm not getting no abortion, so you better man up."

"How do I even know if it's my baby?"

"What ever Beanz it's yours!"

"I ain't doing Shit til I get a blood test if it's mines, I'm gonna play my part but as far as me and you go ain't nothing."

"So, have you told Laysha that you're back at it yet?"

"No, but I will."

"You keep saying that and you still haven't"

"She probably knows anyway."

"She might, but she's not going to say anything until you bring it up. So how is biz-ness doing?"

"Everything is doing really well. I'm glad you mentioned it, we need to up our order."

"That's good news since tha price will be going down to 7,000 a brick."

Tha next few days, me and Diablo caught up on everything. Before we left for tha airport I told tha girls to be on their best behavior and listen to Diablo. On tha plane Lay said she could have stayed for tha whole summer too.

"Why didn't you? I don't need a babysitter,"

"I'm not sure about that."

"You just can't go wit out seeing me."

"That too."

"I wouldn't be able to go 2 months wit out seeing you either. If I said I could I'd be lying."

After we landed and got our bags from baggage claim we headed outside to find Stacks and Layla already waiting on us.

"How was tha weather down there?"

"Unbearably hot."

"Lil Keem looks like a Dominican for real now."

"Anything exciting happen while we were gone?"

"Beanz is expecting a baby and he sent Cheeze's boy to the bone yard."

"He should have been handled that; Jose been owing him that money. I know Whitey ain't claiming to be knocked up? And is Layla," said aughing.

"Anything to try and hold on to him."

"Sounds familiar to me, how bout you Stacks?"

"So, what are y'all try'n to say?" (Ha! Ha! Ha!) We both started aughing.

"I don't find nothing funny."

"Damn, you can't take a joke?"

"Not that kinda joke."

"If you cry what Lil' Keem gonna do?"

"Stacks, I hope that nigga gonna get a blood test?

"He told her he wasn't doing shit til he got one. He even tried to get her to get an abortion.'

"She ain't doing that."

When I got in tha house my phones were ringing off tha hook.

"I bet they been ringing nonstop since we been gone," Lay said shaking her head. I picked them up and between tha 3 of them there were 162 missed calls.

"I don't know why you need 3 phones if you're not hustling."

"Imma keep my Nextel and iPhone but Imma give Shy my Boost Mobile."

"I think since ya son finally went to sleep Imma take a nap; I'm exhausted."

"I'm wit you on that."

2 hours later, we were awakened by Lil' Keem crying.

"Baby can you get him a bottle while I change him?"

"How about I change him while you get tha bottle."

"No problem," she said walking out tha bedroom.

By tha time she came back Lil' Keem was changed and laying on tha bed laughing.

"Do you think that Whitey is really pregnant by Beanz?"

"I don't know, she so damn sneaky. Truth be told, I hope it isn't Beanz child."

"Why?"

"He doesn't need to deal wit tha bullshit that she is surely to put him through."

"You know what I say, better him than me."

"What ever happened to tha girl that Stacks were seeing?"

"Who Key?"

"Yeah, I guess that's her name."

"You know that was Star's ex-girl?"

"Are you serious?"

"Dead."

"Wow, I don't even need to know what happen to her."

"Not if you don't want to lose ya appetite anyway."

"Keem, if me and you wouldn't have got together would you have hollered at Whitey and don't lie?"

"Nah, Whitey been try'n to holla at me for years; even before we first started talkin'."

"Why you ain't never tell me?"

"Truthfully, I didn't think it was important."

"So, you didn't think it was important to tell me she said I was cheating on you?"

"That's probably why you did what you did, isn't it and don't lie?"

"Yup, if she would have told me that tha first 6 months I wouldn't have cared."

"Why not?"

"Well, nobody cuts all their friends off until after tha first 6 months because what if it doesn't work out then you have no friends to fall back on."

"Oh, so you still had friends our first 6 months?"

"Yeah, didn't you?"

"No, I knew it was gonna work; I been wanting you for years."

"So that meant it was gonna work?"

"Yup, you see 15 years later we're married wit 3 kids."

"Laysha I love you."

"I love you too Keem."

"Whose phone is that mine or yours?"

I took tha liberty to call Rachel while Lay was on tha phone.

"What up Lil' Sis?"

"Hey Brother when you get back in town?"

"A few hours ago, are you home?"

"No, I'm in front of Paris house."

"You gonna be there for a while?"

"Yeah why?"

"I got something for Naz."

"He doesn't need any more clothes."

"I didn't get him no clothes; I got him that remote control car he

- 313 -

wanted."

"He asked you to get him one? He has three at home that he doesn't even play wit."

"Actually, he was playing wit mine and asked me if he could have it."

"Let me guess, you told him you would buy him one?"

"Yeah, I wasn't going to give him mines."

"What's so special about yours than tha ones he has?"

"For starters, there are no wires attached."

"He has one wit out tha wire."

"Well, this one I got him is ran by gas and gets up to 40 mph."

"What? That's almost like a real car."

"Exactly, and I got him a Bentley wit dub dueces on it."

"That's why he thinks he supposed to get what ever he wants."

"Why is that Sis?"

"Because you and Cream get him what ever he ask for."

"Rach his dad don't do Shit for him!"

"He got me."

"Yeah, and you got me and Cream to help you, so be a'ight wit it and I'll be by in 30 minutes."

"Who was that Rachel?"

"Yeah, she trippin' cause I got Naz this remote-control car."

"You know how she is."

"I know but she needs to be Ok wit some shit, it's not like his dad is doing anything for him! If I wasn't playin' my part and ya brother was in position to spoil tha girls I hope you would be Ok wit it."

"I would probably feel like Rach."

"Why?"

"Because they would think they can call him when ever they wanted something."

"He can though."

"Well, I won't buy him nothing else then."

"I'm not saying that all I'm saying is that it's a'ight to say no and that applies to tha girls as well."

"Hold on, Hold on tha girls ain't got nothing to do wit this. When you were young ya Mom and Dad spoiled you."

"We not talkin' about me."

"I was just making a point and if ya mom was alive she would definitely agree wit me."

"Baby I'm not saying to stop buying them things, I'm just saying they do not have to get everything they want. It's Ok to tell them no sometimes."

"How did you feel when you were told no?"

"I was upset but you know what?"

"What?" I asked wit a smile.

"I got over it."

"Lay, you buy them just as much as I do."

"I'm going in town," Layla said, "they're Bar-B-Qing, you coming?"

"Yeah, let me get Diamond and Dutch."

"Did you get Naz car?"

"Oh Shit, I would have forgot it if you didn't just remind me. This how you feeling today?" I asked referring to tha fact that she was driving her Lasabre.

"I dont get to drive it that much so I figured why not pull it out and let tha top down."

"Stop over Paris house first."

"You can drop me off then go over there."

Lay pulled up to tha park, it was packed wit people everywhere.

"Keem where you going?"

"I'll be back, I gotta run over my sisters real quick.

Rach, Paris, Kelly, Shonda, and Brenda were on tha corner when I pulled up.

"Pushing wifey car today?" Brenda asked.

"It's always you, anyway, where is my nephew?"

"He should be on his way back from Brown Bag."

I looked up tha street and saw Naz runnin' full speed down tha street. I thought maybe a dog was chasing him so I told Dutch and Diamond to get out tha car. When Naz got to me he was outta breath.

"Uncle Keem," he said panting.

"Boy, I thought a dog was on ya heels tha way you was runnin'."

No, he said he saw his aunty car then took off.

"Where are tha girls Unc?"

"In Miami for tha summer."

"Awe man, they at Uncle Diablo's, ain't they?"

"Yeah."

"Why you didn't take me?" he asked mad.

"Cause he didn't," Rach said.

"Ya Mom said you was going wit ya dad for two weeks."

"Yeah right, he a sucker."

"Naz!" I gave Rach a look that said leave him alone.

"I got something for you," I said.

"What you got for me?" When I was about to pop tha trunk his dad pulled up.

"Naz, Naz."

When Naz didn't answer he said, "Don't make me get out I know you here me."

Rach sensing, I was about to say something said, "Naz you hear ya dad calling you."

"Here cause I got to go," he said handing him a remote control car then pulling off.

"I can't stand him," Kelly said.

"No good Mafucka," Paris added.

"I don't need to give you what I was going to give you now."

"Uncle Keem please." I popped tha trunk then pulled out tha car I had gotten him.

"Oh Snap," he said dropping tha car he had in his hands.

"Naz look what you did."

"Mom that thing was cheap anyway. Look at this Bentley wit 22's," he put it down and it took off, "now this is what you call a remote-control Mom. Thanks Uncle Keem, I wish my dad were like you and Uncle Cream."

"That'll never happen."

Rach gave me "tha look" so I cleaned it up, "Naz no matter how you feel that's still ya dad and you need to respect him. Do you understand that?"

"Yes."

"A'ight cool, you still my favorite nephew," I said giving him dap, "Rach when is he going wit his dad?"

"He's not now."

"Well, is it cool if I can take him for tha summer then?"

"Yeah," Naz answered wit out giving Rach a chance to respond.

"I don't think he was talking to you. Are you sure you want him for tha summer; you just got rid of tha girls?"

"Mommy he's sure or he wouldn't of ask."

"You know if you don't want..."

"No, No," she said cutting me off, "take him." I pulled out my phone and called Diablo.

"Hey, you got room for one more?"

"No Naz."

"A'ight, I'll fly in next week." (Click)

"Well nephew, you're headed to Miami for tha rest of tha summer to chill wit ya cousins and Uncle Diablo."

"Yes, I'm going to tha MIA, to tha MIA, to tha MIA," he sang.

"You know I gotta get some new gear."

"Boy you ain't getting no new clothes."

"Well, can I at least get some Gucci sandals like those ones Uncle Keem got on, they fly."

"Ya uncle think he tha flyest dresser on tha east coast," Shonda said wit a smile.

"Nah, but he come in a close second."

"Who's first nephew?"

"Me of course." We all started laughing.

"Ya Mom gets your style from me Lil' Nigga." Rach didn't say nothing because I was right.

"Let me get back over here before Lay start calling me."

"Uncle Keem, when am I leaving?"

"Friday or Saturday, Rach I'll call you later and Naz don't run that in tha street."

When I got in tha car Kelly said, "You forgetting something?" Talking about Diamond and Dutch.

"I'll be back for them, don't worry they not gonna move."

"Yeah right, as soon as you leave, they gonna chase after you."

"No they won't, I got them trained like that."

"He not leaving his dogs, you can believe that."

"Sis you right, but Imma show you something; I'll be right back."

I pulled off, went around tha block, came back and they were in tha same spot.

I asked, "Did they move?" Already knowing tha answer.

"No." They'll follow me over Westside if I told them.

"Diamond, Dutch let's go!" They didn't even wait for me to open tha door.

"Brother where you get those flops?"

"Miami."

"I was just about to call you."

"Why is something wrong?"

"No, you was just gone for a minute, that's all."

"I'm flying back to Miami Saturday to take Naz."

"I'm going."

"I'm coming right back on Sunday."

"So, I'm still going to ask Layla to keep Lil' Keem. You want me to fix you a plate?"

"Please and bring me some steak or ribs on a separate plate."

"For who tha dogs?"

"Yeah, who paid for tha food?"

"I think Stacks, Jewlz, and Beanz."

"In that case bring them two steaks each."

Summer came and went and tha girls and Naz were anxious to get back to school. Lil' Keem Was about to be eight months and he was walking already.

"Keem I think we should buy a vacation house on Miami Beach, so we don't always have to stay wit Diablo when we go down there."

"I think that's a good idea."

Once the kids were bathed, fed, and in bed I thought it was time to have a much-needed talk wit Lay.

"Baby you sleep yet?"

"No, why what's on your mind?"

"I need to talk to you about something important."

"Hakeem please don't tell me you're cheating, or you have another baby on tha way?"

"Hell no, I would never cheat on you again, but I am hustling again and have been since I've been home. I wanted to been tell you but I didn't know how you would take it."

"Well, I had a feeling you were back in tha game because of how much money we have in tha bank. I know that our stock is doing well, and you said that Stacks hits you off every flip but I'm not dumb Keem. How long do you plan on hustling though, we have more than enough money to last us a lifetime."

"I know and that's not including tha millions I have stashed in tha floor safe in tha basement."

"Hakeem, I need to come clean too; I haven't been completely honest wit you either. Do you remember tha Jamaican guy you saw me hugging when you first came home?"

"Of course, I remember."

"Well, that was tha weed connect tha whole time everybody thought Layla had tha city on lock it was me. I just used Layla as a front so you wouldn't know it was me."

"Wow, I didn't see that one coming. I thought you were sleeping wit him and broke it off that night."

"Me sleeping wit Luddy, Hell No! If you thought that why didn't you just ask me?"

"Because you held me down and if you did something I really didn't want to know. You know that say, What U Don't Know Can Hurt U!""

ABOUT THE AUTHOR

My name is Jerz Toston, I reside in Wilmington, Delaware. First, thanks to my fans for your continued support. This is my 7th book titled Wht U Don't Kno Can Hurt U. My other six books are titled Trust is Ery Thing, Compromised, Street Dreamz: Ery Thing Ain't What It Seems, Da Game Ain't Fair, Betrayal & Deceit and Who Can U Trust? are available now on all on-line-bookstores. Also, you can call my publisher directly at 877.782.5550 x1001 and them shipped to ya door.

Writing books is my passion and I'll continue to give you page turners. Just call me Ya Fav Author.

YA FAV AUTHOR

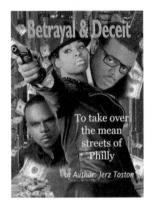

CPSIA information can be obtained
at www.ICGtesting.com
Printed in the USA
LVHW081732130122
708520LV00014B/521